Accolades & Literary Reviews

***** **BEST WESTERN NOVEL AWARD** *****
(Beverly Hills Book Awards, 2013)

***** **BEST LITERARY FICTION** *****
(Kindle Book Review, Best Indie Awards, Semifinalist, 2013)

***** **"DESTINED TO BE A BEST SELLER"** *****
(Lightword Publishing)

"The novel takes the reader back to the turbulent 1890's in central California. Cowboys are vividly depicted as they really were, including their unique jargon ... Monahan's first razzle-dazzle Adventure Series also mirrors the human condition; the karma of acts and events, our unbreakable tie to nature, and our collective inner motivations. Exciting and unique, reading this book is an adventure worth taking."

(The Mindquest Review of Books)

"Adventure, murder, and paranormal activity ... comic humor and satire in this new series of life on a ranch in America's Old West ... Drunkenness, insanity, and murder grab the readers' attention in these first ten pages.

"The colorful characters, engaging dialog, and unpredictable plot twists provide the reader with exciting adventure, danger and humorous circumstances ... create a fast-moving flow of involvement, from side-splitting humor, exaggerated satire, and heartfelt drama.

"Len Francis Monahan has a unique style of writing that captures the heartwarming drama of familial love, the life and death struggles of running a cattle ranch in the early American West with a fictional coming-of-age story. In *Rattlesnakes, Ghosts and Murderers: Volume 1: McKenna and Barnett,* Len Francis Monahan's writing is addictive, entertaining, riveting and rewarding."

(Richard R. Blake, Reader Views)

Accolades & Literary Reviews

"It's a Hoot!"
(Jim Barnes, The Independent Publisher)

"A lot of Humor and Irony, as well as a large amount of Mystery ... [If] you like cowboys and comedy, this is a book for you."
(Christian Price, US Daily Review)

"*Rattlesnakes, Ghosts, and Murderers* is the first novel of a series from Len Francis Monahan, focusing on a wild western setting that presents many curious adventures of the people there, drawing strongly on humor throughout. Exciting and engaging, *Rattlesnakes, Ghosts, and Murderers* is a strong pick for fans of the Old West; recommended."
(Midwest Book Review)

"Funny ... laughing out loud...."
(IndieReader)

"Monahan's quirky characters provide many entertaining moments ... historical events are also referenced in a light-hearted way ... But there are also very tender moments. ...

"Monahan captures the vernacular speaking style of the time, lending an authenticity to the narrative. ... The story is simple and straightforward but engaging throughout, primarily because the characters are so likable.

"Monahan creates much intrigue – and fun – and will have readers looking forward to spending more time with the characters in the next installment, *Volume 2: The Curse Continues.*"
(Maria Siano, Foreward Review)

Excerpts from Articles & Interviews

Native Toledoan Chronicles the American West in New Book (Newspaper Article)

"For many writers, the journey toward a finished novel is often long, laborious and unpredictable. Toledo native Len Francis Monahan's path ... eventually led him into the American West ... where Monahan found the inspiration for his current literary endeavor.

"'One evening, as I sat on a friend's 2,000-acre ranch and watched lights belonging to the Mexican drug cartel vehicles moving up and down the mountain roads, the phrase "Rattlesnakes, Ghosts and Murderers" sprang to mind,' Monahan said. 'At that moment, I realized what a marvelous title it was. This is how [the series] came into being.'"

(Jay Hathaway, Toledo Free Press)

A Dead Ranch Hand, a Silver Picture Frame and a Curse (Radio Program)

"When I first started reading the first ten pages...the first paragraph...I thought, 'This is kind of...odd diction...and maybe a little bit of strange vocabulary.' It took me just a few seconds before I realized – Oh my gosh! – he's speaking to me in a voice of the 1890s...on a cattle ranch. And I thought, 'How cool is this!' You've really captured it!"

(Bill Thompson, The Bookcast (Washington, DC)

Print Interview

Interviewer: *Rattlesnakes, Ghosts and Murderers* is an unusual title. Whatever possessed you to write this book?

Len: "Possessed" is a good word. When people ask why I wrote this book, I tell them that I used to be happily employed in an insane asylum but that, on one particular day, I forgot to wear my white uniform to work. Not knowing who I was, a sadistic guard ordered me to get in the chow line with the rest of the "inmates" – so I did. And I've been standing in this same line ever since. Hence, my inspiration for all my writing.

(Thriller Ink)

Excerpts from Articles & Interviews

Print Interview

Interviewer: How would you define the term "Western" and what does it mean to you?

Len: It's a man being able to walk into a saloon, roll a cigarette and say to some stinkered-up yahoo, "You heard the little lady, partner. Git yer dirty hands off her!"

Interviewer: If you could go back in time and meet one famous person in the Old West, who would it be and why?

Len: My Great Grandfather knew Jessie James, so maybe I'd like to go back and have my old Grandpa introduce me to him. I suppose I shouldn't have picked an outlaw but there it is.

Interviewer: What draws you to writing Westerns?

Len: People of the Old West were free because they were deeply determined to keep it that way. That period in our history is more relevant than ever, especially in light of how our freedoms are now being so severely threatened by advancing technologies, legalized privacy-invasions and a federal government thoroughly mismanaged by a cabal of pointy-heads in Washington, D.C.

(The Western Online)

Personal Note to the Reader

Dearest Bookworm,

Each night, pen in hand and lost in story-fever, I experienced a dash of a time scribing the events of this novel. That is why I'm sure you're going to enjoy the entire *Rattlesnakes, Ghosts and Murderers* Western Adventure Series. All that said, prepare to whoop it up in one of Heaven's rowdier Imagination-Saloons and accept my sincerest thanks for entering this world.

Yours through the Eyes of Providence,

Len Francis Monahan

RATTLESNAKES, GHOSTS AND MURDERERS

VOLUME 1:
McKenna and Barnett

A Western Tale of Adventure

by

LEN FRANCIS MONAHAN

Author accepts correspondence through:

Greta Fox
PO Box 571
California 93614
USA

GF@Greta-Fox.com

Ordering Information:

ISBN: 0615681654
ISBN-13: 9780615681658
LCCN: 2012911535

C O N T E N T S

D E D I C A T I O N

I originally considered dedicating *Rattlesnakes, Ghosts and Murderers* to my eternally ideational, cute-as-a-dumpling Inner-Muse. But after a little consideration and some very judicious counseling, I was persuaded that such a move could give the wholly false impression that I had been involved in some kind of inter-dimensional agape-triangle. I'm sure you can see the legal problems that might entail.

Accordingly, I have decided to dedicate this fictional work to the following folks:

Elaine A. Monahan (my Wife)
Leonard F. Monahan Sr. (my Father)
Theresa M. Monahan (my Mother)
Kathy Gillen (my Sister)
Musette Contemplatia Aircastle (my Typist)

Len Francis Monahan

P R O L O G U E

Life has a way of twisting and turning in on itself, like the rattler in the dry, August grass blinded by its own shedding skin and ready to strike at anything that moves.

What we do, and what was done before us, kindle far-reaching and generally hidden consequences. We are in nature, and nature is in us. The universal source of our lineage is inescapable. And so, the beginning of this story, as far as we are concerned, originated on a ranch in America's Old West and continued on for over 100 years into our own age.

1

1896: THE UNJUST REWARD

Barnett. had worked for Mr. McKenna for just over ten years. Mr. McKenna has a big ranch, thousands and thousands of acres: the largest spread in the entire county. Though, for the past couple of years, Mr. McKenna has been acting sort of strange, more demanding and kind of crazy-like. And sometimes he would make us cowboys do crazy work that didn't make no sense either; like the time he had me – Ole Smoke – use good branding time to skedaddle into town for a bunch of roses, only to have Mr. McKenna rip those flowers up right in front of my – Ole Smoke's – eyes. Or the time he sat by that puddle of shit-mud water next to the barn, just looking at his reflection and making hand gestures. We all thought he was sort of feeling down, with his wife leaving him and all. They used to have some bang-up fights when she was there. Sometimes we'd hear Mrs. McKenna screaming at Mr. McKenna and throwing things. A couple times after a fight, Mr. McKenna would stand out in front of the main house and make a huge bonfire. Now I'm not talking no little-bitty campfire either. Those bonfires were doozy large. They was so big, we was all afraid he might set the main house on fire. But he never did. He'd just sit there for hours, sweating and glowing from the heat until the fire died down and he turned to shadows. Then he'd go to bed and no one would see him for days. Even if he was bughouse mad, he was still the boss – so we all ignored it. Anyways, he acted normal most of the time.

Now for some reason, B.C. (Bald Curley) who is Mr. McKenna's top man and holds the boss' ear more than anybody, took a real disliking to Barnett. He always used to give Barnett the crappiest jobs and bad mouth Barnett whenever he got the chance. And that didn't make no sense to me either because Barnett was a real straight-shooter. He was honest. And he wouldn't lie nor steal nor nothing. And he wouldn't hardly drink nor did he smoke too awful much either. So why B.C. started in on Barnett was always a mystery to me. But Barnett wasn't the kind to let stuff go: He'd tell you right to your face what he thought of you – and maybe that's what got B.C. going in the first place. Then one day it all came to a head: Barnett stormed into the chow house and confronted B.C. He wanted to know if it was true what B.C. was saying about him behind his back, and he threatened to whup B.C.'s ass right then and there in front of everybody. Well, you could see B.C. was scared. Barnett was no little guy and he could've mopped the floor with B.C. So B.C. backed down. He said he never said no such things about Barnett and that he never would. But, of course, we all knew B.C. was lying – and B.C. knew we all knew – because we'd all heard him say that stuff. But here he was quaking in his boots and denying he'd ever said anything bad about Barnett. After it was over, B.C. got real quiet and left the room. It was one of the most humiliating things I'd ever seen. Looking back, I guess this may be what caused it all.

One day Mr. McKenna called Barnett in for a little talk. Barnett had been in Mr. McKenna's office before, and those were always friendly times. Mr. McKenna used to ask Barnett to sit with him and have a drink or two, and they'd talk about the ranch and how things were going. Barnett always liked Mr. McKenna. But this time, when Barnett came in the room, Mr. McKenna told him to keep standing. There was no drinking nor friendly talk this time around. Mr. McKenna simply wanted to know where "it" was. When Barnett asked Mr. McKenna what he meant by "it," Mr. McKenna got real antsy and told Barnett to quit playing "bullshit poker." Barnett said he didn't know what Mr. McKenna was talking about, and

Mr. McKenna asked Barnett for his storehouse key. At that moment, Barnett knew he was fired.

Barnett told Mr. McKenna he didn't have his key on him, and Mr. McKenna told him to go fetch "it" and the key before gathering up his stuff and clearing out. Somehow, Barnett remained calm. He didn't curse, and he didn't press the matter neither. He just turned and walked away, not slamming the door on the way out nor nothing. But he didn't return. And in the morning, all the fellas knew he was gone.

Mr. McKenna was agitated for days afterwards. Nobody knew what was eating him exactly, but he was crazier than usual. He'd yell and throw rocks at steers, and this was something he'd never done before. Then one night, someone said Barnett was at the gate. Mr. McKenna sent B.C. out to handle it. When B.C. got to the big, iron, Mexicali gate, he wouldn't unlock it. He just stared out through the gate at Barnett and asked for the key. But Barnett only smiled and held the key up for B.C. to see, as much to say, "Come out and get it if you want it so bad." But B.C. was no fool.

"I want to see Mr. McKenna," Barnett told him.

"Mr. McKenna's busy and can't be bothered."

"Well, he's going to have to be bothered if he wants to get this key back."

"I said no. Are you stupid or something? Just give me the damn key and get off this property before I come out there and throw you off."

Barnett laughed and said, "You just tell Mr. McKenna I'll be here tomorrow night at this same time. I want to talk to him by himself. And if he's not happy with what I got to say, I'll give him his key and you'll never see me again." Then Barnett walked away, got on his horse and rode off.

"You'd better not come back, you stupid son of a bitch, if you know what's good for ya!" B.C. shouted out to Barnett.

But the next night, around the same time, one of the boys got word to B.C. that Barnett was at the gate. B.C. told the fella to tell Barnett he'd be right there but to wait for him because first he'd have to check with Mr. McKenna. After that fella left, I saw B.C. sit there thinking for about ten minutes before going to the main house.

Now, usually, I ain't all that nosy. But since I knew somebody could get killed, I stood outside Mr. McKenna's office window and listened.

"Barnett's back," B.C. went and told Mr. McKenna.

"Did he bring the key and the silver picture frame with him?"

"I don't know, Mr. McKenna. It's hard to tell with a sneaky son of a bitch like Barnett."

Yep, that's what B.C. called Barnett – a "sneaky son of a bitch."

"Well, you go talk to him, and if he's willing to give me my silver picture frame back, you tell him I'll just forget the whole thing. You tell him I'm not mad at him anymore, and that I understand. It's just a mistake, and everybody makes 'em. You tell him that. Barnett's a good worker, and rugged cattlemen like him are hard to find. All the hands like him, and he really knows his stuff. You tell him I'll make him foreman if he comes back. You tell him that."

B.C. was amazed. How could Barnett become foreman? That was B.C.'s job. "Okay, Mr. McKenna, I'll tell him. But don't be surprised if he turns you down. He's not trustworthy, Mr. McKenna. And once a thief, always a thief."

I – Ole Smoke – noticed that B.C. was taking his good, old time getting to the front gate. B.C. was thinking this one out good and hard.

"Alright, Barnett, Mr. McKenna will see you," B.C. told Barnett. "But first he wants that three hundred dollars back you took from his house."

"So that's what this is all about? He thinks I stole money from him! I never took no three hundred dollars. You get Mr. McKenna right now and tell him I want to talk to him face-to-face."

"Okay, Barnett, I'll go get him, but first things first. He said he wants that three hundred before he says a word to you. And if you don't give it back, he's gonna have you thrown right into jail."

Yep, that's what B.C. told Barnett, and them's his exact words – "thrown right into jail" he told him.

By now, Barnett was steaming. Barnett was a good and honest man and probably never, in his entire life, had anyone ever accused him of stealing. And now, here he was, being called a low-down thief by B.C. Barnett was madder than he'd probably ever been before. And that's when his fiddle-faddle-talking accuser, Mr. McKenna, came walking towards him, shotgun in hand.

"Open the gate, B.C. I want to see this slinky-footed sharpy eye-to-eye."

B.C. did as Mr. McKenna ordered and opened the gate, and Barnett immediately walked forward. When he did, Mr. McKenna raised his shotgun and pointed it right at Barnett.

"You got it with you?" Mr. McKenna asked.

"No, I don't have it. You really are crazy. How could you ever think I'd steal three hundred dollars from you?"

"Three hundred dollars! You stole money too? What about my silver picture frame?"

"What silver picture frame?"

"Don't lie to me, Barnett. You give me my three hundred dollars and that silver picture frame – or I'm going to fill you full of lead hornets!"

"Are you insane? I don't know anything about no silver picture frame? And I never took no three hundred dollars neither."

"Yes, you did. Or how else would you have known about the three hundred dollars? I didn't even know about the three hundred dollars myself until right this very second. So, if you already knew about it, you must have taken it. Guilt got the best of you, didn't it, Barnett? It made you blurt out your crime. Now you give me my money, you no-good stealer, and my silver picture frame too!"

When Barnett apprehended that he had fallen into a trap, he looked squarely at B.C. and yelled, "Why you rotten…!" And as he charged, B.C. ran and squealed for Mr. McKenna's help. A shot rang out.

Next thing I knew, Barnett was dead.

Following day, Mr. McKenna made us take Barnett's body into town. At first, we told folks he was accidentally stuck through by an oak branch; and there was to be a Bible-reading in the far section of the bone orchard. After we gave him his proper lowering, Mrs. McKenna heard tell of what happened and came back home to look after her husband. And, when she saw how peculiar bad Mr. McKenna had gotten, she stayed at the ranch permanent.

It don't seem right now but, at that time, no one wanted to tell the truth about what really happened that night. Sure as heck, none of us who saw the deed wanted to talk about it. To make things worse, on the night of the shooting, Mr. McKenna found the silver picture frame under a pile of old rags in his closet. That must have made Mr. McKenna feel terrible guilty because, before they put the body into the ground, he made sure the box was opened and that silver picture frame was placed on Barnett's chest.

(This "writ-by-hand" entry was found in Ole Smoke's ten-page diary and dated sometime in 1896. It was edited, punctuated and made coherently readable by present day author, Len Francis Monahan.)

2

1898: THE FREEING OF BARNETT'S GHOST

It's been almost a year since Mr. McKenna shot himself. Truth be told, I – Ole Smoke – thought he'd of done it sooner.

But everyone, including myself – Ole Smoke – noticed how much better Mr. McKenna was acting since he took the "holy Word" and got himself baptized. Sober, Mr. McKenna was different than anyone had ever seen before. Even his wife of thirty-seven years hardly recognized him. He smiled a lot and completely quit doing crazy things. He worked hard every day and never had a foul word for nobody. He even fired B.C. and took over management of the ranch himself. So it surprised us all when we heard the shot and found him dead that morning.

There he lay, face down on poop-dirty straw by the horse barn, and that part didn't make no sense to nobody. Mr. McKenna had changed so much for the good that even his wife cried when she saw the body. It was a real good waste of cowboy manhood who had been led to the One True Light by the loving Hand of our most holy Lord.

But even before he gunned himself down, people knew about Barnett's shooting and some folks started saying that Mr. McKenna was maybe feeling Christ-love guilty about what he'd done to Barnett – killing him for no good reason and burying him with that silver picture frame and all. It sure took up a lot of conversation in the saloon, and some of those stinkered-up yahoos started speculating on how valuable that silver picture frame really was. One boozed-up spooney went to blabbering on about how the frame was probably encrusted with rare jewels and worth hundreds and thousands of dollars. And it was just that kind of talk what put the idea into Boo and Jeever's whiskey-soaked heads to go out and dig up the body.

Now Boo and Jeever wasn't nothing but a couple of no-goods who spent all their time drinking and boozing it up with the backroom gals – that is, when they had the money, which, for them, was getting harder by the day to come by. And since those two had gotten themselves pretty much down to nothing – and hearing all that talk about that jewel-encrusted silver picture frame and all – they come up with the idea to dig up bodies for trinkets and scuds – starting with the body of Barnett.

So this one day, I – Ole Smoke – saw Boo and Jeever come into town all dirty and sweaty and walk into the saloon and ask for some drinks. They had some fancy, dress-up jewelry pinned to their coats and was wearing different shoes and coats, so it didn't seem right. But when Big Irish, the bartender, saw that silver picture frame they was trying to swap, he knew right away what they'd done. So Big Irish went and got Sheriff Hagger who made Boo and Jeever empty their pockets, out of which he found contained some fancy buttons and finger rings and such.

Boo cried and said Jeever made him go and do it. And Jeever called Boo a damn, dirty liar and said he didn't do nothing at all but had only met Boo on the road that day when Boo gave him the stuff. Neither Boo nor Jeever had no good explanation for all the mud stains that was on their clothes. And, since everybody knew they wasn't nothing but a couple of no-good, lying, drunken sons a' bitches, people started shouting that we should hang them. So we did. And it was "good and right too," Sheriff Hagger told us before handing them over to be lynched.

Old Lady Maybell, the dear, saintly schoolmarm, was so pisspot mad at Boo and Jeever for stealing buttons off her dead husband's body, that she screamed and cussed and kicked Boo square in the balls before the crowd drug him away. And, angry and bloodthirsty as we all was, everybody just had to laugh. It was kind of funny watching him squeal and hold his balls thataway – God rest his poor eternally hellbound soul.

And so that's how the silver picture frame got loose once again upon the face of the earth. Where it's gone to now, nobody seems to know. But something around here everybody knows for certain – and that is, along with that silver picture frame, out from the open cemetery ground rose up Barnett's righteously vengeful ghost. And, truth be told, I – Ole Smoke – think that's what made Mr. McKenna up and near blast his head clean off thataway.

(This "writ-by-hand" entry was found in Ole Smoke's ten-page diary and dated sometime in 1898. It was edited, punctuated and made coherently readable by present day author, Len Francis Monahan.)

3

SEPTEMBER 1898:
THE OFFICIAL VISIT

It was damp and windy when Sheriff Hagger rode out of town that morning in the taxpayer-owned, high-wheeled vehicle made by the Kenosha, Wisconsin-based Bain Wagon Co. This magisterial conveyance was essentially a spring-seat placed forward and atop a rectangular wooden box on wheels. As he drove the farm wagon up to Mrs. McKenna's ranch, he noticed how deserted the place seemed. Mr. McKenna had only been dead a year or so, and already things looked neglected. The sheriff rode up to the front of the main house. After climbing down from the wagon, he hobbled his horse's forefeet with a torn strip of gunnysack to prevent the creature from wandering far then walked to the door.

He could hear someone moving around inside but no one answered his knockings. Out of the corner of his eye, he caught a slight movement in one of the curtains. Then he noticed Mrs. McKenna peeking cautiously out at him.

"Afternoon, Mrs. McKenna. Sheriff Hagger here. Mind if I come in a spell."

She moved away from the window, and a great deal of time seemed to pass. "Mrs. McKenna," the sheriff said, knocking, "It's me Sheriff Hagger. I come to see how you're doin'."

The door opened a crack and a woman's eye peered out. "I'm doin' fine. What you want?"

"I just come to see ya is all. Folks in town is worried 'bout ya bein' out here all by your lonesome. Mind if I come in?"

"I'm doin' fine."

"Yeah, I know you're doin' fine. But ya mind if I come in? It's been a real hard ride out here, me with my bad back n'all. I thought maybe ya'd let me sit a spell 'n visit."

"I don't want no man to be visitin' me, 'specially no sheriff. You just go on and tell everybody I'm doin' well."

"No, please, Mrs. McKenna. I just wanna talk. It's official business."

"What kind'a official business could you have with me? If it's about what happened here with my crazy, old man, I don't want to talk about it."

"Please, Mrs. McKenna, let me in. I won't take up too awful much'a your time 'n, anyway, it's official business."

Mrs. McKenna opened the door and walked toward the kitchen. Sheriff Hagger followed.

"I was hopin' ya'd be a lot friendlier. Bein' you're so alone out here on this big ole place n'all."

"What's this official business you want to talk to me about?"

"You mind if I sit down, ma'am? My back's been hurtin' me somethin' terrible."

"Sore back from ridin'; you'd think you'd want to stand a piece."

They stared at each other.

"No, go ahead and sit. You want something to drink?"

"That's mighty nice'a ya," he said, taking a seat at the kitchen table. "What kind'a whiskey ya got?"

"I ain't got no kind'a whiskey for no sore-back sheriff. I was talkin' about coffee."

"Yes please; I'd love some coffee, ma'am; thanks."

Mrs. McKenna walked to the stove and lit it.

"It's mighty cozy-nice in here. Real clean 'n homey. Mr. McKenna was a lucky man to get a woman like yourself. Ever'body says so."

"Everybody? So folks been talkin' about me, have they? Since when?"

"Not long, just recent within the last year or so. But nobody ain't said nothin' 'bout you 'fore your husband gone 'n shot himself. That was a real shame, Mrs. McKenna. Now why'd ya think he'd wanna go 'n do a thing like that?"

"How would I know? I was just his wife. Why don't you ask some of his fair-weather saloon buddies?"

"But Mr. McKenna quit drinkin' 'fore he died; ever'body knows that. 'N when he took up with the Lord, nobody seen him in the saloon no more."

"Yeah, I s'pose that's true enough. Sorry, I'm still a little bitter. Deep down, Henry was a good man of sorts. He really tried, 'specially toward the end." Her eyes started to well up.

"Yeah, we all said Mr. McKenna was a good man. But that was your doin'. Without you he'da been nothin'; ever'body says that."

Mrs. McKenna instantly hardened. "There you go again, sayin' everybody's been talkin' about me. What else has everybody been sayin'?"

"No, nobody's been sayin' nothin' 'bout ya, Mrs. McKenna. Not 'cept for when Henry kilt himself; that's the only time I ever heard anythin', 'n most'a that was good."

"Don't lie to me, Sheriff. I know what folks been sayin'. They're sayin' I was to blame; that I was the one that drove Henry crazy. They're sayin' it was me who made him take to drinkin' and go accusin' Barnett of stealin' that silver...." She abruptly stopped. "I got to check the coffee."

"No, nobody's sayin' anythin' like that, ma'am. You ain't hardly bein' blamed for nothin' Mr. McKenna went 'n done. Most'a 'ems been sayin' ya was good for him 'n that he was just naturally touched in the head. Mr. McKenna done a lot'a crazy things, 'n there ain't nobody who can hold you responsible for that."

"Still cold."

"Who? You're cold, ma'am?"

"No, the coffee. It's still cold."

"That's just fine with me. I always liked my coffee cold. Ain't a day goes by I don't say, 'Boy, I sure could go for a drink'a some'a that there cold coffee.' Just give it to me cold, ma'am. I like it that way."

Mrs. McKenna picked up a small, wooden bowl from the counter and poured coffee into it. "Ain't got no cups, Sheriff. You'll have to drink from a bowl."

"That's fine. I like drinkin' cold coffee out'a bowls. Wouldn't have it no other way."

Mrs. McKenna wondered why Hagger was being so overly ingratiating.

"Bedeviled, crazy husband of mine broke most all our cups and saucers and everything else that was expensive and hard to get. I don't miss that handsome lunatic no more. You want sugar with this? If so, I ain't got none."

"No, it's fine without sugar. I only put sugar in my coffee on special occasions; holidays 'n such. Even then, I only do it out'a politeness."

"Good because I ain't got none, and this ain't no holiday," she said, placing the bowl of cold, unsweetened coffee before him.

"Ahhhhh, yes!" he said before lifting the bowl to his lips then taking a loud slurp. "Nothin' like a good, cold, unsweetened, bowl'a coffee to do a man good!"

"So how's your back?"

"Still hurts like the dickens, ma'am. But your coffee's good for what ails it!"

Helen McKenna sat on the kitchen chair beside the sheriff. "So what do you want to see me about that's so official."

"Oh, nothin' really. I just wanted to see how ya was gettin' on."

"So then...it ain't official."

"No, no, it's official sure enough. Seein' how people's doin's a big official part'a my job."

She stared at him, and this made him feel slightly uncomfortable.

"So how ya been doin' out here, ma'am? You 'n the ranch gettin' along okay?"

"'Cept for an occasional tiff, we couldn't be better."

"But I didn't see no ranch hands out here. 'N the gate's been left unlocked 'n opened. Any ole hombre could'a just rode in."

"Any ole hombre just did. Now, what is it you want to talk to me about, Sheriff? I'm kind'a short on time."

"Mrs. McKenna...I mean, Helen...I...."

She looked increasingly wary.

"Ya 'member how when we was kids back at school, you 'n me? We always got along real swell, didn't we? We was just like family, you 'n me was."

"Sure, I remember school, but why should you? You weren't there 'cept for the first grade. Second grade, your daddy pulled you out; wasn't long after that you ran away from home. Still wearin' those long pigtails, I see."

"Yes, ma'am. I braid my hair 'cause I'm proud part-Injun."

"You always did show a talent for hair braidin'. Guess that's why I never figured you for bein' no sheriff. I always thought you'd end up rollin' cigarettes for a livin' or go to workin' on the railroad alongside the coolies."

"Yeah, I know I wasn't in school too awful much but that's not my point. 'N that don't matter much nohow. People can still know each other 'n be like family 'n not spend too awful much time together."

"So what is your point, Sheriff?"

"My point is that...that...just look at yourself, Mrs. McKenna...you stayin' out here all lonesome-like 'n whilin' away your valuable lifetime...you, a perfectly good, healthy, widow woman like yourself. No, you should be out in the world doin' somethin' 'n bein' with folks. This livin' alone way out here 'n not havin' no one to talk to, it's not good. You should be out 'n about. You should go into town once't in a while 'n see some people. That's all I'm sayin'. I sure don't mean no harm by talkin' to ya this way. I just wanna help is all."

Mrs. McKenna was genuinely moved by the sheriff's kind words. "Thank you, Sheriff Hagger. Yes, it has been difficult for me, bein' out here alone since poor Henry died. And the way he died and all...it's been," her eyes glistened with emotion, "more tryin' than a body can express...more tryin' than most folks imagine even."

Sheriff Hagger patted her hand. "There, there, ma'am, I know. I know it's been tough since Mr. McKenna gone 'n blowed his brains out."

She began to softly weep. "Henry going all crazy like that, and strangers gossipin' lies about us...it's been terrible. And me out here with no one to talk to...I feel so guilty about Henry's death."

"Now, now," he said patting her hand sympathetically.

"You know I left Henry for a short spell. He was actin' so crazy and all, I couldn't put up with it. I just didn't understand."

"Now, don't blame yourself. It wasn't your fault."

"Thank you, Sheriff. I can't tell you how much your hearty words mean to me. Guess maybe we really are like family after all. And to think, all these years, I been misjudgin' you. Thank you for listenin', Sheriff Hagger. You're the first person I been able to tell how I truly feel."

"There, there, Helen," he said, still patting her hand. "May I call ya 'Helen,' Helen?"

"Everybody's talkin' now that I'm to blame. But I tried. Lord knows I tried."

"There, there, Helen."

"And Henry tried too. He wasn't at fault for his craziness. It came down from his family; that whole bunch was a little derailed. So what could poor Henry do about it? That's why he drank so much. He really tried, Sheriff, 'specially at the last." Mrs. McKenna wept and fell forward slightly, prompting Sheriff Hagger to pull her to his chest.

"There, there, Helen dear. It's good for folks to cry when somethin' bad like that happens. But nobody's ever gonna blame you again, 'specially not with me around they better not. 'Cause you 'n me, we was always like family, all that time we spent together in the first 'n part'a the second grade. Times like that makes a person feel real close. Kind'a lovey-like even."

"He couldn't help himself, Sheriff! Henry couldn't help it!" she wailed.

"No, he sure couldn't. He was bughouse crazy; ever'body knows that. But things'll be different for ya now, dearie. I'll get all them hired hands workin' real hard like they's s'posed to be workin'. Won't be no unlocked gate when I'm in charge. I'll run it better'n Henry ever could."

But Mrs. McKenna was much too preoccupied with grief to directly apprehend what the sheriff had just said.

"Henry was a good man, Sheriff. People simply don't know how good he really was."

"Oh yeah, he was good enough alright. 'N it's alright with me if ya don't forget him for a while. We can even hire somebody to draw a picture'a him from memory 'n keep it right up there on the kitchen shelf, right there next to the pantry to remind us what a good provider that loon Henry was."

She looked up at him. "Huh?"

"I was just sayin' that it ain't necessary for you to go forgettin' your Henry right away just 'cause ya got me now. No, we'll keep Henry's picture up there three – no, make it six – months 'fore takin' it down 'n gettin' down to brass tacks'a bein' full-time married folks."

"Married? What the devil are you talkin' about?"

He pulled her closer to him. "I'm talkin' 'bout us, Helen love. You n' me. Oh I was hopin' ya'd take me but never in my wildest dream I'd think it'd happen this fast. I love ya, Helen. I loved ya since we was kids in the first grade."

"Love me? I don't even hardly remember you 'cept for those ridiculous pigtails and ugly, baggy britches you used to wear. They made you look like the town orphan. Are you crazy? Let me go, you idiot!" She pushed him away.

"No, Helen, I didn't mean to come on so lovey strong. But when you went to huggin' on me like that, I just thought ya wanted me as much as," he embraced her again, "I been wantin' you."

"Wanted you? Me? Let go, you stupid clown, before I grab my skillet and break your head open like an egg."

"But, Helen, I only meant that..."

"'Official business,' my eye! Let me go, lummox!" Then she pushed him with such force that his chair toppled with him in it. When he was on the floor, she jumped up and grabbed the coffee pan.

The sheriff got to his feet.

"You come one step toward me and this coffee goes right in your face!"

"That's okay. It's cold. 'N like I told ya, I kind'a fancy cold coffee," he said with a big stupid grin.

"You pigtailed halfwit," she said, putting down the pan and grabbing the Winchester Model 1887 lever-action shotgun she kept next to the stove. "Maybe you'd like some of this to go with your cold coffee."

The sight of a shotgun pointed at him immediately caused Sheriff Hagger's expression to turn to fear. "No, Helen! Don't you even think 'bout doin' that! Don't you even think 'bout it! I am the law!"

"I got your law right here at the end of this gun barrel, and I will blow you to kingdom come if you so much as cross your eyes. No jury in the world would convict me. You come to my home and try manhandlin' your way into my heart with some flimsy excuse about 'official business.' I ought to shoot you where you stand."

"No, Helen dear! Don't! Please! I didn't come out here to do no harm! I did come out here on official business, honest!"

"And what 'official business' might that be?"

"Uhhh...it's uh. Oh yeah! It's right here in my pocket. I came out here to give you somethin' that belongs to ya," he said with a foolish grin.

"I'm listenin'."

Sheriff Hagger reached into his coat pocket.

"Easy, Sheriff, or I'll blast that dullard look right off your face."

"No, Helen, don't you go doin nothin' like that! I'm tellin' ya the truth. It's right here! Here it is here, ma'am! I'm handin' it to ya now! Here! Take it! It's yours," he said reaching out his hand.

Mrs. McKenna couldn't quite make out what the sheriff was offering her. "What is that thing?"

"It's the picture frame."

"What picture frame?"

"The silver one. The one Barnett was buried with after your crazy husband kilt him."

Helen McKenna's mouth dropped open and the 12-gauge smoothbore slumped to her side. "My silver picture frame? But...that's impossible. Barnett was buried with that thing. How could you have it?"

"Well, it's kind'a a funny story. You know those two, ole drunks Boo 'n Jeever? Well, them two rascals took to robbin' graves 'n they got this when they dug up Barnett's body? Funny how things work out, ain't it? Lucky for you too, huh? 'Cause'a them two, worthless, ole spittoons, you got your valuable silver picture frame back. Can't get no luckier'n this, can it, Helen dear?"

"Oh my God!" Mrs. McKenna said with astonishment. "That is my silver picture frame!"

"Pretty lucky for you, huh? Here, take it. It's legally yours. Pretty lucky, huh?"

"Lucky! Are you out of your mind? My husband shot poor Barnett down in cold blood because of that picture frame. Then he killed himself out of remorse! No, that silver picture frame is the cause of all my troubles! It's evil! Get it out of here!"

"I don't understand what you're sayin', Helen. It's a beautiful, expensive work'a art you got here. Are you sayin' ya don't want it? I don't see how a thing this valuable could be the cause'a all your troubles. If you turn this down, you're nuts as your poor ole Henry. It's valuable, Helen love! This thing's pure silver!"

"Get out of my house, you fool!" She raised the Browning-designed shotgun and aimed it square at Sheriff Hagger's chest. "If you don't hightail from my house and take that devil picture frame with you, I'm going to....!"

"Alright. Alright, I'm goin'," he said, backing toward the door. "But you just take it easy with that gun, ma'am, or somebody real nice is liable to get hurt."

"No, that somebody is liable to get more than hurt. You don't move out of here – and fast – I'm going to paint your backside with birdshot!"

"Noooo! Don't shoot!" he cried, turning and running out the door. "All I ever wanted to do was marry ya 'n manage the ranch! What's wrong with you, woman?"

"Get out, you baggy pants dummy! And I'll show you what's wrong with me! Let's see how your sore back feels now!" She opened the breech block to discover the 5-round, tubular magazine was empty. "Damnation! Of all the times!" Helen rushed to the kitchen shelf where she kept the number-9 shot, loaded a shell inside the receiver and pressed down the guides, inserting the shell into the loading tube. She loaded in another shell, uncocked the hammer as a matter of habit, and hurried to the front door.

By this time, Sheriff Hagger had unhobbled his horse, turned it around, and was in the process of boarding the wagon when Helen, having reached a suitable position at the porch's edge, levered a cartridge into the barrel and fired an unsettling blast into the air.

"Neeeeeeiigh!" the alarmed horse sounded, rearing up on its hind legs and jarring the wagon forward.

"Ahheeeeeeeee!" the sheriff cried out, falling hard to the ground.

"How's your back feel now, Sheriff Pigtail?" Mrs. McKenna called out.

"My back! Ooowww, wait for me, horse!" he shouted to the runaway equine. "Waaaait, you stupid animal!"

But the startled horse didn't halt and, instead, headed toward the gate.

Helen McKenna, an expert with that shotgun, waited for the sheriff to get within non-lethal range before taking her next shot.

Some thirty yards before reaching the front gate, the horse came to a standstill and obediently waited for the loudly beckoning sheriff to catch up.

"You stupid horse! You ain't s'posed to be runnin' off on me like that! You're s'posed to wait! You stupid....!"

Confused by the sheriff's tone of voice, the horse began moving the wagon forward.

"Wait a minute now, you stupid horse! You're s'posed to wait for me, I said!" Concerned that he might not be able to catch up with the horse, Sheriff Hagger made an all-out effort to climb into the back of the departing wagon.

Seeing the sheriff hanging halfway in and halfway out of the moving wagon with his backside opportunistically exposed, Helen stepped off the porch and walked several steps out to adjust for range.

"Oh sweet Jesus! There it is!" she said before squeezing the trigger.

A loud shot was heard, followed by a man's piercing shriek and the terrified scream of a reared up horse.

"Ooooww! I'm wounded! My ass! I been hit!" the sheriff exclaimed as the horse sped madly away. "Ahheeeeeeeee!

My ass! I'm bleedin'! Ahhhhhhhhhhhh! Aheeeeeeee!"
he screeched out while holding on for dear life.

"You come back anytime, Sheriff, when you got more
official business," Mrs. McKenna called out. And this
was the first time Helen McKenna had honestly laughed
since before her husband's death.

4

THE GIFT OF HEALING

It was about an hour before sunset, and Sheriff Hagger had been unable to hang halfway in and halfway out of the moving vehicle for anywhere near the eleven and one-quarter miles stretch back to town. Mrs. McKenna's expert markswomanship had left the horse entirely unhurt, allowing only the aft of the wagon and Sheriff Hagger's exposed backside to absorb the spreading blast of birdshot. Sheriff Hagger's thick coat had absorbed some of the pellets avoiding any effect to his upper body whatsoever. But the lawman's hind end was another matter altogether. And now, with the wagon turned over and the horse safely escaped, the longhaired sheriff with one braid untidily undone lay on his side on the cold, rocky ground, in too much pain to build a fire or even seek a natural shelter of any kind.

"The woman is a lunatic," he said to himself. "I can't believe I ever wanted to be married to that ungrateful little.... No wonder McKenna kilt himself. He's better off dead, that's for sure. Ooooh, my butt hurts! How am I ever gonna explain this? Me, bein' shot on official business 'n by a woman, no less. Ooooh-hoo-hoo!"

The sheriff remained awake and in pain the entire night. Around 3 AM, he decided to check his wound again so he pulled down his trousers and tried to look over his shoulder at his rear. He couldn't see anything.

"It don't feel like it's bleedin' no more," he said, gingerly touching his rear end then examining his hands for signs of blood. "'N it sure don't look like blood in this light. That's a good sign. I think this air is doin' me some good. It's healin' me. I should try to get more air on my butt."

While still on his side, the sheriff raised his bare butt slightly off the ground so as to catch a breeze.

"Ain't good enough; I need a powerful strong wind. Wind on the butt'll do more good for me'n an onion poultice."

Observing that a bounteous wind was coming from the west, Sheriff Hagger forced himself up on his bare knees and painfully crawled across the rocky ground to a more open area. Once at his new location, the sheriff remained on all fours, spread his legs wide and stuck his bare butt out and low to the ground.

"Oooo yeah! That's feels soooo good! Wind soooo good! God's good wind! Thank You, God, for Your wonderful, healing wind! You are such a good God, 'n I love Ya so much. Good God! You're a good, heavenly, wind-healin' Gaaw....!"

That's when he heard it: the familiar but unwelcome rattling sound.

"What the....? No, please, God! Don't let that be no rattler! Please, God, not a rattler! Not a rattler pu-lee...." The serpent struck. "EEEEEEEEEAAASE!"

Sheriff Hagger jumped up, looked between his legs and saw a 4-foot long rattlesnake hanging from his testicles.

"Noooooo, I been bit! I been bit, damn it! Let go my balls, you rotten snake! Let go, I say! Ahheeeeeeeee! Ahheeeeeeeee! Ahheeeeeeeee!"

The poor sheriff danced and screamed and wriggled and gyrated until, at last, and entirely of its own volition, the snake let loose and crawled away. At wit's end and unable to tolerate any more pain, Sheriff Hagger fell forward and passed out upon a patch of sandy ground. Night turned to day, and the sheriff never moved from his position.

Ten hours passed before Sheriff Hagger awakened to see two figures standing before him. He rubbed his eyes and focused: An old Mexican with his nine-year-old grandson and burro were all looking down on him.

"Hello. I mean, Joe-la. I am the sheriff, and I been hurt. I need your help real bad. I was shot by a...ambushed by a gang'a desperados. Do you speak English – I mean Ingullsass?"

"No se acerque demasiado cerca. (Don't get too close.)," the old man told his grandson. "El hombre no lleva puestos pantalones. Él podría ser un hombre blanco loco. (He's not wearing any pants. He might be a crazy white man.)"

"Joe-la, amigez. Do you speak el lingo Ingullsass"

"Yo creo que él está preguntando si nosotros puede hablar Inglés. (I think he's asking us if we speak English.)," the old man said to his grandson. "Él suena a una persona estúpida. (He sounds like a stupid person.)"

"Leen-go Ingullsass? Do you speak el leen-go Ingullsass?"

"Yes, I speak 'el leen-go Ingullsass' quite well. How come you're not wearing any pants?"

"Oh, thank heavens you're literate. I'm Sheriff Hagger, 'n I was ambushed by a gang'a bandits. You know, 'bandit-ohs'?"

"Yes, bandidos. But why did they take off your pants?" Then the old man turned to his grandson, "Carlos, maybe you should walk away. Some things you should not hear."

"No, it's alright. It's nothin' like that," the sheriff said. "I was shot in the ass durin' the battle 'fore I managed to chase them all away. 'N when I pulled down my pants to mend my wounds, a rattler bit me on the nuts."

"Carlos, you go now," the old man said.

Carlos walked out of overhearing distance.

"Oh my God! I must'a been out for hours. How come I ain't dead?"

"Let me see," the old man said, approaching the sheriff and kneeling next to him.

"You a doctor? Do you know any medicine?"

"I am considered the healer of my village. Please, let me see the snake bite."

Sheriff Hagger got on all fours and turned his behind toward the old Mexican. "This is embarrassin'. I'm a sheriff, for Chris' sakes."

"Don't be embarrassed. My name is Doctor Perez, and I have seen everything there is to see." The old man leaned down and closely inspected Sheriff Hagger's butt and testicles.

"Aaackkk!" the old man gagged. "¡Casi me tocó la caca! (I almost touched poop!)"

"What's that mean? Is it bad?"

The old man rose up, holding his hand over his nose and mouth. "¡Mal bastante saber el gusto de vómito! (Bad enough to taste vomit!)"

"Am I gonna die, Doctor Perez? Give it to me straight."

"No, Señor Sheriff, you will live. Two, teeny-little, teeth marks and just a dry bite. You're fine except for having been shot on your behind. You'll be itchy sore for a while but you will survive. Not too bad."

"Thank you, amigez! I wanna pay you for all you did. How much do I owe ya?"

"No, pay is not necessary. Doing good and healing others; that is my life's calling."

"Good, 'cause to be honest with ya; I don't got no actual cash-money on me. The bandit-ohs got it all. But here," he said, reaching into his jacket pocket and pulling out the silver picture frame. "It's a solid silver picture frame. Must be worth lotsa dih-nuh-row. 'N it's all yours."

The old man accepted the frame and examined it. "This is a very nice frame. Carlos, come here, please! I'll give it to my Grandson, if you don't mind. But first, pull up your pants, por favor."

"Oh yeah. Sorry 'bout that, Doctor," the sheriff said, painfully pulling up his trousers.

"Carlos, come here!" the old man called out again and walked away from Sheriff Hagger.

When Carlos reached the place where his grandfather stood, the old man bent down and showed him the silver picture frame. "Carlos, my Grandson, this is for you. It is of pure silver and was given to me in gratitude. Such valuable things given in gratitude can only bring good luck. And I want to give it to you, so that you may know what wonderful treasures life will offer you merely by being of service to others...and...," he moved closer and whispered, "... pretendiendo ser un doctor. ¿Entienda? (...by pretending to be a doctor. Understand?)"

"Si, Grandfather, I think so," Carlos whispered back.

The old man stood board straight and said in an authoritarian voice, "But first, you must make me a promise that you will always study hard and that you will always be very, very good. You must promise me that."

"Te prometo, Abuelo. Siempre voy será bueno, y siempre que te sientas orgulloso de mí. (I promise, Grandfather. I will always be good, and I will always make you proud of me.)" And with this sincerest of promises, Carlos happily accepted the silver picture frame from the hands of his loving grandfather.

But, contrary to the old man's belief, the silver picture frame could never be the bearer of good luck, for it had been christened in a fit of madness with the blood of murder. And so, by having accepted it, the path of Carlos' life had been changed forever.

5

OCTOBER 1898: THE SEARCH
FOR ATONEMENT

It was the early part of October, and a weak cold front blew across the ranch grounds. A mass of air dropped into the San Joaquin Valley and moved the temperature into the high seventies. Such weather is deceiving to newcomers since it often serves to presage changes toward the lower end of the thermometer. But Helen McKenna was familiar with the seasonal temperature shifts and always kept a good supply of wood on hand to ensure her home remained warm throughout the shawl-wearing times.

In the crisp chill of evening, Helen sat at the fireplace and stared into the flames. Memories of her deceased husband seemed to dance along the flickering embers, and she wondered what the future might have been had he not taken his own life. Her mind raced with an unrestricted interplay of emotions: She felt the harmonic loftiness of love; the soundless abyss of sadness; unrestrained resentments; fiery anger; guilt; shame; remorse; despair and, not least of all, an incessant monotone of loneliness. All ebbed and flowed within her according to various degrees of strength, tempo, pitch and amplitude; a symphony of parts that played together to create an overall sense of despondency.

What am I going to do? she thought. *I got no one to take care of me. No one to take care of. All I done with my life is work. And, after all this hard work, what did I end up with? Nothin'. Why did it happen this way? I wanted God to give us children. And if we had children, I wouldn't be alone right now. What did I do to deserve this? I tried to lead a good life. Where did I fail?*

In this latest and most intense bout of mental turmoil, Helen's thoughts of self-condemnation and victimhood caused her to think about the one person most injured by her rabid husband: the gun-downed Barnett. Helen hadn't really known anything about Barnett. She didn't even know his full name. To her, he had been just one more faceless ranch hand. She hadn't paid any attention to how long he'd worked at the ranch and, up until this very moment, had assumed he was another single, detached, roustabout transient who traveled from job to job.

Following Barnett's death, it was all she could do to attend to the management of her still quite insane husband. But now she found herself wondering if Barnett might not actually have had a family somewhere; perhaps, a wife and children who hadn't even learned of his passing. Then and there, Helen McKenna decided to find out if Barnett left family behind and, if so, to try helping out that family in any way possible, in accordance with Christian duty. Helen's mind at once found ease, and she put out the last smoldering embers in the fireplace and went to bed.

That night, Helen slept better than usual; sleeping extraordinarily sound for half the night and spending the remaining waking hours imagining what Barnett's family might be like. Was there a young wife? Were there sons and daughters? What about brothers and sisters and living parents? There were so many questions Helen wanted to have answered.

Five o'clock finally arrived, and Helen McKenna quickly dressed, drank cold coffee from a bowl, then hitched her horse to a buggy in the pre-dawn darkness and drove off down Town Road, the most direct route from the ranch. The town where she was headed was little more than a dirty, four-block length of ram-shackled houses; a general store; a livery and smithy; a bank with a steel-reinforced concrete strongroom safely secured by a Sargent & Greenleaf Time Combination Lock; a jailhouse made of area wood and stone and having heavy, riveted-iron, lunatic-cell doors; one bullet-holed saloon; a brothel; Jingle Bob's Eatery; and, a half-mile away from this community's edge, a building that functioned as both a church and a school. By standards of the urban American East, this town was desolate. But to a ranch denizen like Helen McKenna, it seemed fairly bustling, if not over-populated; a place she could not abide and could hardly wait to leave behind. That is why she hadn't been there in over two years.

The ride to town was uneventful and, when she at last arrived, she drove her buggy up to the livery and waited for a skinny, dirty-faced kid to come up to her. He looked to be about fifteen or sixteen years old.

"I'm leavin' my horse here for a while," Mrs. McKenna told the boy. "Where's the owner?"

"He's in doin' bookwork. I'll put your horse up for ya."

"I'm not going to be that long. Where's the new courthouse?"

"New courthouse? What's that?" the kid asked.

"The place where they keep the town's records – where you try people accused of crimes. They were supposed to build a new one."

"No, they never got around to buildin' it. You want the jail. Everything's still done there. You lookin' for town records or wanna try a fella for bein' low-down, that's the place it's done."

"You're talkin' about that flea-infested jail of Sheriff Hagger's?"

"Yep, that's it just across the street," the kid said, pointing to the location.

"It's been a while but I remember. What's your name, son?

"Name's Colt."

"Short for Colter, no doubt," she observed.

"Yes, but nobody ever calls me that. I just go by Colt."

"Very good, Colt; you take good care of my horse, and I'll be back before too long, I hope."

"Yes, ma'am."

Helen McKenna mentally prepared herself to meet Sheriff Hagger again as she walked across the manure-laden street to the jail. She knocked several times before she heard, "What are you; crazy? Come in, damn you. I ain't gettin' up."

Upon entering the building, she saw a man stretched out on a cot that had been placed in a corner of the room. "I beg your pardon, ma'am. I thought you was someone else."

The man was bandaged around his waist. He moaned as he tried to sit.

"No, please don't get up? You alright? You been shot" she asked with no little concern.

"No, ma'am, I'm alright. Never better. 'Cept for this sore spot where that sneak, dirty donkey gone 'n kicked me. Ooooooo that hurts!" he cried out.

"You want me to get a doctor?"

"No, ma'am, I'm in good shape. Never better," he said managing to sit completely upright. "Couple a days, I'll be good as new. So what can I do for ya, ma'am?"

"Is Sheriff Hagger around here?"

"Your guess is good as anybody's, ma'am. He ain't 'zactly been hisself since he got waylaid by those bandidos a while back."

"Bandidos?"

"Yes, ma'am, 'bout a dozen or so snuck up on him in the middle'a the night, shot him 'n threw him in a snake pit."

"Goodness. Is he alright?"

"Now he is. But he almost died. You know Sheriff Hagger, ma'am?"

"We're somewhat acquainted."

"One'a those dirty banditos popped up from behind a rock 'n shot Sheriff Hagger in the backside. Sheriff took a load'a shot in the hindquarters."

"In the hindquarters, you say?"

"Yes, ma'am. Then one'a the pit rattlers got him in the higher-ups."

"By 'higher-ups' you mean....?"

"Yes, ma'am. Nicked him real good in the manlies."

"In the manlies? Oooh hooo! Goodness me," she said, turning away and bringing a handkerchief to her mouth to avoid being detected laughing. "What an ordeal to go through. Hooo hooo! Poor man!"

"I'm sorry, ma'am. I can see I upset you. You're cryin'."

"No, I'm alright. Really, I'll get over it," she said with a slightly concealed snicker. "But he's alright now, you say?"

"Oh yes, ma'am. That sheriff we got is one tough hombre."

"He must be," she said, keeping her back to him. "Him gettin' nicked in the manlies and all. Hooo hooo! What a tragedy! Terrible!"

"Our Sheriff Hagger's a real outstandin' person 'round these parts."

"Lord, if that ain't the truth."

"'N you know what our brave sheriff done after being shot 'n snake bit 'n left for dead?"

"No, you mean there's more?"

"When those bandidos wasn't 'spectin' it, Sheriff Hagger found the strength to crawl up out'a that snake pit 'n take 'em all by s'prise."

"He s'prised 'em?"

"Yes, 'n he fought those bandidos good 'n strong too, he told us. Most'a 'em wasn't nothin' but cowards who up 'n runned away once they figured they's outmatched. But the six who stayed behind, he whupped hand-to-hand all by his lonesome."

"To think!"

"Yep, 'n if his horse hadn'ta run off, 'n he hadn'ta passed out from the snake poison, he'da captured the whole lot 'n brought 'em in for hangin'. Yep, that Sheriff Hagger's just the kind'a hero every man 'n boy in this town can look up to."

"If ever there was a hero, it's definitely him," she said, smiling into her handkerchief before looking up. "You know, I always knew Sheriff Hagger was brave but I had no idea anyone could be that brave. Tell me, how did our good sheriff ever make it back to town?"

"Some Mexican fella named Perez found him 'n strapped him crosswise to a donkey. Sheriff couldn't sit so that's how he had to be toted in, strapped belly down on that dirty donkey – same one that kicked me, matter'a fact. Wished I'd never bought it."

"So how's he doin'?"

"Well, ma'am, that's the problem. That ordeal seems to have taken the spirit plum out'a him. Truth be known, he's prob'ly over drinkin' in the saloon right now. Saloon sheriffin's 'bout all he gets done nowadays. But you can't really blame him. You want me to go get him for ya?"

"No, let's not bother Sheriff Hagger. He's got enough to do sheriffin' the barroom. Anyway, I'm just here lookin' for information about a certain deceased person: a Mr. Barnett. He got shot a while back."

"Barnett? Oh, yeah, I remember him. That was a couple years back. He's that yahoo who attacked Mr. McKenna with a hot poker 'n got hisself killed. I think he's buried somewheres out near Potter's Field, ain't he? But why would ya wanna know about him?"

"I'm Mrs. McKenna."

"Mrs. McKenna? From the McKenna Ranch! Here, have a seat, Mrs. McKenna. Would you like some coffee; maybe some hooch n' crackers?"

"No, thanks, I'm not hungry. So tell me, what do you know about Barnett? Did he have any family?"

"Barnett? No, he didn't have no livin' kin 'cept that one boy. Boy was maybe thirteen at the time'a shootin'. Barnett used to have a wife named Emma but she died a year or so after the kid was born. The young'un stayed here in town while Barnett worked out at your ranch. Good kid; worked like a dog, that boy did. Ain't too many really knew his old man though. Barnett was the quiet type."

"So whatever happened to the boy?"

"He's taken in 'n boarded for work. That boy'll work day n' night, if ya let him: cleans stables; takes care horses; mends fences; digs ditches. Good worker, that Colt is; just like his old man used to be."

"Did you say 'Colt'?" she asked.

"Yeah, Colt Barnett. Works like a dadgum mule, just like his old man done."

Helen McKenna walked to the window and looked across the street to the livery. She saw the boy she had met earlier; he was using a pitch fork to throw straw through the rails of the horse corral.

"Would he be that boy who works at the livery?"

"Yep, that's young Colt. Can you see him workin' there? Works just like his old man, Colt does."

"Thank you for the information. You have been most helpful," Mrs. McKenna said, turning and walking away.

"Do you want me to go let Sheriff Hagger know you're here? He'll prob'ly be s'prised to see ya."

"S'prised isn't the word. No, that won't be necessary. Thank you again for your help," she said before walking out the door.

The man sufferingly got up and tried to watch through the window as Mrs. McKenna made her way back to the livery. "Ooooooo my side! That dang, dirty donkey!" he exclaimed, carefully easing back down on the cot and reclining into a supine position.

6

YOUNG COLTER
LEARNS THE TRUTH

Helen McKenna spent some time inside the house of the livery yard owner. As young Colter Barnett worked, he occasionally looked over to watch them through the un-curtained window. She stood, and he sat. Then she reached into her handbag and handed him some folding money. *She must be paying to have her horse boarded,* Colt thought, returning to his chores.

The longhaired, bald-at-the-top, livery owner called through the open door, "Barnett! Get this lady's buggy ready to roll. Then go 'n get all your things. You're goin' with her."

Colt looked at the man and wondered what it was all about, but he did as he was ordered. Colt had neither been close to, nor even particularly friendly with, the livery owner; the demanding, bald man had simply been his employer. So, during the time the boy rolled up his few items of clothing into his bedroll, re-hitched the horse, checked the buggy and straps and buckles, and drove the vehicle to the front of the house, he felt a well-established sense of indifference. After that, Colt climbed onto the driver's seat of the vintage Rockaway Carriage and waited.

Before too long, Helen McKenna came out of the house. "Hold those reins," she directed and began climbing up into the driver's seat.

"Let me help you, ma'am." Colt offered his hand.

"Nope, done this plenty of times before." Mrs. McKenna pulled herself in, sat next to Colt and took the reins. "But thanks anyway. Nice day for a drive," she said and flapped the reins of the small Banker Horse that her husband had purchased from an unscrupulous peddler from the East while the animal was still half-wild. "Go, Lucas!" she called out, prompting the horse to move forward.

During the drive out of the small community and down Town Road, Colt never bothered to ask why he had been forced to leave the livery, and Mrs. McKenna didn't bother to tell him. More than an hour passed before Colt asked, "Where we goin'?"

"We're going to my ranch. I been told you're a good worker. You'll be workin' for me now for board and lodgin'. You'll be treated well."

"Guess I work as good as any full-growed, permanent hand. 'N always better'n them passin'-through waddies 'cause I work more hours than they will."

"You like to work, do you?"

"Workin's good with me."

"Glad to hear that. But I don't expect you to kill yourself. I only want the same amount of work you was doin' for that livery man. And I don't want you runnin' away neither. I paid good money for you, and it'd be a shame to lose it."

"I won't run away. If I do, I'll let you know afore I go."

"That sounds fair enough." She looked out across the bending section of road. "We'll be there in a few hours. I'll make supper. Colter your given name?"

"Yes, ma'am."

"Everybody prob'ly calls you Colt but I'll call you Colter. It's more proper that way. For now, you can just continue callin' me ma'am."

"Yes, ma'am."

They drove on for more than three hours through the cold air without saying a word.

"That's my house way out there," she said when the ranch buildings came into sight.

"How big is this place?"

"Far as the eye can see; only I ain't never seen it all. We've been drivin' on my land for the last couple hours or thereabouts."

"I never been on a place this big."

"Ain't too many places this big, Colter. But it takes a lot of hard labor to make it work. And that's where you come in."

"My Pa used to work on the big McKenna Ranch afore his mortal accident. Ain't never seen the place though. It anywhere near yours?"

Helen McKenna didn't answer. She just glanced at the boy and continued driving on.

Some time passed, and Mrs. McKenna could remain silent no longer. "Whoooa! Hold up there, Lucas!" she shouted, pulling on the reins and halting the horse in the middle of the road.

"Why'd you stop, ma'am?"

She looked thoughtfully at the boy then turned her eyes to the landscape before her. "Look here, Colter," she answered. "I bought you from that livery man so you'd work for me, but I'm not one to start off with no lies. I don't like lies, and I particularly don't like liars. Never will. But, even if I wasn't to tell you about it, once you found out – and sooner or later you would – you'd get resentful and run off. Then I'd be out all that money I spent for you. Course, I'd still expect you to inform me in advance of your leavin'."

Colt looked curiously at her. "I'd find out about what, ma'am?"

"Colter, ain't you been wonderin' why I gone and bought you from that livery man in the first place?"

"No, why would I wonder that?" he answered, looking out at the ranch. "If this place is half as big as you say it is, it's bound to take heaps'a work. Makes sense you'd go 'n hire a good, experienced worker like me."

"Yes, that's true enough. I can always use good help at the ranch. But that's not why I bought you, Colter. Even before I knew you was a good worker, I went into town lookin' for you intentional."

"Lookin' intentional? Why?"

"My name's McKenna – Helen McKenna – and it was my deceased husband, Mr. Henry McKenna, that shot your pa dead a couple years back. Your pa's killin' is the reason I bought you. I set out to find if he had any livin' kin and, when I learned it was you, I paid that livery fella cash-money to buy you out of there. And that's the reason I want you to work on my ranch. I want to make up for what my husband done to your pa."

Colt was perplexed. "I 'preciate what you done, ma'am; you buyin' me to work for you 'n all. But you got it wrong. My Pa wasn't never shot 'n killed by nobody. My Pa accidental-shot his own self with a bad gun he was firin'. Dang thing blew up when he was shootin' at game. Everybody says it was an accident pure 'n simple, so you ain't got nothin' to concern yourself over."

"No, that ain't true, Colter. It wasn't no bad gun that killed your pa. It was my husband that killed him. My husband shot him dead right there on our ranch."

"But everybody always told me otherwise, ma'am. Ever since I was small, they said it was my Pa who shot his own self. He was drinkin' stupid when the barrel'a that ole hog-leg exploded. Gun blew up right in his face; killed him instantly. There wasn't nobody that caused it. It was pure accidental."

"They was protectin' you, boy; that's understandable. But I'm tellin' you something different now, and it's the God's truth: It was my husband that shot your pa. I know that for absolute certain."

"But why would your husband wanna go 'n do somethin' like that?"

"I don't know, Colter. It's beyond all my ponderin'. But, I know that your pa was a hard worker and a good man. Fact is, my Henry even liked him. Henry used to have him up to the house for drinks sometimes. Some nights they'd sit and talk and have a good, old time. And then, for some reason I'll never understand, Henry went plumb out of his head. He went complete maddog crazy and started blamin' your pa for all kind'a things he never done. Your pa was Bible-swearin' innocent of course, and it was all Henry's doin'. Henry went insane through no fault of his own. But for doin' what he did – killin' your pa like that – I am truly sorry."

"But I was always told my Pa shot his own self accidental when he was drunk. Now you're tellin' me my Pa was murdered by your husband Henry? Nobody ain't never said nothin' like that to me afore."

"It's true, Colter; your pa was murdered sure as you're sittin' here. And it was my Henry that done it."

Colt turned his head away from Helen McKenna.

"I know it's a lot to take in, boy, but it's honest-to-God true. And, hard as it is to hear, you deserve the unvarnished facts."

Colt instantly deduced the authenticity of Helen McKenna's tone and testimony. No doubt, she was revealing a factual scenario.

"Wasn't there anything you coulda done to stop your husband?"

"No, Colter, there wasn't anything I could've done. When Henry got too crazy, I left him. I wasn't even livin' on the ranch at the time. But even if I was, there wasn't nothin' me nor anybody else could've done to stop him. The shootin' was completely unforeseen."

"That's...too bad," Colt responded.

"Yes, it is too bad. Because, like I said, your pa was a real good man. And if Henry hadn'ta gone clean out of his mind like he did, you can bet 'dollars to buttons' he never would've done it. He liked your pa."

"So what made you husband go crazy? Did he get kicked in the head by a bull or somethin'?"

"Sure, more than once. But other people's been kicked in the head and they're alright, so I can't say it's bull-kickin' what did it. He just went crazier by the day, and nobody knew what caused it, how to fix it, or where it would end up. It was like he'd been pushed into an open pit by some unseen hand, and he just kept fallin' and fallin'. But his killin' your pa like he did, nobody could've predicted that."

"When did it start?"

"What? His craziness?"

"Yeah, when did he first go crazy?"

"Oh, I don't know exactly. I remember him havin' periods where he started actin' a little odd, but that was early on and it was nothin' too bad. And Henry would always get better. But, eventually, he started havin' full-blown fits; he'd go cussin' at me and throwin' things. Got so bad, I had to leave. Never intended to go back neither."

"Why did you go back?"

"I went back because of what he did to your pa. When I heard about it, I went back to try 'n help out. I always knew it really wasn't Henry's fault. He wouldn't have done nothin' like that in his right mind. So I couldn't help but feel sorry for him – and for your pa too. They both suffered under stars cursed with devil's luck. You understand what I'm sayin' here, Colter?"

"Yes, I believe I do."

"Good. Now let's put all that behind us and try to make something good and sensible out of your pa's death and my Henry's crazy life." She gently touched Colt on the arm. "There has to be some good in the world, young man. Otherwise, there's no reason for us to be on this here earth. And, that's why I bought you, Colter. I'm going to help you find some good in life. I owe you that much. You still understandin'?"

"Yes. I am."

"Good. You got no other kin I was told?

"No, Pa was all I had."

"You must've loved your old pa?"

"Yeah, I guess I must'a. Didn't barely know him though. Pa was good to me 'n all but he was gone most'a the time. Ma died when I was young so I didn't get to know her either. Only people I got to know was the people I worked for. They was the ones that fed me 'n put me up. I always worked hard for 'em 'n they always treated me good."

"Life's been kind'a rough on you, ain't it, Colter?"

"No, not really; I got nothin' to whine about. I eat pretty good. Always got a place to sleep. No, I ain't fond'a learnin' my Pa was murdered by your crazy, dead husband – but what's done is done. It sure wasn't your fault, ma'am. Sounds like it might not be nobody's fault. But I do thank you for tellin' me the truth, ma'am."

"Me and Henry never had no children, Colter. So I'd be proud to treat you as one of my own – that is, if you don't mind?"

"One'a your own? You mean, like I was your son or somethin'?"

"That's right. And maybe, after some time, we could even get to be like real family. I could become the ma you never knew."

"You'd be my ma?"

"So what do you think? You like the idea?"

"I don't know. I ain't never thought such a thing afore."

"Look here, Colter, times are hard and cash-money don't grow on trees. So whether I'm your new ma or not, I paid darn good money for you and I'd appreciate it if you wasn't to go runnin' off on me unannounced."

"No, ma'am, I said I wouldn't go runnin' off unannounced. You been honest with me 'n I'll be the same. I'd always tell you first."

"Good, that's just what I wanted to hear. Course, after all I told you about my crazy Henry shootin' your pa, I'd understand if you run away."

"No, ma'am, I'll prob'ly stay. Got no place in particular to run off to anyway."

"Good." She smiled. "Glad to hear that, Colter. And if things do work out for us, I promise I'll make you a fine ma."

Colt was silent.

"Yeah, I know it's sudden. First you hear about your pa's killin' then I go sayin' I want to be your new ma. But, as you can tell, I'm the forthright kind."

"Yeah, I can see that."

"And, if I was to become your new ma, I'd take real good care of you, just like you was my own son. I'd cook and make sure you got clean clothes...that is, if you're half the worker they say you are. I sure don't want no lazy, do-nothin' son hangin' around the house all day."

Colt was understandably bewildered. "You really wanna be my new ma? No one ever said nothin' like that to me afore. You don't even know me, ma'am. I might end up bein' crazier than your dead husband Henry."

"That's not possible, Colter."

"Honest, ma'am, why would you wanna go 'n do somethin' like this?"

"More reasons than one. Partly because of makin' amends. But amends or no amends, every child needs a mama and every mama needs a child."

"I don't know, ma'am. It's somethin' I have to think on a spell."

"Alright, I'm not one to rush, 'specially on matters as important as this one." She slapped the reins. "You go, Lucas!" she shouted, and the horse began moving toward the main house. "You take your good, old time, Colter. When we get home, you put Lucas up in the barn, then sleep on it and tell me in the mornin'."

"In the mornin'? Yeah, that sounds about right, I guess."

"Now you said you won't be runnin' off without tellin' me so I'm takin' you at your word. This ranch is big but I ain't got that kind'a money to throw away."

"No, ma'am, my word's good."

"I'm bettin' that it is. Looks like you and me are going to get along just fine, young Colter Barnett."

7

THE DECISION
IS FINALIZED

The next morning, Colt awoke to the flavorful air of eggs and biscuits. It had been a long time since he'd slept in a bed – and it felt wonderful. Opening the guest bedroom door, he walked out and into the kitchen.

"Did you sleep well, Colter? Breakfast's near ready," Mrs. McKenna said as she stood over the stove.

"Yeah, I never slept on such a soft bed as that one. Where'd you ever find somethin' like that?"

"It's store bought. And I'm glad you like it because that's where you're going to be doin' your sleepin' from now on."

"I'll be sleepin' in the house?"

"That's right, in the house, just like civilized folks. You like eggs?"

"Yes, ma'am, I do. In the house? I can hardly believe it."

"I've made you a fine, big breakfast. But just don't let that soft bed turn you into a dawdler because I got hard chores for you to do. East pasture fences need mendin'. You do know how to mend fences, don't you?"

"Sure. Done it lots'a times."

"Good, glad to hear that," she said carrying a skillet to the table and spooning a load of scrambled eggs on Colt's plate. "You like coffee? Growin' boy like you could use some coffee in him."

"I drink it when I can."

Helen McKenna walked back to the stove, put down the skillet and picked up a pan of hot coffee. "You won't be drinkin' anything else, I hope. We don't keep no bug juice around here. I won't allow it on the place. Not since that crazy husband of mine took the Lord unto himself and give it up."

"He quit drinkin'? Was that after he shot my Pa?"

"Yep. When he was drinkin' he was totally out of his head. He was out of his head most of the time anyways but drinkin' only made it worse. He said he made his peace with God and truly repented his crazy ways, but it didn't do no good in the end." She poured coffee into Colter's coffee bowl. "You don't mind drinkin' from a bowl, do you? We got a couple cups somewhere but I got away from usin' them."

"No, bowl's fine. Better'n that dirty, ole, horse medicine bottle I usually drink my water from."

"Better than that any old day."

"So his repentin' didn't do him no good, huh?"

"No, not really. Henry was for sure sorry and he changed and went to the Lord, but it didn't help too awful much. In the end, he was still crazy. Ended up shootin' himself right out there by the barn. We found him layin' in his own blood. It was dreadful."

"I'm real sorry to hear that, ma'am."

"So was I." She sat at the table. "Guilt does funny things to a person."

"Like makin' 'em wanna adopt a total stranger?"

She looked him square in the eyes, surprised at his mental acuity. "You impress me, Colter. Yeah, it'll do that alright – and more. So'd you think over what we talked about last night?"

"Yes, ma'am, I did. 'N I came to a decision."

"You did? No, don't tell me now. You eat first. No use spoilin' your breakfast with such talk."

"It won't spoil nothin', ma'am. I decided to let you take me on as kin."

"Now, don't you be sayin' that lightly, Colter. This is a serious decision. We become kin, there's no going back. I ain't takin' on no son what'll be changin' his mind down the road."

"I won't be changin' my mind. Not 'less you be changin' yours."

"Now why would I be doin' that? I paid good money for you, and I don't say things to be flip."

"I ain't bein' flip neither, ma'am; I'm dead-on serious. I thought on it all night long. Couldn't help but think on it. 'N I judged it could be real good for us both. I'd have me a good place to work 'n someone I could help 'n look out for. 'N you'd have yourself a son. I liked the idea better 'n any I ever come across."

Helen McKenna's eyes glistened then her expression abruptly hardened.

"Now you won't be holdin' against me what Mr. Henry McKenna done to your pa? You can't never do that, Colter."

"No, I won't never do that. What your husband done, he done on his own. You didn't have nothin' to do with his craziness. 'N what you're tryin' to do for me now is real good; good like I never knowed afore. I never thought such good things could ever happen. It's kind'a like... true churchliness or somethin'. I don't know; I ain't no good at expressin' it. Am I talkin' sense?"

He looked intently into Mrs. McKenna's eyes.

"You cryin', ma'am?"

"Yes, I am cryin' a bit. I do that sometimes when I get real happy. And I'm real happy right now, Colter Barnett."

She reached over and hugged the boy. "You want some of those sourdoughs now, son?"

"Yes, ma'am, I sure do."

"Good. And you're going to like them too." She walked to the stove. "Jumpin' Jillshorseisfat! These biscuits gone and burnt on me a little. I'll see if I can't scrape a couple good ones off the fry pan for you."

"No, no, it's alright. I truly like 'em burnt."

8

HENRY MCKENNA'S GHOST

Colt spent the greater part of the morning surveying the eastern pasture. The ranch was impressive in both size and scenery. A mountain range enclosed the freehold estate on three sides, and this eastern pasture sloped gradually down to a valley rich in gold-colored grassland that extended for miles until reaching the thin, dry plants of the desert range. Everything served to captivate Colt's young eyes, and the wind and sun made him feel independent, free and alive. Even the desert scorpions, cactus and rattlesnakes would have appeared beautiful to Colt in this magnificent natural theater, especially with this being only his fifth workday on the ranch.

Arriving at a corner section of a fence, Colt pulled a roll of barbed wire from the wagon. He used a fence-puller to tighten the wire in place, wrapping small lengths of wire through twisted eyes of fence and using pliers to tightly secure them together. Some of the fence posts had fallen or were near fallen, and he used a shovel to dig them down farther into the ground. He also used heavy rocks to help hold posts in places where the ground was too stony to make deep enough holes. Colt pulled fresh wooden posts from the back of the wagon to replace those that had been cut through by seasonal streams or had rotted to a dry brittleness. Mineral hard, fall ground intensified the work, and Colt labored without break until daylight became so faint as to make continuing impractical. With his day's work at an end, Colt loaded up the wagon with barbed wire and tools and drove towards home.

It was cold and dark, and the various passageways between hillsides, boulders, drop-offs and rainwater-cut gullies were sometimes impossible to distinguish. Fortunately, the horse knew the way, and Colt trusted the animal to act as chief navigator. It was a long, wearisome journey back to the ranch, and for indeterminate periods of time Colt sensed himself fumbling to fight off sleep.

At long last, Colt caught sight of the main house. Smoke from the chimney rolled across the gray-colored, moonlit sky as Colt drove the wagon through the opened and broken, iron gate. He backed the wagon up inside the barn, unhitched and tended to the massive Shire Horse. "Good boy, Samson." He lovingly patted the horse on the side of the face. You done good work today."

Ready to go up to the house, Colt put out the Dietz "Victor" oil lamp and walked toward the barn door. That's when the strange sounds began: muffled talking, mumbling, ranting, self arguing, followed by the blast of a single gunshot. Colt momentarily froze in his tracks. "Who's there? Who are you 'n what do you want? Whoever you are, you're not s'posed to be here so put down your gun 'n show yourself."

All was silent.

Colt picked up the Yerkes & Plumb Machinists' Ball-Peen Hammer sitting next to an anvil and walked slowly forward. "You better move on out'a here. I may not be fully growed but I can handle myself pretty good in a dustup. So, 'less you're intendin' to shoot me for no good reason, you better skedaddle. Go on now; move out! Now's your chance."

Remaining hidden in the shadows, Colt passed through nearly the entire length of the barn's interior; still, there was no one to be seen. With one hand, he quietly slid open a door leading to the arena and cautiously walked outside.

There, in the darkness, Colt saw what appeared to be two legs sticking out from just beyond a corner of the barn. As he cautiously moved closer, it became clear that someone had been shot and was laying face down on the ground. The wounded party twitched wildly while Colt scanned the area for an armed assailant. Colt knew he had made himself an easy target for any gunman lurking in the shadows and so, listening and watching for the slightest sound or movement, Colt backed away toward the arena fence.

Hammer in hand, Colt easily slid his body between the wooden, corral rails and scrambled to a nearby tree. Sheltering himself behind the timber, he appraised the situation before continuing to move toward the house.

Once at the house, it occurred to him that a gunman could have managed to get inside so Colt moved silently up the steps and onto the porch. Finding the door unlocked, he threw it open and rushed in. A shadow moved toward him from out of the corner; and Colt raised the two-pound hammer, preparing to land it dead-center on the intruder's skull.

Mrs. McKenna stood before him completely startled. "What the....? What in heaven's name is going on?"

"Shhhhh," Colt warned. "You alright, ma'am? Anybody else here?"

"No, no one else. What's wrong?"

"Bad goings-on out there. Looks like a fight. Got a gun?"

Helen McKenna hurried to the kitchen and retrieved the Winchester shotgun next to the stove. Colt rushed up next to her and took the gun. "Got any shells for this thing?" he asked.

Mrs. McKenna pulled four, shotgun shells from the shelf. "It's all the buckshot I got," she said handing the ammunition to Colt.

"It'll do. Any other weapons here? Pistol? Anything?" Colt asked, loading the shells into the shotgun.

"I got a loaded pistol under my bed."

"Good, you go get it 'n lock yourself in. I'm goin' back out."

"No, don't go out there. You're liable to get yourself killed."

"We're both liable to get ourselves killed if I stay here. Don't worry now; I'll make certain nothin' happens to you. You can count on that, ma'am."

"No, you're too young to go gunhuntin' brushpoppers. You just stay right in this house with me, boy."

"Sorry, ma'am, can't do that. We don't know how many's out there, 'n if we both stay here we'll be like denned rabbits waitin' for badgers to break in. No, I gotta take the fight to them."

"Then I'm going out with you."

"No, ma'am, it'll be safer for us both if you just stay here. But don't fret none; I'm plenty familiar with guns, 'n I can scrap like a cornered mama sow when I have to."

Colt peered through the window then moved to the door and turned the handle. "Just make sure you keep this thing locked. Else somebody might take it as an invite to walk in."

"Don't worry. I won't allow no guest in here tonight."

Colt opened the door, listened and looked around, then stepped outside and closed the door behind him.

Helen McKenna locked the door then rushed to the bedroom and pulled a pistol from beneath her bed. After checking to make certain it was loaded, she hurried back into the living room and peeked through the window. She could see Colt moving across the yard; and he appeared to her to be like some wiry shadow blending into the cover of night as he furtively glided between the dark concealments of trees and brush.

Colt arrived at the barn, glanced in every direction then peered inside the structure from ground to loft before making his entry. Proceeding quietly, he ducked inside behind some nearby hay bales where he waited and listened awhile.

Failing to detect anything that alerted him to immediate danger, and vaguely thinking that any person or persons responsible for the shooting would most likely be long gone, Colt relaxed and breathed easier. But then he remembered that he hadn't seen or heard anyone riding away from the ranch and grew nervous again.

Colt held his Winchester ready for action as he walked through the wide, center aisle and looked into each of the stalls. He observed that none of the horses showed any signs of being particularly upset, and that seemed strange to him.

He climbed the ladder to the loft where he checked for lurking gunmen who could have been hiding behind bales of hay or stacked up stores of feed, tack and assorted supplies. He even looked up into the louvered cupolas and, finally, over the railings to ascertain that the first floor, side-entry doors had remained closed. No one was in the barn; Colt was now certain of it.

Bracing himself to deal with confronting a dead human body, Colt descended the ladder and walked through the opened door that led to the arena. Colt looked out to where he had seen the person convulsing face down in the dirt and was surprised to see no one there.

He must still be alive 'n crawled away, Colt thought, driven forward by curiosity though half expecting the injured form to pop out at any moment and start shooting.

I don't get it? he questioned, as he stood near the spot where the paroxysmic person had lain. *Where's the marks in the dirt? Where's the blood? There's no sign a person was ever shot 'n fell here?*

"Is that where you saw it?" a voice from behind Colt asked.

Colt swung around and aimed the shotgun in the direction of the questioner.

"My God, I coulda shot you!" he exclaimed, upon seeing Mrs. McKenna standing there and holding a pistol at her side. "You should be inside, ma'am, where it's safe."

"This the place?" she resumed inquiring.

"Yeah, this is it. But he's gone now. Somehow, he must'a got away. Only I don't see no slither marks in the dirt 'n, the way he was twitchin', he must'a been hurt real bad." Colt knelt to examine the ground. "This just don't figure. How come there's no blood?"

"You won't see any blood. Nobody ever does."

"What do you mean by that, ma'am?" Colter asked, looking guardedly over his shoulder while still hunched over the place where he'd seen the thrashing body of an injured man."

"I mean this's happened before. Many times. It's the main reason a lot of men quit this place. They're superstitious and think livin' persons can be hurt by a dead ghost."

"Whose dead ghost? My Pa's?"

"No, not your pa's; my Henry's. This is the same exact spot Mr. McKenna shot himself. I found him layin' dead there," she said pointing to the ground, "Right there, layin' face down."

"But that wasn't no ghost I saw, ma'am. I heard the gunshot, 'n he was layin' there clear as day, all alive 'n twitchy-like."

"What you saw may have been twitchin' but it sure as Jesus wasn't alive. A lot of people seen the same thing you just did. They'd hear a shot and see him movin' around face down. And that's exactly how I found him. It's Henry for certain; it's got to be. And it's got to stop!" she called out into the darkness.

"Maybe you could just ask him to leave us alone," Colt suggested.

"And that's exactly what I'm intendin' to do," she answered. "Alright, McKenna," she shouted into space, "Enough is enough! No more of this ghostin' nonsense, understand? This here's young Colter Barnett, son of the man you shot dead for no good reason and the man whose death caused you so much grief that you went and shot yourself just to be free of the guilt. But I guess you still ain't free of the guilt because you just keep hangin' around killin' yourself over and over again. But now it's got to stop, Henry. Now! Tonight! You hear me, Henry? I want this spookin' of yours done and over with. Young Colter's here now, and I'm going to be his new ma. So no more of this guilt and penance stuff you keep doin' to yourself. You got to stop it now!"

"You think he hears this, ma'am?"

"Sure he does." And she continued addressing the spirit, "First of all, you crazy fool, you was out of your head when you shot Barnett so nobody's holdin' that against you – not me and not young Colter here. You're free of that terrible sin, you understand? And now I'm adoptin' this boy as my own. Young Colter's workin' for us now, and I'm going to give him a good life. This boy was Barnett's only kin, and I'm doin' right by Barnett. And like I said, young Colter ain't holdin' no grudge against you; he's already told me that. Come here boy," she said to Colt. "You tell this crazy fool ghost of Henry's. It'll help if he hears it from you."

Colt stepped closer to her and looked solemnly into the vagueness of night.

"Go ahead and tell him, boy. Tell him you ain't holdin' no grudge. Once he knows Barnett's only livin' kin forgives him, we can get this spookin' business over and done with. Go ahead, boy, Henry'll listen to you."

Colter gazed into the air and spoke with solemnity, "Henry...I mean, Mr. McKenna...your wife's told me what you done to my Pa. But I don't hold no grudge against you. None at all. She told me you was crazy out'a your head when you done it 'n you couldn't help yourself. 'N now she's tryin' to do right by me by givin' me this here ranch job. So I forgive you, Mr. McKenna. I ain't mad at you in the slightest. If Mrs. McKenna says it wasn't your fault, then it wasn't your fault. So I forgive you like the Good Book says I should. So now if you wanna do right by me, just don't come around here no more. I ain't afraid'a most things but I truly don't like dealin' with no dead people. Nothin' personal. So please, just go away 'n don't never come back. Amen."

"Alright, you heard the boy," Helen McKenna added. "Young Barnett here don't have no bad feelin's toward you. I ain't mad at you. God ain't mad at you. And you know Jesus: He don't never hold no grudges. So you go away now and leave us be. We don't want your kind hangin' around here. You just go wherever it is you dead people are s'posed to go – heaven or whatever – and don't you be comin' back. It upsets me. It upsets young Barnett. And it's harmful to maintainin' a well-run ranch. You go now, Henry, understand?"

Helen McKenna moved a small distance away from Colt where she paused and looked down at the ground. No little sadness came over her. "I still have feelin's for you, Henry," she whispered tenderly, Always will. But now you got to leave us be so we can live in peace. You go now, Henry, please. And no more of this ghostin' tomfoolery, alright?" Mrs. McKenna waited quietly, as if half expecting her dead husband to answer.

In the silence of darkness, Colt and Helen McKenna stood patiently, neither wanting to miss any penetrating, final message from the other side. And though an audible answer or visible sign did not occur that night, the angst-ridden, spasmodic ghost of Henry McKenna was never seen nor heard from again. The bonds of contrition had been inexorably broken, and the ranch was, at last, enduringly exorcised of Henry McKenna's spectral presence.

9

SEPTEMBER 26, 1899:
A DAY TO REMEMBER

Summer had passed, and the range grasses had seasoned tall and bountiful. This was due, in large part, to the isolated, mountain ranch having been neglected the year before; thereby, allowing ungrazed forage to accumulate in nutritive quality and availability. McKenna bovines were of the highest reputation. The ranch's free-range cattle had grown large, and this year's cows had produced a multitude of healthy, well-formed calves.

Helen McKenna hadn't invested much in cattle the year before due to the trouble she had keeping manpower at the ranch. This was partly due to her relative inexperience in management and partly because of stories regarding murderous, mad-Henry's ranch-bound ghost. But, whatever the causes, this failure to invest turned out to be quite auspicious. The devastating, Southern California droughts, and the heavy winter of '98 that extended into February of '99, had created a downward trundle of livestock mortality estimates, influencing cattle market prices and, therefore, the personal fortunes of many speculative cattlemen. Ranchers who were unable to meet their financial obligations had simply gone out of business.

It was Mrs. McKenna's judgment that, due to the unfortunate events of the past, the timing had become right to plunge headlong into cattle investment debt. Fewer ranchers meant fewer cattle; fewer cattle meant increased demand; and increased demand meant conditions of greater profit. As far as she was concerned, there was simply no way she could lose and, moreover, the year's prospects just felt good to her. Young Colter had broken the haunting curse, and the superstitious cowboys were no longer averse to staying at the ranch. Colter's presence had definitely changed Helen McKenna's luck to an upswing course and she, in turn, was determined to make use of that providential trend to make both rich. So, it was in this frame of mind that Helen McKenna took a leap of faith, investing most of her savings – along with tens of thousands of additional dollars she had borrowed from the bank – into this new herd. Helen envisioned herself becoming a cash millionaire and felt she would have been a fool not to take advantage of such great opportunity. In the year of 1899, life had once again become an exciting and happy adventure for this widow of the guilt-ridden, lethiferous Henry McKenna.

And to be completely fair to Helen McKenna, during good times, turning a single dollar into ten was not unheard of; and an "all or nothing" gamble based upon a solitary season, though perhaps reckless, was neither illogical nor impossible. Unfortunately, circumstances were not as "good" as Mrs. McKenna had desired them to be. Lawlessness had gotten so out of hand that cattle rustlers seemed to be nearly as numerous as their pirated cattle. And cattle prices had not yet recovered from the year before. Things were still very tenuous despite Helen McKenna's audacity, rationales and dogged optimism. But this rancher woman had vowed to become rich beyond young Colter's wildest dreams – and that's all there was to it.

It had been nearly a year since Colt had been taken in by Mrs. McKenna and, riding his horse homeward off the range, Colt wondered what Christmas present he could buy for this woman he now called "Mama Helen." Thoughts of presents and money casually led Colt to recollect Mrs. McKenna's stated business plan: Sell the cattle before Christmas, if the market reaches her ideal price – or – let the cows winter ration on cheap roughage and straw, permitting more cows to birth calves, and then sell the cattle in the spring when prices peak. According to Helen McKenna, this strategy was perfect and with no possibility of failure. Mama Helen had told Colt, "There's no way we can lose," so often that even he had come to believe it.

Colt recollected celebrating the previous Christmas of '98 with Mama Helen and what a wonderful day that had been. For the first time he could remember, that holiday made Colt feel like he had family and that he truly belonged somewhere. That was also the day Mrs. McKenna asked him to call her "Mama Helen." It felt strange calling her that in the beginning but, by this time, he'd grown comfortable saying it.

On the morning of this September day, one of the ranch hands had relayed the message from Mama Helen, "You be sure to get home afore dark," he communicated to Colt, "Them's your mama's strictest orders." And, before leaving the ranch four days previous, Mama Helen had instructed Colt to, "Be sure to get back home before dark," on that particular Tuesday night. She said she had some important ranch business for him to attend to and that it couldn't be put off till the following day. True to his nature, Colt didn't ask any questions. He just figured the ranch must have been getting some new horses or some additional breeding bulls. Either way, he told her he'd be home.

As he rode through the mountain rain, Colt continued to think about Christmas and what gift he might buy Mama Helen. A rush of cold air prompted him to contemplate buying her some mittens. But then, he remembered that she already had several pairs of those. He rode his horse down-slope and slogged across a muddy creek. *Maybe I could get her a new pair'a winter boots,* he wondered. But then, how could he know if they'd fit properly without her having tried them on beforehand. He shrugged off all thoughts of Christmas; it was still some three months away, he figured. So Colt considered other things and estimated he'd be home around sunset.

The young man rode for hours on a horse fit enough to travel a hundred miles in a single day. But Colt had learned to be sensitive to the subtle communications of horses and stopped occasionally to give the animal a rest, looking for places sheltered from the rain and with fall forage. Recognizably close to home, Colt shortened the final rest period and rode the last leg of the journey home.

That day, Helen McKenna had been busy preparing food for a surprise party she was throwing for Colt. This was Colter's sixteenth birthday and, even though she had pretended not to be aware of the fact, she had been planning this party for months. Mama Helen had cooked stacks of fry bread and covered them with towels. A large pot of chili thick with meat, beans and peppers had been set on the stove to be kept warm until supper time. A metallic bean pot was filled to the brim with hot coffee and a skillet lid was used as a makeshift cover. For dessert, several batters of ash cake had been baked up with blueberry jam made available as a spread.

A rider galloped to the front of the main house. "I seen him on the trail, ma'am. Won't be long now," he told Mrs. McKenna. So the cowboys all hid away in the horse barn as Mrs. McKenna waited outside for Colter's arrival.

Before long, she saw him riding through the opened gate. "Hey there!" she called out.

Colt acknowledged Mrs. McKenna with a wave of the hand. Once at the front porch, he pulled his horse to a stop.

"How are the cattle doin'?" she asked.

"We're in for a cold spell but, otherwise everything's fine. I'm goin' to put my horse up."

"No, don't put your horse up yet," she said, preventing Colter from taking the horse to the barn. "Tie him there, to that rail at the far fence."

"Why the far fence rail?"

"Food's ready to eat, and I don't want horse poop smell next to the house. Come in soon as you're done. Got something to show you."

Colter dismounted and walked the horse across the front yard to the tie rail near the far fence. "That's odd," he wondered aloud. "What's so darn important she don't want no horse poop by the house? Not like we're havin' a party or nothin'."

He walked across the yard then wiped his shoes thoroughly before going inside the house. "What's that? That cornbread I'm smellin'?"

"Yep. Thought we'd have something special tonight. But first, I want you to see this." She unfolded a two-page document and handed it to him.

He stared at it. "What's it say?" he asked, wiping trail dirt from his eyes.

"Don't be so lazy, boy. Read it."

He took a few moments to look it over. "It says here, these are some kind'a adoption papers. What's it mean?"

"It means you are now officially my son. I had these papers drawn up special by my attorney. You and me are now legal kin."

He smiled and looked at her. "But these papers ain't necessary, Mama Helen. I already told you I was gonna be your son."

"Yes, I know you did. But these here are necessary. I want everything done up proper. Here," she said, handing him more documents.

"What's these? More adoption papers?"

"Read them, lazy boy."

He looked the front page over and let his eyes move from the bottom of the page to the top as he read aloud, "Courthouse...proved under oath...estate of said Helen Bethany McKenna...to my son Colter Barnett and all his heirs...to take title to all my lands and possessions upon death...Last Will and Testament of Helen Bethany McKenna. Last Will and Testament!" he said with alarm. "What's wrong, Mama Helen? You sick?"

"No, I ain't sick. I'm healthy as a horse."

"Then why did you make out this will for? I don't want none'a your stuff."

"I know you don't. That's not the point. Everybody needs to make a will – just in case."

"'Just in case' nothin'. I ain't gonna let nothin' happen to you. Forget these papers."

"I know you won't, Colter. But everybody who owns property's got to have a will. It's just common sense. Otherwise, the state or some bank's going to end up gettin' it all, and we worked too hard our entire lives to be givin' it to them. That's why I'm legally adoptin' you. I don't want nothin' standin' in the way of you inhertin' my fortune. And I am going to have a huge fortune after this year. When we sell our cattle, I'm going to have more than a million dollars cash-money."

"But I don't want your money. I only want you to be alright."

She took his hand. "I am alright, Colter. Shoot, I ain't never felt better in my entire life. But when the time does come – a long, long ways from now – I want everything to be in order for you. You're my son now, Colter, and I got to take care of you."

"I am your son, Mama Helen. 'N that's why I ain't never gonna let nothin' or nobody hurt you. You're the only true mama I ever known."

"Happy birthday, Colter," she said, smiling and holding tightly to his hand.

"Dang, I plum forgot. Today is my birthday, ain't it."

"Well, I didn't forget. And neither did nobody else." And she swung open the front door to reveal the crew of hired hands standing in the front yard.

"Happy birthday, Colt!" they shouted out, rushing toward him. "Happy birthday, boy!" a cowboy said, patting him on the shoulder and shaking his hand.

"Thanks, fellas. I plum forgot about this bein' my birthday. Nothin' like this ain't never happened to me afore."

"Come on everybody!" Helen McKenna called out. "Let's eat!"

All the men rushed into the kitchen for some good tasting grub and cornbread.

"Arbuckle Coffee's in the bean pot. Everybody help yourselves. Sorry, boys but we don't drink no liquor around here no more. Just Ariosa ground now. This place's completely dry."

No one was particularly surprised by Mrs. McKenna's "no liquor" announcement, and no one expressed any disappointment. But, true to the behavior of range hands, when the "cookie" calls, everybody comes a'scuttlin'; and a'scuttlin' they did.

"Man at the pot!" someone hollered, and the cowboy there at that moment became obliged to serve anyone who wanted coffee poured into his bowl.

This party was a celebration of Colt's birthday but it was also about getting some good eatin' done, and everyone wanted to get as much food into him as his stomach could hold. So little talking went on as the men filled their plates, coffee bowls and bellies. Jawin' could be done later – after eating – outside on the porch where they could all sit and smoke.

Once all the men were outside, Colter and Helen McKenna sat across from each other at the kitchen table. "Thanks, Mama Helen; nobody never gave me no birthday spree afore."

"You're more than welcome, boy. Happy sixteenth to you!"

10

COLT ENCOUNTERS THE MIXED NATURE OF HIRED HELP

Less than an hour into the party, Colter decided to take his horse from the tie rail and put the animal in the barn before mingling with the men. As he opened the front door to walk outside, he heard the voice of Big Dingles, one of the newer hired hands. "Biddy makes up a good stew, don't she? I wonder if that little boy'a hers wasn't really from one of her husband's knocked-up whores? Why else would she take in that little mutton-puncher? He sure don't look like much to me."

"Don't talk like that, Dingles," Ole Smoke said. "It ain't right ya talkin' like that. Anyways, ya ain't been here long 'nuff to know nothin' from nohow."

Colt heard every word.

"I been here long enough to get a good look at that woman what owns this ranch. 'N I tell you this, boys, I wouldn't mind pairin' up with that cow afore she gets too old 'n all biggity catawampus." Big Dingles laughed aloud and alone. "'N when I was done, if ya was all to ask me real nice, I jus' might let some'a you barn cowboys get crossbreedin' privileges."

"Uh oh," one of the hired hands uttered after noticing Colt standing in the open doorway.

"You done gone too fer this time, Dingles," reproved Ole Smoke. "Not only is what you said a load 'a prairie coal, but you done said it right in front'a the boy."

Big Dingles, who was sitting on the edge of the porch, was disturbingly surprised when he turned and saw Colt staring at him. "Him? Hell, who cares 'bout that little weaklin'? He ain't nothin' but a cow poodle. Now you jus' go back inside, little doggie, where ya belong. We men is busy out here talkin' man talk."

Colt walked outside, down the steps and stood directly in front of the large man. He evaluated the situation while looking directly into Big Dingles' eyes.

"What do you want out here, little jenny? You get back to your mama afore I have to turn ya over my knee 'n give ya both a good whuppin'."

Colt remained silently analytical. He wondered how this sober oaf could have eaten their food and then insulted Mama Helen like that: It was inconceivable. He carefully weighed his options.

"Maybe you don't hear too good, mutton-puncher. I jus' told ya to get back inside."

"Nobody talks like that about my Mother, least'a all no ass-scratchin' sidewinder like you. Go get your things 'n clear out. You're fired."

"Fired! Who the hell is you to fire me, you short-legged little....?"

At that moment, Colt spontaneously chose the most compelling course of action and kicked Big Dingles in the knee with every bit of force he could muster.

Dingles screamed in pain and immediately grabbed his knee, prompting Colt to rapidly move in and pull Big Dingles' pistol from its holster. After lodging the gun within the inside of his own belt, Colt walked alongside the house to a pile of firewood and thoughtfully selected a piece of hardened oak cut to about two feet in length and two and one-half inches in diameter. Then, calmly walking up behind Big Dingles, he swung the log and hit Dingles hard on the right ear.

Again, Big Dingles screamed. This time the large man fell to the ground holding both his knee and bloodied ear. "What's wrong with you, boy? Ya gone 'n clouted me! You're plum loon-crazy like your old man McKenna? I was jus' funnin' when ya gone 'n sneak-clouted me!"

"I seen you work, Dingles. You're lazy 'n you're worthless. You didn't never earn your pay, 'n you got a big, nasty mouth. I ain't said nothin' afore but I'm sayin' it now." Colt pulled out the pistol and held it at his side. "You go down to the louse house, pick up your raggedy things 'n move on. 'N if you ain't out'a here in the next five minutes," the boy aimed the gun at Big Dingles, "I'm gonna blow a hole in that big, pig-lard gut'a yours. You hearin' me, Dingles?"

"But I'm bleedin', boy. 'N I can't walk neither. My ear's ringin' 'n ya done messed up my leg real bad."

"That ain't all I'm gonna mess up if you ain't on your horse 'n riding out'a here in the next five minutes."

"But I can't walk, you illy-jitymit mutt, so how'm I gonna ride? Ya done gimped up my knee."

"You think this is funny?" Colt asked one of the men who was snickering at Big Dingle's plight.

"No, Colt, not too much I don't."

"You go get his horse. 'N make it real fast or I'm gonna give you somethin' even funnier to sniggle about. 'Cause big man here's close to findin' himself aerified. 'N you," he said pointing to another man who had also been giggling, "You run to the louse house 'n get Dingle's dirty clothes 'n things. 'N do it now!" he ordered the men.

Both men scrambled to do as they were told.

"My knee. Ya done broke my leg."

"Quit complainin', Dingles. If you was a horse, I'd shoot you where you lay."

Big Dingles moaned and mumbled but no one went to his aid. A short time later, the two dispatched men returned.

"Now help Mr. Dingles here on his horse, 'n walk him to the gate. 'N make sure he's ridin' away from here or both your cattlin' jobs are done."

The two men helped the wounded man onto his horse. "But I can't ride." Big Dingles complained. "I need me a doctor."

"Just keep ridin' till you find one."

"But what if I can't find no doctor?"

"Then the buzzards are gonna have themselves a big meal'a Dingles tallow."

"But even if I do find a doctor, I ain't got no money to pay him with. I need me some money."

"In that case, find yourself some tender-heart vet. 'N when he asks what happened, tell him you was bit by a cow poodle. Now move!"

"Oh yeah, I'll move. But when I'm well n' fit, I'm comin' back for you, you little Arkansas toothpick," Big Dingles threatened as he rode away.

"I still got your gun so you best quit chewin' cud if you wanna keep your lamps on."

The men now looked at Colt in a new way. If there had ever been any doubt, this young man just established himself as their undisputed, ranch boss.

"Party's over, men," Colt said. "We got work tomorrow."

The ranch hands immediately and quietly dispersed and left the main house yard.

When Colter entered the house, Mama Helen looked at him intently. This was a side of her adopted son's nature she had never seen.

"Thank you for the birthday shindig, Mama Helen. I'm sorry about the trouble out there. I know you must'a heard some'a the goings-on. It was just somethin' had to be done."

"What was it about, Colter?"

"Nothin' to speak of. Just somethin' had to be done is all."

No more was said about the incident, and neither Colter nor his mother ever mentioned it again. But from that day forward, Colt never left the house without carrying a sidearm.

11

APRIL 1900: FORTUNE, MISFORTUNE, AND THE AGE OF THE AUTOMOBILE

The ending period of 1899 had not been as cold as the beginning months, nor had that year been as harsh as the blizzard of 1898. In accordance with Helen McKenna's hopes, prayers and idealistic calculations, most of the cattle had actually managed to survive the winter. And though existing market prices did not permit her to sell the cattle, she was confident that premium prices would be achieved in the year 1900, more than enough to compensate for the herd's overall loss in poundage.

In February of 1900, a supply of large, highly prized, breeding bulls from Texas had been delivered to the ranch, and Colt had instructed his men to introduce them into the herd. The McKenna Ranch had some of the most knowledgeable ranch hands around; men who knew that managing aggressive bulls was not only dangerous work but that it meant more than just randomly herding bulls into this or that cow pasture. A healthy bull is aggressive by nature and another bull's mere proximity will cause a fight to ensue. Therefore, ideally, bulls should be separated by sufficient distance from each other to avoid competitions that could lead to their injury or death. Animals like these new Texas bulls were so large and muscular that they could easily take down a horse and kill the rider. Weighing over a ton, these bulls were also capable of destroying fences and going through buildings. And, should a bull break a leg in a fight, that would be a complete loss because a cowboy would have no choice but to put that bull down.

Bulls also had to be inventoried and evaluated according to age, size and soundness and then placed accordingly into designated cow herds. The process on the McKenna Ranch was not at all scientific but relied instead on the intuition and experience of the cowhands. And, once bulls were put into their groups, the cowboys would have to watch the bulls for several days to make certain things got all sorted out proper-like.

Female cattle have a leadership hierarchy also, with the dominant females initiating movements that lead their group from one feeding area to another. Cows usually come into heat every twenty-one days or about six weeks after calving. They act restless and tend to group with other females undergoing estrus. With their genitals swollen and discharging a thick, clear mucous, the bawling receptive cows give off a sort of "yoo-hoo" odor that the bulls find so utterly delightful.

Older bulls tend to be more dominant, territorial and aloof and will generally attempt more mountings. Cattle are social animals that form sub-herds, maintain comfortable social distances and will participate in the defense of each other. To the cowboys' satisfaction, once herd harmony is established, there's not too awful much to do than stick on a pair of mud boots and get ready for the calvings.

Colt oversaw the cattle operation and spent most of his time riding the range. But, at his mother's request, he was to spend this particular day at the main house. It was around ten thirty in the morning, and he sat in the living room near the lit fireplace and rocked in a chair.

Mama Helen sat on the settee and was going through her accounting book and calculating percentages.

"Things look good, Colter. We're going to make us enough money to pay off all our debts and have plenty left over. I been readin' about the automobile, and I think it'd be nice to get us one."

Colter laughed. "Automobiles! Those things ain't nothin' but high-dollar dogcarts with the dogs ridin' inside. Few years from now, you won't be hearin' nothin' about no automobiles. No, no automobile's ever gonna replace the good, ole, reliable horse."

"Don't be so sure, Mister Smarty. Some people think that someday we're going to have roads all over this country that'll be 'specially designed for automobiles."

"Nope, don't think so. How you gonna ride automobiles up rocky hills or across streams or around some big, downed log? Nope, ain't possible. Never will be. I'll stick with my horse any day."

"Says otherwise in this article here," Helen McKenna said holding up her magazine. "It's got a picture of the Winton Motor Carriage. Made in Cleveland, and it's gas powered.

"Gas!" Colter laughed. "'N just where in heck you s'posed to get gas?"

"It's got one cylinder and two forward speeds. And it goes in reverse too. Says here, Mr. Winton drove one from Cleveland to New York in forty-seven hours, thirty-four minutes. That's seven hundred and seven miles in less than forty-eight hours at a speed of fifteen and a half miles per hour. That man was near flyin'!"

"Flyin' or walkin', where'd this Winton fella get his gasoline?"

"Maybe we could take our money and invest it in Mr. Winton's motor carriage company. I think it's going to be real big in the nation's future."

"Somethin' don't sound right, Mama Helen. I heard about these horseless carriages, 'n they all need fuel. No way Mr. Winton coulda drove over seven hundred miles on one load a' fuel? He must'a had some horse-drawn vehicles ridin' along with him to carry all his gasoline. So what's the sense'a havin' some fancy, horseless carriage if you gotta have horses to carry all your gasoline? That don't make no sense."

"Maybe he had some extra buckets of fuel on board with him."

"Maybe, but somehow that don't seem too practical neither. No, I don't think nothin's ever gonna replace the horse."

"Says here they only cost a thousand dollars, and we'll have a whole lot more than that before the year's up."

There was a hard knocking at the door, and Colter got up to answer it.

Helen McKenna looked out the window. "Looks like Ole Smoke," she said.

Colter opened the door and Ole Smoke peered in. "Yer mama home?" Ole Smoke asked. "'Peers like we got us a 'mergency."

Colter stepped outside and closed the door behind him. "You just rid' in from camp?"

"Yep, 'n good thing the moon's near full," Ole Smoke remarked. "I rid' Camptown Road the hour 'tween moonset 'n sunrise."

"What's the problem, Smoke?"

"The cattle. They's sick."

"What do you mean 'sick'? How so?"

"It come on 'em sudden-like. The calves been dyin' 'n some'a the cows's weak."

"How many cows?"

"Can't say but it's an awful big bunch. Them cows afflictioned their sickness to some'a the bulls even – 'cept fer them Texas bulls yer mama bought; they's the healthiest'a the lot. Them Texas bulls's probably the strongest stock we ever seen in this county. But we been separatin' 'em out so's they won't all come down with it."

"Good; that was smart. Now we gotta try 'n keep it that way. I need you 'n the men to separate out all the healthy stock 'n put 'em out on fresh range where there ain't too much poop nor cow-bit grass."

"But it's all been pooped or cow-bit."

"No, it ain't neither," Colt corrected him. "That low-valley range just west of the river ain't been used all season. That tract'a land ain't hardly seen any cattle for the last two years."

"Yep, that's true," Ole Smoke said in agreement. "We sure could range 'em there aw'right."

"I'm gonna ride into town tonight 'n get the vet out there. We need ourselves a real doc to see this firsthand."

"I'll take care ever'thin'," the old cowpoke said, walking to his horse.

"'N we don't need nothin' said to no strangers about this neither," Colt reminded. "Last thing we want is to be scarin' off buyers afore our stock gets well."

"I'll make certain nobody says nothin' to nobody," Ole Smoke offered reassuringly then climbed onto his horse.

Colter waited a few minutes, watching Ole Smoke ride away, before going back inside.

"What'd Ole Smoke want? Anything wrong?" Mama Helen asked anxiously.

"Ain't sure yet. Some'a our stock's come down with somethin'. I'm gonna get the vet to ride out with me."

"How many are sick, and how bad is it?"

"Won't know till I see for myself, Mama Helen," he said, tying on his sidearm. "But Smoke said some calves's died 'n some'a the cows has gotten sickly. But I won't know nothin' positive till the vet looks at 'em."

Helen McKenna moved forward in her chair. "Calves dead. But we can't afford to have any of our stock die now – not when we're just gettin' ready to sell them."

"Now, don't hold on to that worry too much, Mama Helen. It may be just some'a them cows has got hold'a some bad drinkin' water. 'N they might'a just passed it on to the calves through their teat milk. You always gotta expect a certain amount'a losses out on the range. It's normal."

Helen McKenna walked to the kitchen cupboard. "Here," she said handing a cloth sack to Colter. "You can eat these hardtack crackers on the way. And be sure to fill up your canteens before you leave town for camp. Old Doc Barnes's dead now so you'll have to get that drunken, fool Walters. Here's some cash. Folks say this new doc won't work 'less you pay him first."

Colter accepted the hardtack and cash and walked to the door. "Don't worry, Mama Helen, it's likely just some bad water. I'll be back soon as everything's taken care of."

"You be careful now," she cautioned Colter.

Doorways are monumental places. They are where you stand when you watch your loved ones leaving and returning. As times previous, Helen McKenna now found herself standing in the same dispassionate doorway, looking out and worrying. And, as before, she could not help but shudder slightly as she watched her young son riding off into the foreboding uncertainty of that wild and potentially baneful, indifferent night.

12

IS THERE A DOCTOR IN THE SPORTING HOUSE?

It was around three thirty in the afternoon when Colter stood outside the saloon, looking in through the window. "Doc Walters in there?" he asked a drunken man coming out.

"Who?"

"The vet."

"Nope, he ain't in there," he said wiping his mouth on his sleeve. "He's prob'ly over there," he said, pointing to the building across the street. "Likely got ole Mule Face in there with him."

"Ole Mule Face? What's that?"

"Can't tell ya, kid. Ya just gotta see her firsthand."

"Well, whatever she is, if the doc's not in the saloon, there's a good chance he's sober," Colt commented.

"Don't be so sure 'bout that!" the drunk laughed. "Ole Mule Face's so ugly it takes a whole lot'a red nose-paint to get into that bed. She's the ugliest strumpet we ever seen. And she's fresh from Bostontown too. God must make them whores real ugly in Bostontown."

Colt ignored the drunk and walked across the street to the ramshackle building the drunk had pointed out. He knocked on the door; no one answered so he knocked again. After waiting several minutes, he opened the door and stepped inside. Colt found himself in a dust-ridden parlor with walls colored gaudy red and faded in places by the incoming sun. The room contained several chairs and a table, all covered with some type of frilly material of a lusterless red color.

A middle-aged woman in a food-stained, cotton nightgown entered the room. "What's your pleasure, sonny boy?" she dryly greeted.

"Doc Walters here?"

"Yeah, but he's kind'a busy right now."

"Yeah, I s'posed he would be. But we need him for an emergency. Can you get him out here for me?"

She stared at the boy a few moments. "Hey, Rosie!" she shouted, keeping her eyes on Colt. "Somebody out here wantin' to see Doc Walters!"

"He's biiiizzzeeeey!" a rough sounding woman loudly shouted from a backroom.

"I told him that but he said it's a witness-bearin' emergency!" She turned to Colt, "It is witness-bearin', ain't it?"

"Yeah, it's witness-bearin' for sure."

"It's for sure witness-bearin', Rosie! You tell the doc to put his pants on and get out here!"

"All Riiiiiiight!" the voice angrily shouted. "You don't have to screeeeaam!"

"Mule Face always thinks somebody's screaming at her," the lady whispered to Colt. "She's got some kind'a vexation inside her."

"Mule Face? Is that what everybody calls her?"

"No, and don't you be callin' her that neither – 'less it's behind her back. She's a real stickler 'bout not bein' made fun of."

"He's coming out now! And you make sure he pays for the extra!" Mule Face demanded from a backroom.

After a couple of minutes, Doc Walters opened the backrooms' hallway door and walked into the parlor. He reeked of alcohol. "What's this powerful big emergency?" he asked, tucking his shirttail into his pants.

"Kid here's lookin' for ya. Mule Face says you owe extra."

"What's the problem, boy? Do I know you?"

"I'm Colter Barnett, from the McKenna Ranch. We need you to come out 'n take a look-see at our stock."

"Colter Barnett? That name sounds vaguely familiar.... So what's wrong with your stock?"

"Can we talk outside?" Colt beckoned.

"Something you can't tell me here, boy?"

Colt walked toward the door and indicated for the doctor to follow.

"What is it, boy? Some kind of big secret?" the veterinarian asked as he followed Colt outside.

Once the door was closed, Colt turned and said, "We got some sick cattle, Doc. I don't know how many or how bad. But I was told some'a our calves died 'n we got some ailin' cows. I came outside because we need to keep this quiet. We don't need to be spookin' buyers for somethin' that might just end up bein' a whole lot'a nothin'. The bulls we got from Texas are still healthy so I figure it's prob'ly tainted water what's caused it. But whatever it is, we need you to come out 'n do your trained vettin' on 'em."

"Whose place is this again?"

"The McKenna Ranch."

"Oh yeah, I know the McKenna Ranch. Those folks always hired Doc Barnes to do veterinary work for them. Guess now that Barnes is dead, they'll be coming to me."

"Guess so."

"That'll be thirty dollars."

"Thirty dollars! But that's more'n a month's pay for one'a our ranch hands," Colt objected.

"Not if you're counting his room and board it's not," Doc Walters countered.

"You plannin' on movin' in, are ya?"

"It's still thirty dollars, whether I move in or not. Pony up fifteen now and fifteen after I examine the herd."

Colt reached into his pocket, carefully pulled out no more than twenty dollars, counted it then handed fifteen dollars to the veterinarian.

Doc Walters counted and re-counted the money.

"Alright, it's all there. Let's go over to my office, boy, and get some necessaries. Oh, wait a minute," he said, as if remembering some small detail, and walked back inside the bordello.

Colt waited outside and watched through the open doorway.

"Here you go, darlin'," the doctor smilingly said to the woman in the food-stained nightgown and handed her a coin. "Fifty cents. That's for all my extra with Rosie."

"Lordy me! A whole fifty-cent piece? Why so much?" the woman asked sarcastically.

"I know. But there's a little extra in there for the last couple of times too."

"Fifty cents! Heavens! What in tarnation's been goin' on back there?" the woman said with a laugh as she walked across the room with the coin. But, after putting on her glasses and examining the coin, she protested, "Hey! This here's Mexican!"

"And worth every centavo, I might add," the doctor magnanimously declared as he left the establishment.

Colt walked alongside the slightly staggering doctor to the veterinary office. The boy was upset at having been charged the outrageous sum of thirty dollars and at having been forced to make an advance payment of fifteen dollars. He considered this veterinarian to be little more than a professional thief, and Colt told himself he wouldn't try catching the teetering sot should he fall.

It took a good, long while for the doctor to gather up all the "necessaries" from his office; and Colt, being true to his nature, put aside his irritation at having been "overcharged" and carried out all the supplies for the sobriety-impaired medical man.

The veterinarian asked Colt to saddle up a horse and wait outside while he attended to his own "very private and personal medical condition" before embarking upon "that physically strenuous journey into the wilderness." While accomplishing this chore, Colt occasionally peered in through the window and observed the doctor slowly finishing off the contents of his "medicine bottle."

The young man worked at keeping his anger in check solely because he needed the services of the trained, medical practitioner. So Colt waited patiently. The consequence of this toleration was that the doctor didn't finish self-administering the curative elixir until a little after six in the evening. With everything ready to go and the veterinarian at last, outside, Colt managed to get Doc Walters onto a horse; then the responsible adolescent and carefree adult rode out toward Camptown Road, the most direct route to the McKenna rangeland.

For more than a half hour into the ride, the two said nothing because the drunken Doc Walters was obviously in no mood to talk. After that, the vet began to make light but sporadic comments, such as: "Night's gotten chilly," and "Road's not too fearfully dark." Actual conversation didn't begin until after the doctor belched loudly and said, "Nothing like a good belch to clear the head," followed with his waving the air in front of his face and exclaiming, "Whooooooeeey, that's stinky! What on God's good earth did I ingurgitate?"

"You might wanna clean the spill off your latchpan," Colt said, not bothering to conceal his disgust.

The vet felt his mouth. "Oh, you're so right. Sorry, boy. This is what happens when you drink too much medicine." And he pulled a handkerchief from his coat pocket and wiped his mouth.

"You told me you got some bulls from Texas. Have they uh....?" Again, the doctor belched loudly. "Whooooooo, pardon me!" he said, waving the air from the front of his face. "Lord, that's revolting!"

Colt felt strong repugnance toward this ill-mannered medical man but tried hard to ignore it. "They're the healthiest'a the herd, I been told," Colt responded. "Right now, them 'n the other good stock are bein' drove to fresh pasture to keep 'em all from sickness. Seemed like the best idea."

"Yes, it normally would be. Oh God, this is vile!" Doc Walters said, still waving the air by his nose. "Believe me, boy, I don't customarily smell like this. It's the medicine."

"Glad to hear it. But what do you mean by 'normally would be'? Ain't it a good idea to separate out the herd?"

"Too early to speculate, boy. Once I have a good look at them, I'll know. Moon's bright enough to read by," he said, changing the subject. "We've been out here a while, and this night air's making my innards cold. Got any whiskey?"

"No, only water. Want some?"

The doctor wiped his mouth with his sleeve. "No, no water for me. Maybe later."

"I was with the herd for the last couple'a weeks 'n only left a short while. How could they'a gotten sick so fast?"

"It could be anything. Like you said, it might even be bad water. Speaking of which, are you sure you haven't got anything more powerful than water to drink?"

"Nope, water's it. I got an extra canteen."

"No thanks, I can wait," the doctor grumbled then abruptly changed the subject. "Damn, now I remember! Colter Barnett – the guy who accidentally shot himself or got killed in a gunfight or something! Yes, I remember him now. You're Colter Barnett's boy."

"Yeah, I'm him. Most folks call me Colt."

"What a coincidence. Your father and I were kind of friendly... sort of. At least, I used to know him a little before he worked for McKenna. He always seemed good with horses. He'd get in a corral and spend hours with some fired-up killer just so it'd get used to him. Some folks said it was a stupid waste of time but I'd say he had talent."

"I'd say he had talent too."

"Sure wish I had some whiskey, Colt. I don't suppose....?"

Colt changed the subject. "You really like goin' to those places, Doc?"

"By 'those places,' you're referring to....?"

"You know: that place back there where I met you."

"Oh, you mean whorehouses." Doc Walters became suddenly peevish. "Sure, I like going in there. What's wrong with that? I haven't got a wife anymore. She up and ran off with some manure-smelling cowboy just like the pig she was. So what am I supposed to do, sit home and cry?"

Colt was surprised by Doc Walter's reaction. "Sorry. I shouldn'ta asked."

"No, you can ask. You're never too young to learn, boy. But, in truth, I don't see anything wrong with a man going to a whorehouse if he needs companionship. At least you know what type of woman you're dealing with – not like my pig wife who hid it from me for all those years."

"Yeah, I s'pose that makes sense."

"But don't get me wrong, boy. I'm not saying it's good all the way around. No, someone your schoolboy age should never be caught dead in a sporting house. Those are for dirty, old, drunken doctors like me to go to," he said jokingly. "Anyway, nobody cares what some roostered-up, old reprobate like me does. I could take a goat to a barn dance and still be popular as President McKinley."

"The president goes to barn dances? But ain't he married?"

"You're missing the point, boy. But, yes, of course he's married. He's married to Ida. Ida McKinley. Now there's a fine woman! How devoted those two are to each other! Why couldn't I have found a woman like Ida instead of that pig wife of mine?"

The doctor's perseveringly inebriated mind turned to politics. "And President McKinley is still the best president this country's ever had or is ever going to have. He got Cuba straightened out once and for all, and he whipped Spain's colonialist butt at Manila Bay. We never lost even a single man at Manila Bay! Did you know that?"

"No, I sure didn't. Where's Manila Bay?"

"You don't know where Manila Bay is? Boy, I'm surprised at you. Manila Bay is in the Philippines."

"The Philippines?"

"Next you're going to tell me you don't know where the Philippines are located. Boy, you need to forget about whorehouses and go back to school."

"So we didn't lose a single man in that fight. That's good to find out."

"No, we didn't. And all the credit goes to the great President McKinley. What an exemplary man he is. Did you know that President McKinley is the most popular Republican across all forty-five states? The working man likes him. The newspapers like him. Even the Democrats and that low-down, water-guzzling Prohibitionist Party secretly like him. God really looked out for this country when He sent us Willie McKinley, and God won't ever let anything bad happen to that man. McKinley's here on a divine mission! Good strong tariffs; that's the answer to this country's problems. And just like McKinley beat that religion-hating, tea-drinking, "cross-of-gold" carrying William Jennings Bryan, he'll beat the pants off him again – if Bryan should get nominated, that is. Come November, Willie McKinley'll whip "The Great Commoner's" pants right off!"

Colt didn't know anything about politics, and no one he knew ever talked about much more than cattle and grub. In fact, he had forgotten the name of the president until Doc Walters mentioned the word "McKinley." But Colt was now mightily impressed with this politically brainy, worldly knowledgeable, doctor – even if that same person were also a talk-too-much, drunken, money-grubbing, smelly, gas-belching slob.

"I guess maybe I shouldn't have mentioned William Jennings Bryan's pants, especially after making reference to our sweet and refined First Lady, Mrs. Ida McKinley." And he returned to the theme of whorehouses. "But, as I was saying, yes, I do go into those places. But I'm old and experienced so, naturally, I'm allowed. But you – you on the other hand – you're way too young to be in those kinds of places. No, it wouldn't do at all for a boy your age to be hanging around some delightfully seductive, sensation-pleasing cathouse."

"Don't worry. So far, I got no plans to."

"Good for you, boy! So are we finished talking about this or does your young and curious mind have any more questions?"

"Just one, Doc."

"Well, now's your chance. Ask wholeheartedly."

"I was just wonderin', Doc: Why do them cuddle-parlor gals always have such different soundin' names? Like your girlfriend, f'rinstance. Why do they call her that mule name?"

"If you're referring to the insulting sobriquet of 'Mule Face' heaped upon her by the rude townsfolk and her Jezebel colleagues, personally, I find it despicable. If anyone should be allowed to call a person by an animal name, it would be me because I'm a veterinarian. But I'm much too much of a gentleman to call any lady 'Mule Face' – not even in reference to those indolent wastrels she shares that house with. Why, I didn't even call my no-good, cheating wife 'Pig Face' – and she was an actual pig!"

"I see."

"No, boy, never assign that moniker to my sweet Rosie. 'Mule Face' is a disparaging 'nom de guerre' and no way to address a lady. To me, she'll always be just 'Rosie'; my kind and thoughtful, petticoat princess. Sure, she yells a bit too much but that's to be expected in her line of work. Other than that, I thoroughly enjoy her company. And just because she's employed at that bawdy-house doesn't mean we do any depraved or untoward acts together."

"You don't?"

"No, most certainly not. With Rosie, all I ever do is talk. It's all we've ever done – just talk. And that's all I pay her for. Of course, I always walk out tucking in my shirttail so nobody ever gets the wiser. But we just talk is all."

Colt considered Doc Walter's admission a bit of an eye-opener but said nothing in response.

"Speaking of tucking in the old shirttail, my Rosie gal sewed me a pair of drawers last month made entirely from feedsack. It says 'American Sugar Refining Company' on the back." He laughed. "Of course, they're way too tight but she's still such a sweet, sweet lady to do that for me."

"If she's sewin' you up in sugar britches, you bet she's sweet. You ain't sportin' them things now, are ya?"

"No, of course not. Why would you ask me such an insulting question as that? A man's drawers are his own personal and private business."

"You brought it up. I'm just sayin' don't go flashin' any sugar britches in camp. The cowpunchers won't like it."

"Now, hold it right there, boy. My Rosie was simply having a little fun with me. Of course, I'd never put on a pair of feedsack drawers! It's unthinkable! I'm a doctor, for Christ's sake! How insulting you are! Don't talk to me anymore."

And so on they rode for over an hour without saying a word to each other. Doc Walters occasionally mumbled to himself but Colt never interpreted that as a signal to communicate.

In the course of time, Doc Walters abruptly opened up. "Look, Colt," he said with a somewhat sober but agitated expression, "what I told you earlier about us – my Rosie gal and me – about our only talking and not doing any uh...any you know...that's just something between you and me. Alright? Let's not go telling anyone else. You agree?"

"That's fine," Colt said.

"No, I mean it, Colt. What my lady and I do in the privacy of some unkempt backroom of some nefarious house of ill repute is entirely confidential. Now, I need your bonded word on this."

"Okay, Doc, I won't say anything."

"Because it's nobody's business what somebody does – or does not do – in that den of iniquity. That's private between two people – although, I have heard there are sometimes more people involved. Still, no matter how many participants are implicated, it's all sacred in the eyes of inviolable intimacy and must remain our secret for all of eternity."

"For all eternity? Don't worry, Doc, I ain't interested in talkin' to nobody that long."

"If you must know the unvarnished truth, Colter, it could be very embarrassing for me if some people were to find out that Rosie and I were just talking. Right now, all the saloon louts think I'm this great, big lover – and that's how I want it to stay. I wouldn't have opened my big mouth to you about it except for all this stinking, alcohol-based medicine I dumped into me. Normally, I...bwaaaaaaap!" the doctor loudly belched. "Oh Lord! Where'd that come from? So that's what's been doing it," he observed, waving away the odor from his face.

"What you 'n Rosie don't do in that place is your business; not mine nor nobody else's."

"And...how about those feedsack drawers I mentioned?"

"Look, Doc, I'd rather talk about cattle. Least it's somethin' I know about."

"Good boy! That's just what I wanted to hear from you!" The vet's spirits picked up. "So you say you got some bulls all the way from Texas? Why Texas of all places?"

"Shoot, Doc, everybody knows them Texas ranches have the best breedin' stock."

"Yes, that's what they say. So what about your family, Colt? Where did the Barnetts hail from originally?"

"Sorry. I can't say, Doc," Colt answered.

"Can't say; hmmmm? Oh, this is too interesting. Could it be that maybe you've got a few skeletons in the old cupboard yourself? Why don't you just ease your burden, boy, and share them with me?"

"Heck, I ain't got no skeletons, Doc. I just don't know is all."

"Oh, I see. Well, I'm glad we had this little talk, Colt. It's important that we uh...that we trust each other and uh...uh...." Doc Walters put his hand to his mouth and released three short but nearly connected belches, followed by one tremendously long but disconnected one. "Oh God, this is worse than most horse farts," he complained, turning his head away from the odor.

Once again, Colt had the strong desire to verbally manifest his point-blank annoyance with the fume-eructing veterinarian. But he remembered the sick and dying cattle and controlled himself.

Another period of no talking ensued. Thereupon, about ten minutes of on-the-trail, uninterrupted belching occurred before Doc Walters sobered up sufficiently to ride composedly alongside Colt and talk about everything and anything – everything and anything, that is, except his intimate whorehouse conversations with a certain vociferous tart possessing the byname of "Mule Face."

13

REDWATER AND FIRE

---

iding toward main camp, Colt was first to notice something in the darkness. Approximately thirty feet off the road and sticking out from behind some brush was something black and large.

"What's that?" the doctor asked.

They halted their horses and looked out.

"Appears like a downed cow," observed Colt. "Let's go see."

They dismounted and walked through the brush and low grass. When they were close enough, they observed it to be a cow, dead and laying on its side. Ten or fifteen feet behind the decomposing mother lay a dead calf and, several yards farther, yet another dead cow.

"What's happened here, Doc?"

"Don't know," the veterinarian said, bending over the cow and visually inspecting it. "But it's not good. Clearly, this animal wasn't attacked by a predator, and I doubt if the other two were either. No, this looks more like disease – maybe Redwater – but I can't say in this dark."

"Redwater? Does that mean they got hold'a some bad water like I guessed?"

The doctor felt the dead animal. "No, it's something else; kind of like malaria in humans. Redwater Fever's killed a lot of stock. How far to camp?"

"Prob'ly mile 'n a quarter I'd say," Colt answered. "Can people catch this Redwater?"

"No, not as far as we know. No reported cases in humans up to this point anyway. So we're probably safe. Still, I wouldn't tell the men to be touching cattle carcasses like I just did. I need to wash. Would you get me some water?"

"Sure." Colt walked to his horse and retrieved a canteen.

"I need you to pour some of that on my hands."

Colt opened the canteen and poured water over the doctor's hands.

"I don't like taking chances with this stuff," the doctor said. "Though, it'd sure be a lot better if I had some whiskey to clean up with. You certain you can't come up with any alcohol, Colt?"

"Sorry. Not if I was the Savior, I couldn't," Colt answered.

Doc Walters rubbed his wet hands together as he walked away from the dead cattle.

"Well, have you got any food then? All at once, I'm feeling kind of hungry." He shook his hands then wiped them on his pants.

"Got some hardtack crackers. Or we can wait till we get to the grub wagon," Colt suggested.

"No, I'm hungry now."

The two men saddled up and rode towards camp, gnawing on hardtack and drinking canteen water.

After riding about one-half mile, the veterinarian asked, "What's that out there? Looks like it might be more carcasses."

"I hate to say it but I think you're right."

"It certainly looks like a mass of dead animals out there. I'd be surprised if we didn't ride out tomorrow and find most of your cattle already goners."

Colt became dispirited by the veterinarian's "already goners" remark and felt immediate concern for Mama Helen's future; it showed in his countenance.

The doctor, incorrectly interpreting Colt's response as a vulnerability of character, felt inclined to take advantage of the moment.

"Don't go getting all faint-hearted in the saddle there, baby boy. It's only cattle and much too early for any of your childish poltroonery."

"Any'a my what?"

Colt didn't know what "poltroonery" meant but it was clearly an insult.

"Look here, Apple Jack, I don't know what you think you just read in my face but I don't take kindly to that kind'a talk."

Doc Walters was momentarily stunned.

"Now, don't go flying off the handle, Colt," the doctor backed off. "I'm just saying that we don't know what the problem is yet or how far it's progressed. It might just be restricted to those few cows or it might be something worse. But it's way too early to let ourselves go wilting. I'm just trying to buck up your spirits, boy."

"My spirits don't need no buckin' up, thanks."

Doc Walters wondered if this gun-toting, temperamental, young boy had the potential to be dangerous. That thought was followed by remembrance of local barroom tales regarding the legendary Billy the Kid and of the argumentative drunks who had credited the Kid, incorrectly or otherwise, with having killed upwards of twenty-one men.

"How far is it to your cowboy camp?" the doctor asked nervously.

"Just up over that ridge; maybe three-quarter mile usin' hawk wings. But since we ain't birds, we gotta climb some."

They rode up the ridge made less steep by the turnings and twisting of a path cut into the hillside.

"All this catty-cornering gets kind of hard on a man's gut," the doctor complained.

"Yeah, well what do you think it does to the horse?"

When they reached the hillcrest, they could see the campfire below. This cattle ranch encampment looked falsely utopian against the backdrop of mountains and clear night sky.

"There she is, Doc," Colt pointed out, "Home, sweet home. Okay, let's head down."

The doctor felt nauseous and shamelessly choked the saddle horn during the steep moonlit descent to the plain.

"I hope there's some good strong drink in your camp. I really need something to settle my guts."

"Somebody's always got somethin'. Look, I think I see a couple cowhands standin' out there."

The two cowboys stood watching the shadows of horsemen riding towards them.

"Hey, it's Colt," one of the men shouted. "And he's got that new doc with him."

Colt and Doc Walters rode up but only the doctor dismounted as the two cowhands sauntered up to them.

"Ooh, that saddle's a killer!" the doc complained, rubbing his sore backside. "It's not natural for a man to ride on a horse. Christ I'm thirsty! Find out if they got anything to drink, Colt boy."

"Hey, Colt," one of the cowboys greeted. "See ya got the new doc there with ya."

"Yeah, this here is Doc Walters."

"Howdy, pards," Doc uncharacteristically drawled, attempting to sound cowboy-like.

The cowboys looked at each other quizzically.

"So how's it been goin' out here?" Colt asked.

"Well, we got most'a the healthy ones cut out 'n drove to the river valley. But we still got a lot'a sick ones on our hands," the cowboy said. "Passed a bunch a sick ones three-quarter mile south'a here on the East Wind Flats."

"Lot of sick ones, eh?" the doctor responded. "Christ am I thirsty! Which one of you cowpokes has got some whiskey to drink?"

"How many sick 'n dead?" Colt asked.

"Oh...prob'ly two-thirds. Maybe more," the man responded.

"Two-thirds!" Colt exclaimed. "Let's go look at 'em now, Doc."

"Now? But I'm thirsty – and it's way too dark out there."

"We'll make our own light. You men get together a lot'a burnin' wood," Colt ordered. "Then meet us at that flat piece just afore goin' down into the river valley. Let's go now, Doc. You'll get your drink later."

The veterinarian recognized that he was dealing with a "won't take no for an answer," headstrong adolescent.

"Oh, alright. What the hell. I rode this far."

Reluctantly, Doc saddled up and followed Colt toward the flats, which ran in the direction of the rich, low-valley pastures that stretched out and across a wide and free-running river system.

As they rode, Colt and Doc Walters were intermittently confronted by sightings of lifeless, adult cattle and calves scattered out alongside the trail. In the distance, they sometimes made out dark forms that they surmised must be even more dead cattle.

"This is astounding," the doctor remarked, "so many animals here. How many cattle does this ranch have?"

Colt gave his routine answer to that question. "We figure forty thousand, give or take a few dozen."

"Forty thousand! My God! Just how big is this place?"

"Right around twelve thousand acres. It's got a lot'a rock 'n mountain 'n over-growed places – nice to look at but no good for nothin'. But at least five thousand's in useful, grazin' land."

"I knew the McKenna's Ranch was big but I had no idea. I've never been out here before."

"That place there is where a considerable amount'a stock should be," Colt said, pointing into the distance. "I see a lot'a somethin' out there but I don't see no movement." Colt knew that "no movement" implied another mass of dead livestock but he just couldn't bring himself to say it outright.

The riders rode onto the flats along a line of dead and deathlike bovines. It was a shuddersome sight, compounded by darkness of night under the light of a bright moon. They steered their horses between the animals, maneuvering back and forth to avoid stepping on carcasses. The sickly smell of decaying flesh surrounded them, and they tied bandanas around their faces to keep from breathing in the noxious odors.

"Whew! That is one magnificent stench! Now you see how they got the term 'malaria,'" the doctor touted. "It's Italian for 'bad air.'"

"Let's get out'a here till the wood comes in," Colt said to the doctor.

Doc Walters' horse followed Colt's horse away from that far-flung group of bodies and to a clearing atop a hill. From there, they surveyed the woebegone land below.

"It won't be long before sunup. Maybe we should just wait," the doctor suggested.

"Daybreak's still five, maybe six hours away yet. Wonder where they are with that wood?" Colt asked himself aloud.

"Here they come," Doc Walters said, pointing to the silhouettes of oncoming riders.

Some ranch hands rode up the hill to Colt's location. Ole Smoke approached. "Where ya gonna be wantin' this wood, Colt?"

"See that open spot out there?" Colt pointed out. "Have the men make a fire in that."

"Let's go, boys!" Ole Smoke beckoned the others to follow. "We's firin' up the open spot!"

"We'll have good light in no time," Colt informed Doc.

But Doc didn't want to wait for the firelight. Spying an isolated, dead cow some sixty feet away, he dismounted from his horse and walked over to it. Seeing this, Colt also dismounted and walked up to the doctor.

Doc Walters slowly walked a complete circle around the animal before getting down on his knees to perform a more critical inspection.

"This is a real shame," the vet opined. "This cow was well fed and good for market. She appears to have calved not too long ago but there's no dead calf anywhere nearby. Probably died somewhere else and mama had to leave it. This is a real tragedy, Colt."

The veterinarian carefully inspected the cow's mouth and nose, checked its head and behind the ears, then he ran his hands over the body, feeling for signs or cause of disease.

"I can't make out anything in this light. If there's a tick here, I sure can't feel it."

"You think a tick is able to do all this?" Colt asked.

"Some people don't think so but, if it's Redwater, that's what did it for sure. Those ticks'll get on an animal and hang on for days and weeks, biting, and feeding on the blood. Their bites spread the disease throughout the animal and, before long, you got yourself an infested herd."

"What can we do about it?"

"Not sure. It might depend how far it's gotten into the herd and how sick your animals are. The cattle here are either dead or so near-dead that nothing can be done. First, we have to determine what the problem is. It may be Redwater. It may not be."

"You men, we need that fire now!" Colt shouted anxiously. "Hurry it up there!"

Doc Walters picked up on Colt's worry.

"No forget the fire, Colt. There's nothing I can do here now. I'm going to need more light. Let's just go to camp, get something to drink and wait till sunup. Five hours or so won't make any difference one way or the other. Your boys got any whiskey back there?"

Colt didn't want to hear that there was nothing that could be done at that time. He wanted immediate answers, immediate actions, and an enemy to fight right there and then.

"Let's go, Colt. I'm telling you; this is a waste of time."

Colt hesitated. He looked at the moon, guessed the remaining hours until daylight, and then resigned himself to accepting Doc Walter's ostensibly sensible opinion.

"Forget the fire, men!" Colt shouted out. "We're goin' back to camp!"

"But it won't take long to pile this all up 'n set to flame," Ole Smoke called back.

"I know but Doc can't work here tonight. It's too dark. So just leave the wood 'n get everybody back to camp," Colt ordered.

"O.K. Yer the boss," Ole Smoke complied.

The men quit piling the timber and mounted up. Colt and Doc Walters walked back to their horses.

"Sun comes up close to five thirty. Guess five hours, give or take, won't change things too awful much," Colt stated and mounted up. "Anyway, this place smells bad. Let's ride out'a here."

Doc Walters smiled slightly; and, although he despised having his judgment second-guessed by a mere teenager, he managed to conceal his irritation by way of amiable dialogue. "Boy, if you think this place smells bad," he said, climbing up onto his horse, "you ain't been around much. I could give you a first-class education on bad smells."

"S'that right," Colt responded skeptically.

"Yeah, that's right. Once you've been a veterinarian as long as I have, you'll have smelled everything. Why, I've smelled smells I never even thought possible to smell; smells so bad that, after a while, I found myself longing to breathe in the good, clean, wholesome smell of rotten shit."

Colt snickered involuntarily.

"That's right, boy, go ahead and snigger. But, you start hanging around me and go where I go and, after a while, shit'll get to smelling to you like some kind of elegant, deluxe perfume."

"Now I'm really hearin' somethin' here. You tellin' me you think shit smells like perfume?" Once again, Colt couldn't help but laugh. "Now see what you made me do. You gone 'n made me laugh. I shouldn't be laughin' out here under these conditions. Now I feel like I gone 'n committed a sin or somethin'. This is way too serious for any laughin' to be goin' on."

"Your right, boy; this is nothing but serious. But you're going to have to take life as it's thrown at you. And laughing's one way to learn how to handle it."

"Glad you waited for your 'medicine' to wear off afore you got to preachin'.'"

"I'm not preaching, boy. I'm just telling you how I see it. Because it seems to me that, no matter how bad it gets, a normal person just can't keep from laughing in the face of tragedy. And the worse it gets, the more you want to laugh. I think laughing might be the only thing that keeps us from going completely crazy."

"Maybe you're right," Colt agreed but then he grinned and added, "Crazy laughin' cure – now there's a fine Sunday sermon."

Doc Walters wanted to backlash at Colt but didn't. He interpreted the boy's remark as rude, insulting and demeaning to his higher station in life – and he also didn't find it to be one bit funny. The doctor quietly seethed as they rode downhill then uphill and steered their horses back and forth through the animal bodies and toward camp. Although, in actuality, Colt hadn't intended to be offensive and was even quietly considering the meaning of Doc Walter's theory regarding the healing effects of laughter.

Once outside the herd, Colt asked, "'N just what kind'a treatment we gonna use on this Redwater Fever?" but then couldn't help himself and jokingly added, "You think laughin' might be able to keep our stock alive?"

The doctor really didn't appreciate the apparent cynicism of the remark, especially coming from one so deficient in years and so seemingly volatile. The vet was especially concerned about the volatility aspects of Colt's personality so he chose not to pick up on the lad's comments and endeavored to retain a professional demeanor.

"This many cattle, I don't know. Some places they dip the cattle in a mixture of crude oil and water to kill off ticks. But even if you were set up for such an operation, it's too late for that now. Then again, sometimes the fever just clears up on its own. And no one knows why." Doc Walters weighed the alternatives in his mind before speaking again. "And then there are those who say dipping is just a big expensive waste of time. Nobody knows for sure. Your boys got any whiskey in camp?"

Colt was experiencing heightened frustration with this drunken doctor, a man who had demanded to be paid in advance and yet didn't seem to be able to provide any solid answers.

"Well, does anybody know anything about this illness?" Colt asked impatiently.

"Not a whole hell of a lot, boy. But one thing's for certain; I've got to wait for better light to make a meaningful diagnosis. So I'm asking you again: Any of your cowboys drink Old Tom?"

Colt felt a momentary sense of despair, an emotion foreign to his nature. *How will I tell Mama Helen the bad news?* he wondered. *She was so sure this season would make money. 'N now this.* It was almost more than he could bear.

"How about Old Towse? Any of your boys drink Old Towse?"

"Yeah, a couple, I guess. You think it's safe to take down our neckerchiefs?"

"You probably won't die if you do but I'm keeping mine on," the doctor answered.

It was unnatural for Colt to find humor in misfortune but, on this day, he was not feeling altogether typical. "So tell me, Doc, you ever try bottlin' that shit-smell perfume'a yours 'n givin' it to your lady friends?"

Doc Walters took this as Colt's attempt to set things right, and the vet's well-seasoned gallows humor immediately picked up on Colt's comment. "No, I can't say as I have. Of course, most of the low-down, lady friends I used to cavort with wouldn't have had any need for it. They had plenty of shit smell of their own."

Colt laughed loudly then tried to contain his amusement. "How far do you reckon we should be afore we take these kerchiefs off," Colt asked.

Doc Walters looked back and checked the distance. "Think I'll keep mine on awhile longer. One good whiff of that shit smell, and I go all sentimental."

Colt laughed again. "We'll see if we can't get you some'a that Ole Tom when we get back to camp," he said, speaking through the bandana tied across his face.

"Now you're talking! Old Tom and I always like to sing when we get together. And tonight, we'll be performing 'In the Bright Mohawk Valley' for our very first song." The doctor happily began to vocalize: "Oh they say from this valley you're going. We shall miss your sweet face and bright smile...."

No more discussion of whiskey, women, shit-stink perfume or Redwater Fever took place on their ride back to camp. Colt's concern returned to Mama Helen and, for some reason, listening to Doc Walter's rendition of "In the Bright Mohawk Valley" seemed to cause Colt to re-experience his strangely alien sense of despondency.

14

THE HARD MORNING LIGHT

Since arriving back at camp, Colt, Doc and the men had remained awake. They all sat near the Studebaker Roundup-model chuckwagon designed by Colonel Charles "Chuck" Goodnight and drank coffee as the light from the rising sun fired up and over the ridgetop and pierced through the residual darkness.

"This Arbuckle's good n' strong. But I like it like that," one of the men said.

No one responded. Everyone was tired and dreaded going out into fields of dead cattle.

"Light's getting' pretty good now," the cowboy said.

Colt sat holding a coffee mug and staring at the ground. Doc Walters sat leaning against the wagon; his eyes were shut but he was far from asleep.

"I guess we better get this over with," the doctor said, his eyes still closed.

Colt drank the remainder of his cold coffee then stood upright. "Bad luck; I hope it ain't."

Doc Walters opened his eyes and stood, then poured cold coffee from a tin mug into his cupped palm and patted the coffee into his eyes. After shaking the liquid from his face and wiping his eyes with his sleeve, he said, "Yes, coffee's a real pie-opener alright. But now I need a little drink before we go out there. Anyone got some more whiskey?"

"Let's get at it, men, afore this thing turns to night duty," Colt said. "Anything we need to bring with us, Doc?"

"Just a weak nose and a strong stomach. How about a little drink before we go? I surely could use a drink."

No one found any humor in Doc's "strong stomach" remark, and the men began preparing for the ride.

"Just one, little drink, old-timer?" Doc asked Ole Smoke, who was standing near his own horse and getting things ready. "I need it to keep my doctoring hands steady."

Colt nodded to Ole Smoke who retrieved a bottle of whiskey and poured some into Doc's mug.

"Ah, yes! Thank you, my friend!" the doctor said appreciatively to Ole Smoke before guzzling it down. "Ahhhh! Sweet morning nectar! Better than any mother's milk I ever had! How about another one, compadre?"

"That's enough for now, Doc," Colt said.

"But just one more will make my morning bright and beautiful."

"Prob'ly would. But now there's work to do. There'll be more hooch here for ya when the job's done."

Doc Walters sneered at what he felt was this young boy's high-handedness.

The cowboys moved at their usual pace, and it wasn't long before most of the men were mounted up and riding away. Colt led his saddled horse and Doc's unsaddled horse over to where Doc was standing.

"Let's get at 'er, Doc," Colt said.

"Yes, of course, sir. Whatever you say, sir," Doc scorned.

"You're bein' paid. No need to salute'," Colt smoothly countered.

"Like a little drink is going to make any difference," Doc Walters commented lowly to himself, "I should have made him cough up the entire thirty dollars up front."

Colt waited patiently for the vet to saddle the horse. Afterwards, Colt and Doc Walters climbed onto their horses and followed languidly behind the cowboys.

It was the professional, yet unspoken, opinion of the alcohol-tippling doctor that this herd was most certainly afflicted by Redwater Fever. Colt had also secretly resigned himself to the worst. There was plenty of light left in the day and neither person was in an all-fired hurry to get to that location where their suppositions would be decidedly confirmed.

The men were traveling to the area where they had been ready to set a large bonfire some scant hours earlier but the ride out, now, seemed like a death march. Cowboys rode apart from each other, and no one talked. The hired hands were psychologically tired, stemming, in large part, from their feelings of disgust with the way things were turning out. It wasn't simply that they were losing their livelihoods; this place was their home. It's where they worked and lived. They had strong attachments to this range and were understandably concerned with the welfare of the herd.

The cowboys rode somewhere around three-quarters of a mile from camp before arriving back at the East Wind Flats, a place containing an especially large group of "goners," as Doc Walters would have bluntly referred to them. The workers could not help but feel sickened by the sight: acres and acres of dead or fallen cattle stretched as far as the eye could see. The cowhands unambiguously recognized that they had been effectively beaten down by those calloused antagonists known as Death and Disease. But defeated or not, it was part of their cowboy code to see a job through to the end; and see it through, they would. So all the men tied bandanas over their mouths and noses, waited for Colt and Doc to catch up, and prepared for the worst.

By and by, Colt and Doc Walters reached the assembly of riders.

"Let's start over here," Doc Walters directed through his bandana.

Doc Walters got down from his horse, and all the men followed suit.

The vet walked over to a dead calf and visually examined it from head to foot. Then he ran his fingers over the carcass and examined its genitals. "Hmmm. It's red down there. Bloody urine. That's not a good sign."

"S'that why it's called Redwater?" Colt asked.

"That's exactly why," the doctor answered. "And I believe that's what we've got here. And look at this," he said, walking to and into a puddle-sized pool of red-colored liquid. "This is blood and urine mixed together. Yes, this is probably Redwater. Now we just need to find the culprit to prove it."

Doc Walters walked over to a dead cow and started feeling behind the ears. "Some people aren't entirely convinced it comes from a tick. But it sure looks that way to a lot of us. No, nothing here."

He walked over to another dead cow and felt behind the ears. "These ticks move from cow to cow and are often found around the ears. That's because they climb aboard when the cattle bend down to feed. Ah, here it is!" he said, removing it and holding it up for examination.

He walked to another dead animal and felt its head and ears. "Some folks are so dead set against dipping that they've been dynamiting other folks dipping vats. They think it's just a lot of expensive hooey and say they'll fight this tick idea to the death. But most of them change their minds when their cattle start dying. Yes, here's another one!" he said, pulling a tick off the animal and holding it in his hand along with the first tick. "As far as I can tell, these two appear alike. Both are hard shelled. Yes, these are most likely the cause of your problem right here."

The vet walked to another dead animal and discovered another tick. He held all three ticks in his hand and inspected them. "Yes, these look like the culprits to me. Anybody want to see them?"

A few of the men stepped forward to look at the ticks. Colt also stepped forward.

"Those itty-bitty, little things did all this?" one cowboy asked.

"Those itty-bitty, little things are dragon killers." The vet threw them on the ground and stepped down hard upon them.

"Don't you need to take those back to your office, for study or somethin'?" Colt asked.

"No, there's plenty more where those came from. But I am going to be performing some external, postmortem inspections on a lot of these cattle; rudimentary stuff really but there's nothing any of you can do to help. So you cowboys don't have to hang around taking in all this rotten smell. You men all get back to camp. Take it easy. Have a drink. Colt and I'll tend to everything."

"Doc Walter's right," Colt countermanded. "It's better that you men go out to the river bottomland 'n check on the culled herd. If you see any sick ones, cut 'em out'a there."

Doc Walters had been trying to convey the absolute hopelessness of the situation when he told the cowboys to go back to camp. Once again, he felt that this impertinent youngster has devalued his esteemed, veterinary authority. Even though he had listened to and disagreed with Colt's instructions, the doctor sullenly said nothing.

"O.K., Colt," spoke up Ole Smoke. "Aw'right, boys, yuz heered the boss," Ole Smoke called out. "Let's cowboy up!"

Colt stood watching the death-weary cowhands mount up and ride toward "greener" pastures.

"At least it'll give their guts a rest," Colt said.

There was no reply.

When Colt looked around, he saw Doc Walters walking out into the field of dead cattle. Not knowing how to be of assistance, Colt followed along and silently observed the doctor inspecting one decaying carcass after the other.

Standing amidst the dead animals, Colt felt the breeze on the uncovered part of his face as he studied the clouds moving across the sky. It was technically spring yet, despite the season, mountain weather incorporates a natural potential for unpredictability. Nevertheless, Colt concluded that this day was going to be a warm one.

Doc Walters was preoccupied with his work, moving rapidly from animal to animal and cursorily performing his "external, postmortem inspections," and was far from aware of any tedious discomfiture that Colt might be suffering.

The doctor's dartingly non-comprehensive, postmortem investigations bothered Colt greatly. For it seemed to Colt that this veterinarian was planning to spring from one dead animal to another until he had looked over every single carcass on the range, and Colt just wanted this whole disgusting business to be over. At one point, the smell was so strong that Colt had to fight off the impulse to jump onto his horse and gallop away from that field of malodorous flesh and ride to a place where he could rip the bandana from his face and breath freely again.

After what seemed to be a cow-hair's breadth short of infinity, the doctor approached the end of his tasks. So, after examining the same animal twice to achieve a measure of certainty, he turned to Colt and said, "I need some water for my hands. Would you fetch me some water please?"

"Sure thing," Colt answered walking over to his horse to retrieve a canteen.

Doc Walters slowly followed behind. "I'm exhausted, boy," he spoke out. "This is a lot of work for a mere thirty dollars. You're getting quite a deal."

Colt walked up to the doctor, opened the canteen and said, "Hold out your hands, Doc."

Doc Walters held his hands out as Colt poured water over them.

"I've seen enough to determine what killed these animals." Then he made his long awaited pronouncement. "It's

Redwater alright. No doubt about it; it's Redwater Fever for certain."

"But what about the healthy ones, Doc? What're their chances?"

"Chances?" the Doc insolently replied with a smile. He shook the water from his hands and walked toward his horse. "I need some air. There's nothing more to be done here."

"Glad to hear you say that, Doc. I was ready to go a long time ago."

Colt and the veterinarian saddled up and rode in the direction of the river valley pasture land.

"So what are their chances, Doc?"

"Not now. I've got to breathe."

Neither spoke. But when they were far enough from the actual odor of corpses, both removed their bandanas to find the aroma of death still clinging to them. Death was in their clothes, hair, eyes, mouths and nostrils.

"I can still smell them dead cattle," Colt said.

"And you will," Doc offered. "Smells like that hang in the memory long after you've cleaned yourself up."

The pair rode quietly along for some time over uneven hilly ground until they descended into a rocky corridor that led to some of Helen McKenna's most fertile, river bottomland. Eventually, they could see distant cowboys cutting out cattle from the herd. At their high-up perspective, they also saw cowboys at herd's edge driving healthy animals farther down the river valley.

When they were close enough, Colt waved at the ranch hands. A couple of the men saw him and waved back.

"Looks like they're cuttin' out some good ones. Huahy!" Colt shouted. "There's a sight finer'n cream gravy! We'll save this herd yet; right, Doc?"

Doc Walters didn't acknowledge Colt's overly sunny assessment. Neither book learning nor real world practice had ever shielded this medical man's fragile psyche from the unrelenting assaults of nature such as he had just experienced. Doc Walter's congenitally flimsy, thin veneer of concern and objectivity had washed away a long time ago; exposing little more than self-centered survival interests, deep unfounded apprehensions, plenitudinous uncertainties, psychological coarseness and a general malaise of the soul.

A sight finer'n cream gravy! What a bumpkin! the veterinarian thought. At that moment, Doc Walters became re-acquainted with his stop-and-go cravings for the good, strong taste of whiskey.

Colt wondered about the doc's failure to reply and apparent lack of vigor. The young man thought the veterinarian would have been happy to see that so many animals had successfully survived the ordeal. But, obviously, this was not the case, and Colt was curious.

"Christ I'm thirsty!" the doctor barked.

"How the cattle doin'?" Colt asked an approaching cowboy.

"Soon's we spot a goodun, we cut it from the dyin' ground. Lots'a gooduns too. 'Specially them Texas bulls; they's nothin' but healthy. Sure wish they's all like that."

"Thank the Lord for Texas! Hear that, Doc? We're gonna save this herd after all. I'll drive some wagons into town 'n get us some crude oil." Colt turned toward the cowboy, "Go tell Ole Smoke we plan to dip the cattle, 'n everything'll be back up 'n runnin' in no time."

"Will do," the cowboy happily said and rode off.

"What do you think now, Doc? Good news, eh!"

Doc Walters, who had been concealing his contempt for Colt's opinions, kept his head down and said nothing. He wanted to wait for the ranch hand to be out of hearing range before speaking openly to Colt.

"What's that ya say, Doc? Can't hear ya," Colt goaded.

"Won't work, boy." The vet raised his head and looked Colt square in the eyes and said, "They've all got to be shot."

"What!" Colt exclaimed. "Ain't you been listenin' to me? We still got us some good stock."

"Yes, I've been listening."

"So you should know there ain't no reason for us to be shootin' down this herd – not when we still got a good supply'a healthy cattle left. Yeah, we'll have some delay in our plans but we'll build this herd again – especially usin' those big, healthy, Texas bulls we will."

"Those 'big, healthy, Texas bulls,' as you refer to them, will have to be the first to go. They are the ones who caused this entire mess in the first place."

"What are you talkin' about, Doc? They ain't even sick."

"That's right, they're not sick. But they're carriers."

"Carriers? Carriers'a what? Every one'a 'ems healthy."

"So it would appear. But this disease didn't start yesterday, and I know one hell of a lot more than you do about it, sonny boy. So try putting your learning-ears on and listening to me for a change. In Texas, they call it Texas Fever. But call it Texas Fever or Redwater Fever, it's one and the same. And I guarantee you, if I did a tick count on those bulls, they'd be chockfull of those little devils. That's just the way it works, sonny boy."

"But they're healthy."

"Listen to me. No, they are not healthy. For some reason, some Texas bulls have managed to get themselves immune from this disease – that's a known fact. They catch it and won't show any signs at all. But then they'll go on to infect every cow and calf they come in contact with. No, I know you're the big boss of this place, Colter, but, on this matter, you are going to listen to me. This entire herd has got to be exterminated."

"But how do you know these particular Texas bulls even got Redwater in the first place? Why don't we just dip 'em, put 'em all in quarantine 'n see what happens? Then if none of 'em shows any signs'a disease, we can send 'em on to market."

"First of all, boy, that is not going to happen - not while I'm in charge."

"You're in charge? In charge'a what?"

"As a veterinarian, I have certain legal powers and influences. And if I were to contact the State Board of Health, this operation would be shut down right now – right now! – no questions asked."

"Is that what I paid you for? To turn us in to the authorities?"

"You haven't paid me for anything yet – at least, not altogether you haven't. But that's neither here nor there. Right now, I'm trying to make you understand that your cattle have all been contaminated – all of them. So it's just a matter of time before the rest of your cows start showing signs."

"But how do ya know that? What's it gonna hurt to put 'em all in quarantine 'n see if they stay healthy?"

"It doesn't matter if they stay healthy. You can't put this herd to market. You could spread this infection throughout the entire county, maybe the whole state even. No, I can't allow you to do that. It's going to end right here and now. I have a legal obligation, and it's the right thing to do."

"But it'll mean complete ruination for my Mama Helen. She'll lose the ranch. She'll lose everything she's ever worked for. Near every cent she's got's in these animals."

"Well, I'm sorry, sonny boy, but that's too bad for her. I think the public interest is just a little bit more important than your family finances. So your Mama Helen is just going to have to go bust because this herd is being put down," the doctor said coldheartedly.

Colt's right hand unconsciously moved to the pistol at his side, and he stared intently at the doctor.

"What...what are you doing there, boy?" the doctor asked.

Colt stared blankly at him.

Doc Walters recognized he was in danger and that he'd better say just the right thing to avoid taking a bullet. "You think it's easy for me to do this, Colt? Well, it's not. Yes, you could shoot me dead right here, and maybe nobody'd ever be the wiser. But that won't change things. Your cattle will still all be sick, and most of your cows will still die before there's a chance to breed them. So, in the end, all you'd be left with is a bunch of worthless, disease-carrying, Texas bulls and my dead body. I'd sure hate to see you ruin your young life when all I'm doing is trying to help you here – especially since your shooting me won't make a bit of difference, Colt; not one little bit it won't."

Colt's harsh expression toned down some, and he seemed to be snapping out of it. Moving his hand away from his holster, Colt took the reins and slowly rode off.

The doctor, not wanting to lose the advantage of persuasive speech, rode up alongside. "Look, boy, I don't enjoy being the bearer of bad news. But truth is truth. Your cattle are all infected, and there's no way around that fact. They've all got to go."

Colt brought his horse to a halt, put both hands on the saddle horn and looked at the doctor. "What I was thinkin' back there was automatic. I felt like you was attackin' Mama Helen, 'n your words set me off. Ain't sure if I'd actually plugged ya or not. But if I had, I'd been real sorry afterwards."

"I suppose I'm kind of glad to hear that."

"Nothin' personal, Doc. I know you're doin' what you think's best. But this spells the end'a Mama Helen's cattlin' business."

"Apology accepted and no offense taken," Doc Walters adroitly lied, although now feeling increasingly wary of Colt's capacity to react violently and despising the authority-bearing boy all the more for it.

"I know we can't put these cattle to market. But Mama Helen's gonna lose everything. I just can't help but worry about what's gonna happen to her."

"Don't be so sure your mama will lose everything, Colt. The McKennas have had this ranch a long time, and ranchers are used to weathering hard times. But first things first: You shouldn't be wasting any more precious manpower herding those cattle. Do you have a good store of bullets on hand?"

"Yeah, sure we do, but not enough to kill this many animals."

"Well, you're just going to have to get some then because it's got to be done. I recommend you start with the Texas bulls then dispatch all the healthy-appearing ones after that. Nature'll help take care of the rest. And you should have your men get at it right away, while there's good daylight."

Colt hesitated. He didn't like this vet's insistence on having the herd immediately destroyed, and he wanted to ponder things first. Colt needed to consider if there might not be some other possible alternative.

"So what's it going to be, boy? Tempus fugit. Time's flying, and we're just sitting here."

"Yeah, well time's all I got once I listen to you. Right now, I'm askin' you to leave me be, Doc, so I can do some thinkin'."

"Alright," the doctor agreed. "Just don't think about it too long. It still has to be done."

Colt rode about twenty yards away and brought his horse to a halt. He sat there for some time, weighing consequences and searching out possibilities. Colt knew that any verdict he made would have life-altering finality and that it, at least, required some respectful modicum of time to think through. With no little difficulty, Colt arrived at the only decision he could reasonably attain, and he waved over Ole Smoke.

"Smoke, I need you to get the men together. 'N have 'em load up their Winchesters. We gotta kill off the herd."

"What? S'ya done gone crazy?" Ole Smoke cried out. "E'sterminate this herd! Why do that? There's some pretty dang good 'n healthy ones out there! A whole big bunch'a 'em is."

"Sorry, Smoke, we got no choice. Doc says even the healthy ones are sick. They just don't look that way yet."

"This's crazy."

"So now I need you to have the men load their '94s 'n lead pushers 'n bring all the ammunition they got. Then get 'em all here for a meetin'. Can ya do that?"

"Most'a the guns 'n bullets they own, they's already got with 'em. But ya fer sure on doin' this, Colt?"

"You know me, Smoke. I wouldn't do it if I didn't have to. I got no choice."

Ole Smoke shook his head, shrugged, then turned his horse and rode off.

Doc Walters rode up alongside Colt.

"Men ain't gonna like this," Colt said.

"So what if the men don't like it?" the doctor countered. "Who's the boss of this place, you or that boodle of countrified yacks?"

"Mama Helen's boss'a this place, Doc. Only she ain't here now so the decision's on me. But it ain't about who's boss. These are good men. Naturally, they don't wanna be killin' off the herd nor do nothin' to hurt this ranch. Some'a 'em been workin' here a mighty long time."

"I'll take care of it, boy. I've got no problem telling a bunch of dirt-eating, range riders what to do. You just leave it all to me."

Colt looked at him. "You know, Doc, I'm thinkin' maybe I shoulda shot you."

The doctor laughed nervously but, at some level, he suspected Colt wasn't kidding.

Both men got down from their horses and waited for the men to arrive. Colt surveyed the scenery while Doc Walters rested against a boulder and, every now and then, rubbed his hand across his mouth in longing for alcohol.

Ole Smoke assembled the men and gave them his own private and lengthy view of events. Arguing continued amongst the group for over an hour before the men reached an unsatisfactory conclusion. A half hour or so after that, all the cowboys rode up together to Colt's meeting place.

Seeing the men riding in, Doc nervously recoiled from the boulder and ambled over to where Colt stood.

The cowboys dismounted and gathered in front of Colt and Doc Walters.

"Men, I know this is gonna be hard for you to hear – maybe even harder for me to say. But we got no choice here. We gotta kill off the entire herd," Colt spoke out.

It was apparent that Ole Smoke had warned the men of what Colt was going to tell them because they didn't react as they otherwise would have. A few of them did look with murderous contempt at the veterinarian, however.

"I can see you're all loaded up 'n ready to go. So what I just said, you most likely already learned from Ole Smoke. But now – today – we gotta start killin' off every last one'a these animals."

The men grumbled.

"Hold down!" Ole Smoke commanded, "Hold down now!"

The grumbling quickly subsided.

"Doc here says it's Redwater. Turns out, if we was to keep workin' this herd, we'd just be wastin' our time. Worse yet, we'd risk spreadin' it to every bull, cow 'n calf in every part'a the county, 'n we can't do that. So now Doc's gonna say somethin' to ya. You go ahead 'n talk, Doc."

Doc Walters stepped forward, cleared his throat and "heroically" spit on the ground; then he assumed, what he believed to be, his most virile, outdoorsman-like stance.

"Look here, pards. These cattle all have Redwater Fever; also known as Texas Fever, Tick Fever and probably some few other names none of you ever heard of. Now I know most of you cowhands haven't got any education to speak of. Some of you, no doubt, are unable to even read and write your own names. So take it from me – Doctor Walters – a real-life-experienced, highly educated veterinarian – that these animals have that disease called Redwater Fever – every one of them does. And believe me when I say that there's no cure for it. So no matter how deficient you may be in your intelligence and schooling, you should all be smart enough to understand what I have just explained to you."

"You go to hell!" a voice rang out.

"Now, boys, yuz gotta listen to the doc," Ole Smoke admonished the group. "He's the vet; we ain't."

"Thank you, Mr. Smoke, for your most wise endorsement of my scholarship. Now, as I was about to say, even those so-called 'healthy looking' Texas bulls have been completely infected by this disease. The fact is, Texas bulls are known carriers of Redwater Fever, and they're probably the ones who gave it to your animals in the first place. So there's no other alternative but to kill off the entire herd. There; that's all there is to say on the matter. So please don't waste any more valuable time, and just get on with it. They all have to be killed now."

"But what about jus' puttin' 'em in quarantine instead?" asked a cowboy. "Why don't we jus' wait 'n see what happens 'fore we goes killin' 'em all off?"

"I already asked that question," Colt answered for the veterinarian. "Doc says...."

"Quarantine, my ass! Don't you think I'd have already thought of that?" the doctor interrupted, and then raising his voice with an irritation likely activated by alcohol withdrawal, he added, "I'm a veterinarian, for Christ's sake! What are you? Quarantine's not the answer, man! Haven't you been comprehending? All of these animals have been thoroughly infected. Just how many times do I have to tell you cowhoos that?"

"Cowhoos? What's a cowhoo? What'd you jus' call me?" the cowboy reacted, feeling possibly offended and taking a step forward.

"It's alright, Doc. I'll take it from here," Colt interrupted the exchange, regaining control of the group. "Men, I'm sorry to say that I have to agree with Doc Walters here. Quarantine won't make no difference nohow 'cause Redwater always wins in the end. One way or another, all these animals are gonna end up dead; it can't be helped. No, there ain't no use in us draggin' this out any further. Plus, like I said, if some'a these cattle was to cut loose 'n make their way into another herd.... No, Doc's tellin' us the unpleasant truth. It's not somethin' we wanna do but, still, it's gotta be done. Now Doc here's gonna tell you what to do first. Everybody listen to him real close now. He's tellin' it for your own good. You tell 'em, Doc."

Once again, the doctor cleared his throat and assumed his champion-like pose.

"At the outset, I would like to apologize for having appeared a little harsh in my preliminary address. As a humanitarian and dedicated veterinarian, I have always considered myself to be a true friend of low-down cowpokes like yourselves. But, as most of you no doubt know, presently, we have all been experiencing some considerable distress. So I'm sure you'll take that into consideration when you forgive any unintentional rudeness on my part."

"Get to it, tangle-foot. Yer makin' things worse," one of the cowboys shouted.

"Yes, of course. So now the first thing you'll have to do is to kill all of those Texas bulls. Then go after the healthiest looking cattle and work your way down. The rest of them – the sick ones, the calves and the ones that pee backwards – they can all be clubbed to death once you run out of bullets. And you should get at it right away before it gets dark."

Every cowboy, save Colt and Ole Smoke, stared resentfully at the doctor. They didn't like his flippant "ones that pee backwards" comment. It was insulting to the cows.

"Look, cowboys," the doctor said, trying his best to win them over, "if there were any other way, I'd have you do it. But there isn't. And if you don't do it now – humanely – these animals are just going to suffer prolonged and painful deaths. And none of us want that to happen, do we?"

The cowboys continued to stare with hostility at the doctor.

"Men," Colt stepped up, "I know each 'n every one'a you feel like I do. We don't none'a us wanna be doin' this. We all worked hard 'n long to bring this herd to market, 'n now this thing has hit us. It's a terrible way to end up."

Colt stopped talking for several moments.

"But it's just somethin' that's gotta be done is all. So let's just get it behind us, 'n go 'n do it."

There was an uncomfortable silence.

"But we bin workin' this herd day 'n night fer months! It don't seem fair somehow!" a cowboy protested.

"No," Colt replied, "it ain't fair at all. 'N if I coulda saw the future, I'd killed every one'a them Texas bulls afore they ever had a chance to get into this herd. But I didn't see it comin', 'n what's done is done. So let's just get this over with, men. Least we can keep them cattle from sufferin' more'n they otherwise will be."

Colt walked to his horse and mounted up.

"I spoke my piece. Whoever follows, follows. I can't help what any'a ya do."

Without looking back, Colt rode off alone toward the diseased herd.

During Colt's talk, Doc Walters had seized the opportunity to slip away from the unfriendly throng and find sanctuary behind a large tree.

"What a bunch of ignorant, dirt-eating rabble," Doc lowly said, "I hope they all shoot their own asses."

The veterinarian hid from view but could hear the men grumbling and talking amongst themselves. He knew these cowboys had an utmost reluctance to take any action which would harm the herd and that they especially hated the magnitude and methods of his proposed killing. Doc could hear the men arguing and saying that, once the McKenna herd was gone, it would mean an end to their way of life on this range. At core, and for reasons unknown even to himself, the doctor remained unsympathetic to their plight.

"I knew I should've collected the thirty upfront. I hope they shoot their own asses," Doc Walters said to himself."

Fear of their uncertain futures, intermixed with the knowledge that annihilating this herd would mean an immediate loss of employment, made each man's decision-making emotionally and rationally clouded. Some were more stubborn than others and said aloud that they would "never" kill the herd. But, with varying rates of progress, each man eventually arrived at his own conclusion and, in the end, each felt compelled to come around to Colt's point of view. According to the individual's readiness to act, every cowboy mounted up, one by one, and followed his young boss out to the sorrow-filled, grazing land.

15

SANDERS CANYON

C olt stood just outside the herd and waited for his men. He felt certain that all the men would eventually join him, and he was right. Sometime after one thirty in the afternoon, the last man finally made his decision and rode out to join Colt.

As they stood near the border of the herd, all the hands felt listless and none of them wanted to talk. Talking required energy, and no worker wanted to waste precious strength talking about killing cattle. Anyway, what would have been the point? They had already argued the subject with Ole Smoke, and it didn't amount to a hill of beans. As usual, all their talking had been in vain, reinforcing their notion that talking seldom makes one whit of gainful difference to a cowboy's lot.

In addition, these cowboys recognized that, in their group's disheartened state, any fool-angry comment might induce a fellow cowhand to erupt into fracas and perhaps even quit, making them one man short and the slaughtering work that much harder to accomplish. No, these men found that, as a rule, talking only seemed to make life more difficult and generally served no good end.

Colt began his instructions. "Accordin' to Doc, we should cut out the bulls first 'n shoot 'em dead. Then he said to cut out the healthy ones 'n kill them. But this bunch here ain't too weak to run, 'n we sure don't want 'em gettin' spooked 'n stampedin'."

"N jus' how we s'pose to 'complish that?" Ole Smoke asked. "Soon as we start firin' they's all gonna run. 'N what's that doc know about cuttin' out bulls anyways? He ain't the one lie'bell to get killed out here."

"You're right about that, Smoke. Got any ideas?"

"Danged if I know," Ole Smoke said. "I ain't never tried killin' no wallopin' large herd'a cows afore 'n don't know anybody what has. What about runnin' 'em off a cliff or into a ditch or somethin'?"

"That's what I been thinkin' too, Smoke. Or we could herd 'em into Sanders Canyon. It ain't more'n two mile southeast; 'n once we drive 'em in there, we could shoot down on 'em from above. That seems like it might be a good way to handle this."

"Yep, smart as a cricket, that idea is!" Ole Smoke agreed. "Glad I thunk it up!"

"Alright, men," Colt directed the cowboys, "We all gotta work together on this. Five'a you stay back here with Smoke while the rest'a us trail down to Sanders Canyon."

The men indicated they understood.

Colt gave his attention to Ole Smoke, "Smoke, you take your men 'n the dogs 'n cut out as many cattle as you can. But give us some time to get up-top that canyon afore you go runnin' 'em in there. 'N don't nobody go shootin' 'less you have to. Last thing we wanna do is unsettle the herd 'n cause a stampede."

"Yuz heered that, boys?" Smoke called out. "There's ain't to be no shootin' along the trail!"

"Speakin'a which, we're gonna need most'a the bullets your men got," Colt said to Ole Smoke.

"You, you, you, you and you – yuz'll be stayin' with me," Ole Smoke selected his crew. "Boys, give Colt's men most'a yer bullets. They's gonna be needin' 'em more'n us."

Ole Smoke's crew handed over most of their bullets to Colt's men.

Colt turned to Ole Smoke. "After you cut out the cattle, only use three cowboys to herd 'em into Sanders Canyon."

"I'll be one'a them three," Ole Smoke said decisively.

"Fine. Then leave the other three behind to go back 'n cut out a second bunch. 'N make sure those men wait a proper spell afore they go movin' that second herd in to us. We sure won't need more'n we can handle."

"I get it. Ya want me to be splittin' up the congregation."

"Well, since nobody here's got any experience doin' this sort'a thing, it just seems like a good idea to be splittin' up the animals to make it less burdensome."

"I 'gree. But jus' make sure these animals's drove in real close to yuz afore yuz commences to shootin'. We don't need no bullets droppin' in on us from above."

"So how 'close' do you figure them cattle should be to us afore we start firin'?" Colt asked.

"Well, let's see now...." Ole Smoke put his hand to his chin and thought.

Every cowboy on this range acknowledged Ole Smoke was *thee* man to consult with any serious questions of ballistics and firepower. Ole Smoke had more experience with guns and munitions than anyone they knew, and this was especially true when it came to shooting thirty-thirties from a Winchester '94.

"I figure them canyon walls to be 'bout hun'dert foot high," Ole Smoke continued. "Them thirty-thirties's prob'ly accurate to 'bout hun'dert twenty-five, hun'dert thirty yards. So if yuz shootin down from above, jus' make sure yuz don't target out no more'n say...two hun'dert fifty feet, to be safe. Yuz shoot out any further'n that 'n bullets's lie'bell to stray down 'n plug a feller. Thirty-thirties can travel five hun'dert yards afore they hit ground, ya know.

"I understand. You're tellin' us not to target out more'n two hundred 'n fifty feet from where we'll be standin' on the cliffs. Is that right?"

"Yep, no more'n two hun'dert fifty feet – at most!"

"Okay, Smoke, I got it. Good luck to you 'n your men," Colt said to Ole Smoke before turning his attention to the cowboys in his own group. "Alright, rest'a you deadeyes, mount up 'n follow me. We got work to do."

The cowboys climbed onto their horses and followed Colt out toward Sanders Canyon.

Ole Smoke and his men remained behind and shortly went to work cutting animals out of the herd.

About this time, Doc Walters, who had felt nervous and angry at having been left alone by the cowboys in that strange place, decided to make the trek from the river valley back to camp.

"Those ignorant, inconsiderate cowbums," Doc talked to himself as he rode along, "leaving me by myself like this. I could've gotten surrounded by coyotes or attacked by savage, rogue Indians in this godforsaken place. I can't wait to get back to civilization and see my sweet, little Rosie again. And, Lord, if you let me get back alive and with my hair, I promise I'll do more than just tuck in my shirttail next time."

Several rocks slid naturally off the side of a hill, making some noise on the way down.

"What in hellfire was that?" Doc stopped to listen for a moment then spurred his horse in an effort to achieve fleet speed in the northern direction of camp.

"Fly boy! Fly like the wind!" he cried out to his merely fast-trotting horse.

Back at the river valley: cows, calves, heifers, steers and bulls had intermingled into one large herd. Actually, this "herd" was simply a collection of naturally segregated subgroups residing within specific social-spheres all geographically located within a larger sphere on that rich, pasture land.

Contrary to Doc Walters' highly unrealistic suggestion, the Texas bulls were neither the first to be cut out nor removed individually. These animals were the most dangerous and sometimes near impossible to manage. Next in the hierarchy of hazards to a cowboy's life and limb would be the recently calved cow, since a frightened mother protecting its young may not hesitate to attack a rider or maul a man to death.

All of the cowboys in Ole Smoke's group were highly experienced cattle-handlers who recognized bovine threat-displays and knew how to react accordingly. If, for example, a bull were to demonstrate any sign of aggression, such as standing broadside to show how large and powerful he was, a cowboy might carefully withdraw to a safer distance and let that animal's anger subside. A tucked position of the tail; a change in the arch of the back; a lowering of a head; a hunching of the shoulders; a pawing of the ground with the forefeet: all of these behaviors meant something to the experienced cowhand.

Sometimes there seemed to be a virtually telepathic communication going on between a cowherder and his cutting horse. The Western-style-trained equine not only possessed a natural "cow sense," giving it an ability to think on its own, but was conditioned to respond to neck-reigning cues, leaving one of the cowboy's hands free for use.

Cowboys and their horses cut out cattle by maneuvering between animals and continuing to "push" out the animals from the main group. The object was always to keep pressure on the separated animals while holding the herd. Some animals, however, naturally migrated out with the separated animals; e.g., mothers and calves had a tendency to stay together while being moved.

The cowboys labored to move the animals en masse while trying to avoid any high-risk encounters. And, as a matter of habit, each cowboy maintained an unspoken yet predetermined exit-strategy according to his ever changing environment and trail conditions. In other words, cowherders were required to think defensively in order to survive.

After a while, the men had managed to cut out approximately five hundred head of cattle from the main herd when Ole Smoke, who had a highly developed sense for intuiting the passage of time, guesstimated when it was right to take to the trail. At that point, Ole Smoke and two others began driving the separated cattle towards Sanders Canyon.

Ole Smoke took the lead or "pointer" position, the rider who stayed at the head of the herd and guided the cattle toward their destination. Any man who rode the highly coveted "pointer" position was a cowboy respected for his experience and advanced capabilities.

The other two cowboys worked as "flank riders," men who rode toward the back and kept the animals herded up. These drag riders had to eat a lot of dust and were chiefly responsible for chasing the occasional stray. But the importance of these men cannot be overestimated because, although cattle mentally followed the direction of the rider in the lead position, they were actually being driven forward from behind by the "flank riders."

It should go without saying that, no matter which herding position the individual riders occupied, all of these men were first-rate cowboys who applied their backbreakingly acquired lessons in herding science in a careful and methodical manner. Accordingly, each greatly contributed to successfully driving the animals toward the box canyon without disrupting that herd's critical forward momentum.

Sanders Canyon was a wide-open, rocky landscape surrounded on three sides by adjacent, vertical, hard-rock cliffs. Wind and water had carved this walled structure leaving behind an ancient river bed within a magnificent natural enclosure. The cattle had no way to get in or out of this box canyon except for the canyon entrance and one narrow opening located far-off and at the approximate center of the cliff walls, an area that had been breached by the unrelenting flow of a seasonal stream.

Colt's plan was to have herders drive cattle into this gorge while he and nine other gunmen, positioned around the top of the hundred-feet-high cliff walls, would shoot the cattle down. He explained Ole Smoke's mental calculations to the men and said they mustn't shoot out more than two hundred fifty feet from where they were individually located. Colt and the men reckoned that distance by pointing out landscape markers. Colt also placed one man at ground level just outside the singular, narrow, cliff cut-through to prevent any animals from getting through that juncture.

"You fellas be sure to make every bullet count. Otherwise, that's one more we gotta do by hand," Colt told them and then reiterated, "'N make sure you only shoot those drove in close. We don't want nobody down below gettin' shot."

The gunmen on the cliffs engaged themselves in analyzing how and from what positions they could get their best shots. After familiarizing themselves with their surrounding conditions, they sat and waited for Ole Smoke and his men to arrive.

Having been close to the stench of dead animals, Ole Smoke and his men had pulled their bandanas up over their mouths and noses as they cut out cattle from the main herd. And, during this entire first drive to Sanders Canyon, they had kept their faces covered.

"Here they come!" one of Colt's gunmen shouted.

The men got themselves into position and readied their guns.

"'N don't forget to shoot in close so no cowboy gets killed," Colt re-emphasized.

Along with Ole Smoke's gang ran a pack of cattle heelers, short-legged herding dogs capable of avoiding a lethal kick after nipping at the heels of cattle. A "bear dog" also ran with the pack, a compact, curly haired, aggressive fellow who was not only good at herding cattle but had been seen on more than one occasion to be yapping at the heels of bear.

The men herded the animals into the gorge and as far toward the cliff walls as possible. Ole Smoke had explained to his men why they shouldn't get within "three hun'dert feet of them walls." He told them that, even though the gunmen above would be trying to limit their shots to animals no farther than two hundred fifty feet from their elevated positions, a single, overly long shot could kill a rider below.

And then it began. Two, three, four, eight shots or more rang out followed by indeterminate lengths of silence while the herders ran the frightened cattle back toward the cliff walls. More gunfire was heard and, distraught with the knowledge of impending doom, the animals went completely crazy. Some tried charging up the walls.

A portion of the terrified herd tried running back to the entranceway, and Ole Smoke and his men rode to head them off. Ole Smoke's horse ran smack into the side of the lead steer, managing to turn the steer back and redirecting the course of its followers. The dogs were also invaluable in keeping the cattle from running back toward the entranceway.

"Dang! A bullet just flew by me!" one cowherd exclaimed as the cow to his left took the shot in the leg and fell sideways.

"Get yerself out'a there now!" Ole Smoke hollered at the cowboy who had inadvertently been maneuvered by frenzied cattle to within the two hundred fifty feet range of fire. "Ya wanna get yerself killed?"

That cowherd shot three cattle dead as he rode through the herd, managing to escape the enclosing animals and get back to a safer position.

"Colt!" a gunman called out over the gunfire. "Hey, Colt, over here!"

Colt looked over.

"He's in trouble down there! A bull's gettin' through!"

Colt ran and dropped to his knees, sliding on loose gravel to nearly the very edge. He put his right hand down against the rock to keep from going over. Looking down, he saw a bull struggling to escape through the narrow rocky opening in the cliff.

The cowboy below took a step back to get braced for his next shot, tripping over a rock and falling backward. As the cowboy fell, his gun discharged into the air and he hit his head on a boulder becoming temporarily stunned.

The bull charged.

"Son of a...!" Colt exclaimed, aiming his Winchester '94 and firing three shots in rapid succession.

Having taken one of the bullets directly through the skull and into the brain, the thundering bull slammed unconsciously into the ground, landing a few feet short from the stunned gunman below.

"You get down there," Colt ordered the cowboy at his side. "Make sure he's alright 'n keep those animals at bay."

"Will do, Colt," the cowboy said, rushing off and down the cliff.

It was a hectic and frightening, first-time experience for all the cowboys in the canyon. The herders were afraid they might either get mauled by the horrified cattle or shot by their friends.

And the gunmen above were also concerned. They worried about accidentally shooting one of the men below or about missing a critical shot that could prevent a possibly toppled herder from getting trampled. One gunman, moving to take a shot that wouldn't injure Ole Smoke and his men, nearly fell to certain death as he slid down loose rocks some fifteen feet to a narrow shelf that, most favorably, jutted out from the side of the cliff.

When the shooting finally ended, the gunmen looked down to inspect the results. All the cattle lay dead, and every man there felt disgusted at the sight. But their emotions also included a huge sense of relief that they had managed to get through the harrowing experience without any wounding or fatality of their friends.

During the initial slaughter, Ole Smoke and his men had boldly herded the cattle into the gorge and, a few times, found themselves trapped within a ring of panicked animals. Naturally, they were somewhat shaken by the ordeal but ultimately no worse for wear.

The gunmen waited on the cliffs as the riders below left to meet the second group of animals that were about to reach the opening of Sanders Canyon. This time there would be six herdsmen available to work the approximately two hundred fifty cattle that would enter the gorge, and the herding and killing efficiency would improve noticeably.

One-half hour before sunset, they finished the day's bloodbath. The gunmen climbed down from the cliffs to meet up with the herders, and they all rode back to camp together.

The end of the workday having finally arrived, all the men lay or sat congregated near the chuckwagon. An exhausted Cookie, who had been on the cliffs with the rest of the gunmen, was still busy as he worked to whip up grub for the men. All the other cowboys took the opportunity to rest and discuss the events of the day.

The men calculated that they probably killed eight hundred or so cattle that first day, and admitted to having used up nearly all of the more than twelve hundred fifty bullets they had with them. They allowed it was impossible to "keep track of" how many cattle were downed with a first shot and how many animals had to have two or more bullets fired into them. These men never claimed to be professional marksmen; and a targeted beast within a moving group is hard to keep visual track of, let alone managing to kill it with a single shot. Admittedly, some of the cattle took upwards of four bullets before they dropped. The men all agreed that they seemed to have gotten the "hang of it" towards the end and discussed ways to improve on future slaughters.

But a thing of interest should be mentioned here that requires some little digression and a chronological movement of events backward a bit. And that is, during the time when the cowboys had cut out their first group of cattle from the herd and were endeavoring to drive those animals toward Sanders Canyon, Doc Walters had made his way back to camp where he was looking high and low for something strong to drink.

Doc's main concern had been with trying to uncover places where those "low-down cowboys" might have "selfishly hid" their whiskey; and, to this end, Doc searched the bedrolls, under rocks, beneath bushes and other possible places of concealment. To his outright delight, the empty flask he always kept on his person was able to be filled from individual cowboy's whiskey bottles and in such a way as to prevent the theft from ever being discovered. Doc had also found two opened and partially filled bottles Cookie kept in the food wagon for purely medicinal purposes. Unable to control his drinking urge any longer and feeling compelled to consume the entire contents of one container, Doc downed the whiskey in one prolonged drink. Realizing afterwards what he had done, and becoming fearful of being found out, he urinated into the whiskey receptacle, bringing it back to its original half-full state before returning the bottle to its proper location.

Now move forward in time and back to the camp of dead-tired cowboys.

With the food finally ready, Cookie yelled, "Grubslingin's done! Grub's up! Grub's up! Grubsling's done! Get yer vittles! Grub's up! Grub's up!" causing the cowboys to jump to their feet and descend on the chuckwagon as if they had never eaten before.

"We ain't got that many bullets left," Ole Smoke informed one of the men. "Somebody's gotta ride out for more."

Colt, who was passing by and eating grub from a plate, overheard Ole Smoke's comment. "You men worked hard enough for one day. I'll ride out tonight and get us some more bullets."

"Better go to the tradin' post then," Ole Smoke suggested. "They's got more in stock'n town ever does."

"You're right as usual, Smoke, 'n that's exactly where I'll be goin' to. If everything goes alright, I'll be back tomorrow – late in the day sometime."

"Obviously, there's no use in me staying here any longer than necessary," spoke up the unusually quiet but highly inebriated Doc Walters, who had been sitting on the ground and holding a tin plate full of beans." "I'll ride back with you after I'm finished eating."

"I'll get as many rounds as I can. Figure we got prob'ly five...six days, maybe a week of killin' ahead of us. While I'm gone, you men can go to the low pasture 'n kill off some of the sick ones by hand."

"And jus' how we s'posed to do that?" one grizzled cowboy asked. "Shootin's one thing but killin' by stick's another. I ain't never stick-killed nothin' in my life. I don't even know how."

"I know something about killin' by hand," a young cowboy interjected. "I use ta work at a abattoir."

"A what?" the grizzled cowboy asked.

"A abattoir," the young man answered.

"Dang it, boy, I knowed ya fer four years," Ole Smoke said with obvious disgust, "'N ya ain't never told me ya done worked in no cologne-stinky aba-twa. Ya should oughta be ashamed'a yerself."

"What is a aba-twar anyway?" the grizzled cowboy inquired. "Ain't that some kind'a fancy place for meetin' ladies?"

"No, it ain't neither got nothin' ta do with no ladies," the young cowboy answered with earnestness. "Abattoir's a big-city French name for slaughterhouse. That's where we put down livestock."

"Aye-baw-twaar," the grizzled cowboy practiced his pronunciation.

"At the slaughterhouse, we used ta hit 'em o'r the heads 'n slit their throats."

"S'that what ya say we gotta do?" Ole Smoke asked.

"I don't know. There, they was all in pens 'n couldn't move none too much. It's gonna be lots harder ta do with animals what can move 'bout on open range – even if they is all weakly sick. 'N we's all gonna be on foot so it's gonna get real messy. Blood, snot 'n shit all o'r the place. It's dang dirty work."

"How long's you been at that there...aye-baw-twaar?" the grizzled cowboy asked.

"Not long. I never much cottoned to it. But we had us some dangerous types who really enjoyed that kind'a killin'. Them's the ones you didn't want ta make mad."

"I ain't never signed on to work in no aba-twa," Ole Smoke complained. "Bad 'nuff we gotta be killin' with bullets. But slittin' throats all day'll drive a man crazy."

"Alright, I'm converted," Colt said. "Forget doin' any killin' by hand. We sure don't need none'a you goin' crazy on us."

"Thank heavens fer that!" Ole Smoke said with relief.

"I'll ride out tonight 'n be back tomorrow with bullets. Tradin' post ain't more'n fourteen miles one-way but I prob'ly won't make it back sooner'n late day. But we'll do it the complete bullet way, not the stick way."

"Colt, you mind pickin' me up some lead plumb for my Derringer while youse in town?" a cowboy asked.

"No, I ain't pickin' up no lead plumb for nobody's Derringer. 'N don't nobody be askin' me to get no handgun bullets neither. It's enough I gotta pay for the ammunition for all them Winchesters you been assigned. Anyhow, don't nobody need to be carryin' no pocket pistols out here. Them knuckle-buster sneak-guns ain't good for killin' calves let alone full-growed cattle. You men get your rest. There's gonna be plenty'a hard, dirty work to do when I get back."

Colt ate a couple spoonfuls of beans. "These are good beans, eh, Doc? Put hair on your pants."

"Yes, my sincerest compliments to the bean master," the doctor insincerely endorsed with a besotted sneer. "But now I need a good, strong drink. Anybody got some 'family disturbance' to help wash down these Pecos strawberries?" he called out.

"Cookie, give the doc here a drink," Colt called out. "After all, the man rid' all the way out here 'n done everything he's s'posed to do."

Cookie retrieved a whiskey bottle from the chuckwagon and handed it to Doc Walters. "Here ya go, Doc."

"Thank you, my good sir, for your kindhearted consideration – for which I shall be eternally grateful."

'Ain't nothin'," Cookie replied.

The drunken, short-term-memory-impaired doctor took a long, generous swig from the bottle before erupting into an anguished, "Ptttuuuuuuuuueeeey!"

The veterinarian spit and coughed repeatedly then dashed the bottle against a rock and yelled, "What kind of low-grade rotgut do you buy? It's got horrible, putrid impurities in it! That stuff tastes worse than monkey piss!"

"Well, I'm sorry if it ain't s'pensive falutin' enough for ya," the insulted cook retorted and walked away.

16

THE TIRED TRAIL

Doc Walters and Colt left camp somewhere around quarter to four in the morning. They had been on Camptown Road about an hour and a half but, because both were so extremely tired, few words had been spoken between them.

Shortly before sunrise, and feeling the need to stay awake, Colt decided to talk. "You're prob'ly gonna be glad to get back to ole Mule Face, huh, Doc?"

"Always glad to get back to my little old Mule Face," Doc listlessly answered. After a few moments, he added, "And please don't call her that, boy. The lady's name is Rosie."

"Sorry, Doc, I forgot. No harm meant. Guess I'm too tired to think polite."

"As am I. And that cheap whiskey of Cookie's has still got a grip on my stomach. That low cost batch-alcohol probably had enough impurities in it to give a body a permanent nervous gut. The worry alone could make a man vomit."

"Try not to brood on it too much."

"But returning to the subject of Rosie: yes, my Rosie is actually quite beautiful. 'Mule Face' is just something those jealous, working gals started calling her. Those rivalrous shrews! But I think I already told you about them, didn't I?"

"I'm too worn to remember. Say it again if you want."

"Well, it was those green-eyed she-wolves she works with. They were all jealous of Rosie's natural beauty so they called her all kinds of mean names. But 'Mule Face' is the one that stuck. And since my little Rosie is too much of a lady to scratch their envious eyes out, she puts up with it. I don't know how she does it? If she weren't employed in carnal commerce, she'd almost be a saint. Here, let me prove it to you. You want to see how beautiful my darling Rosie is?"

"No, I believe you."

The doctor reached into his jacket and pulled out a locket, "I want you to take a look at this picture, boy." He opened the locket and handed it to Colt. "Here, take a look at that. That's her there. I dare you or anyone to say my Rosie's not beautiful! She is beautiful, isn't she, boy?"

Colt took hold of the locket. Looking at it under the twilight sky and by light of a full moon, he winced slightly. The long-faced woman actually did appear to have the countenance of a mule. "Kind'a hard to say in this light, Doc," Colt responded. He attempted to hand back the locket.

"No, no, hold it closer. Sun's coming up. Take a good look now. You ever see a better looking woman in your entire life?"

Colt squinted as he held up the photo for closer inspection. "Yeah, I can see it now. She's a real looker alright. 'N that's some hat too."

"Hat? Rosie's not wearing any hat. That's her hair – and it's all hers too! That's one reason those gals all got so jealous of her. You ever see real hair that thick and sumptuous and piled up all nice and high like that?"

"No, this is the first."

"You should be able to see that. Take another look."

Colt reexamined the picture. "Yeah, you're right. Guess bein' tired 'n lookin' at it in moonlight, the eyes kind'a play tricks. But, I think I see it. She's real handsome. 'N she's got some real nice, authentic, hair headdress too. You're a lucky man, Doc." He handed the locket back to the vet.

The doctor looked at the picture and smiled warmly. "Yes, I am lucky. Rosie is the joy of my life! My every happiness!" he gushed. "Every breath of air that I enjoy, I enjoy because of her."

"Hmm."

"I even wrote a poem about her. Do you like poetry?"

"I don't know much about it."

"Would you care to hear my Rosie poem?"

"Tell you the truth, Doc, I really ain't too much for poetry."

"But it's a wonderful poem, Colt. It's about life and love and nature...I'm sure you'd enjoy it. It's entitled 'Rosie,

Rosie, Love's Dear Little Posy.' Would you like me to recite it to you?"

"Sounds kind'a private, Doc. Maybe it's not for public hearin'."

"No, no, it's not private at all. Poetry is never meant to be private. Poetry is to be shared with the world and read aloud and embraced by the listener. Poetry is the perfect art form, Colt. And isn't art what we really all strive to live for?"

"I don't know. I never thought about it."

"I'll recite a bit from memory for you."

"Yeah...okay."

"Now, when you listen to the work, boy, I want you to put yourself in the shoes of the writer: a very passionate man who loved bravely but lost; a man who suffered for years under a bad marriage with his cheating pig wife but who, after searching and searching, at last, found his one, true truly-fair. Do you think you can put yourself in those shoes, boy?"

"I don't know nothin' about findin' no lost truly-fairs but I'll give it a hearin'."

"Pull up here, boy. Pull up here."

They stopped their horses.

"Now when you listen, boy, try listening with your feelings. Try to open up your mind and let your heart fly. Become the world. Become a tree. Become a bird."

"Prob'ly easier you becomin' a bird than me. You bein' a vet 'n all."

"Now listen attentively, boy. Here it is. I call it 'Rosie, Rosie, Love's Dear Little Posy.' Oh first, I should mention: don't let the title fool you. It starts off simple then takes on a more classical form; much in the way of John Milton, I suppose – but completely different."

"Who?"

"'Rosie, Rosie, Love's Dear Little Posy'...."

"Rosie Rosie, Love's dear little Posy,
How you make my heart swoon!
When you talk to me at long past noon,
With Rosie face, cute as yon lovely moon.

"Rosie, her breath is sweet like morning nosegay that riseth to meet the day,

Where happy sun and charmful, singing birds doth bring.
For Rosie is thine name ere heavenly gems in herbful fields,
With fiery love tempests possesseth you,
Liketh chaste, burnt heart from goddess Venus herself
above.

"Rosie Rosie, Love's dear little Posy,
How you make my heart swoon!
When you talk to me at long past noon,
With Rosie face, cute as yon lovely moon."

"Well, what did you think? Pretty good, huh?"

"That's some writin'."

"You think so?"

"I know I sure couldn'ta done it." Colt made a clicking
sound to start his horse moving again.

The doctor rode up next to Colt. "Don't feel bad, boy.
Most people couldn't write at that level of acumen and
sensitivity. Writing's a gift, and poetry's been my hobby
since I was a young child. I'm planning on getting my
work published some day."

"That'd be somethin'. Do folks get rich writin' stuff like
that?"

"Certainly, they do! A published poet with a loyal audience can become unbelievably wealthy; like uhm…like Edgar Allan Poe, for example. And what did you think of my line: 'With Rosie face, cute as yon lovely moon'? I purposely didn't say 'Rosie's' face – an avoidance of the possessive case – so the reader would be forced to think of a beautiful, peach-colored face in warm contrast to the lovely moon. That's pretty good, isn't it?"

"Sure sounds like it must be."

"And it's true too. My Rosie's face is 'cute as yon lovely moon.' 'When you talk to me at long past noon, With Rosie face, cute as yon lovely moon,'" he recited. "Now tell me the truth, boy. You've seen it. You think it's pretty, don't you?"

The sun had moved up off the cusp of dawn, and Colt gazed at the setting moon that appeared to have been gracefully painted upon an illuminated morning sky. "No doubt about it, Doc. That is one pretty thing to look at," he said, in reference to earth's satellite.

"So you agree! See, you really are a poet, boy. Poetry recognized is poetry composed."

"I ain't sure what you just said but it sounds like somethin' that belongs in a book."

"And so it shall be."

"So how come you ain't never married this woman, Doc?"

"Married!" the doctor protested. "Are you mad?"

"But why not? You just said how much you love her."

"Well, of course I love her. How could any rational male keep from loving someone as wonderful as Rosie? But love's got nothing to do with it. I already married one pig, and I'm not going through that again. And I am certainly not going to marry some man-ravaged, soiled dove, no matter how beautiful she is!"

Colt looked down at the road and shook his head with puzzlement.

"Ahhhhhhh!" Doc exclaimed after taking a long drink of whiskey. "Anyway, poetry is my only real love. Everything else is insignificant by comparison."

Colt looked over and saw Doc holding a flask and wiping his mouth on his sleeve.

"Where'd you get that?" Colt asked.

"Never you mind, boy. Nobody's going to miss it back at camp. This is the good stuff which I desperately need to ease my clinically foul stomach. So just consider it my due reward for a job well done. Which reminds me, how about paying me the rest of my money you owe me?"

"I'm plannin' to. It's in my saddleback. When we stop at the Fork Road, I'll count it out there."

"Excellent, just as long as I get paid. I don't like being flimflammed."

Colt didn't appreciate having his honesty questioned but let the drunken vet's remark pass nonetheless.

"I really enjoy being out here in the open air. But truth is, boy, I possess a touch of claustrophobia."

"What's that?" Colt asked.

"Claustrophobia? It's a medical term I came across it in an old article printed up by the British Medical Association. Apparently, some man by the name of Benjamin Ball introduced the term in 1879. He defined claustrophobia as 'a morbid fear of closed places'; and that's what I think I must have – claustrophobia. 'Claustro' comes from the Latin 'claustrum' which means a 'shut in place.' And 'phobia' comes from the Greek word 'phobos' for 'fear.' Claustrophobia: that's what I've got for sure."

"Clawster-phobia...is that how you say it?"

"Yes, claustrophobia. Although to be honest, I'm also a little afraid of being out in these wide-open spaces like we are. I don't know why but I have this terrible fear of being attacked by Indians. Claustrophobia! Maybe that's why I drink so much." Doc Walters took a quenching swig from his flask.

"You ain't gotta worry about no Injuns out here, Doc. We don't have those kind'a problems in this country no more."

"Not since the Civil War; I know. But I'm older than you are, and I remember it wasn't that many years ago when George Armstrong Custer and his 7th Cavalry were viciously slaughtered by those bloodthirsty Sioux near the Little Bighorn River. It was hideous!" The doctor took another satisfying drink from the flask.

Colt had to smile. "So what do you think is worse, Doc? You havin' clawster-phobia or you havin' Custer-phobia?"

The doctor didn't think Colt's remark was particularly funny and became instantly bad tempered. *Is this kid making foolery of me?* he thought. *That bossy little mongrel! He's laughing at me!*

"So how much longer before I get the rest of the money you owe me?" Doc Walters brusquely asked.

"What?"

"My fifteen dollars? How long before I get it?"

"I told you; when we get to the fork."

"And just how much longer is that going to be?"

Colt realized that there was no being friendly with this ill-tempered boozer. "I'll let ya know when we get there," he replied with some irritation.

Time passed and neither rider spoke to the other. It was somewhere around quarter after seven that morning when they arrived at the intersecting roads of Camptown and Fork, which is where they stopped their horses.

Colt climbed down off his mount, opened his saddle bag, reached in and pulled out a wad of paper money. "Twelve...fourteen...fifteen dollars," he counted, walking over to Doc Walters. "Here ya go," he said, reaching up and handing the veterinarian the money. "Count it if you like."

Doc Walters sat on his horse and stared at the wad of cash Colt still held in his hand. "That's quite a sum of money you've got there."

"Supply money," Colt stated as he put the cash back into his saddle bag.

Doc counted out the money, whispering each number to himself. "Yes, fifteen dollars. It's all there," he concluded, his dark mood seeming to have lifted. "It's been a real pleasure doing business with you, Colt."

"Yeah, I could tell."

"Now any time you need a veterinarian, you know exactly whom to come to."

Colt decided to overlook Doc Walters' previous remarks, dismissing the vet's irrational moods as being entirely alcohol fueled.

"Thing's have been working out pretty good for me, boy – financially that is – now that old Barnes is dead. Too bad about old Doc Barnes though." He smirked but then, catching himself, added with apparent staidness, "God rest his saintly soul."

"This is where we split up, Doc. I'm gonna walk my horse a while."

"It's farther to the trading post. You sure the store in town won't have enough bullets for you?"

"Pretty sure. I never found 'em to carry all that much."

"Well, I'll take your word on that but I do wish you'd reconsider and ride to town with me. I'd truly like to have the pleasure of your company."

"Still scared them Injuns might get ya?"

Doc Walters was provoked to silence.

"Sorry about my jokin', Doc. 'N what you told me about you havin' clawster-phobia won't go no further'n my ears. Speakin'a which, we sure don't need nobody learnin' about our herd neither. If folks was to find out...." He cast a cautionary glance at the doctor. "I need you to promise me that you won't be sayin' nothin'."

"Me! Talk about your private business! Boy, you never stop misconceiving me. A man of my personal character and professional integrity automatically keeps things on the hushful side. It's also part of my veterinary code of conduct. No, you don't have to worry about Doc Walters saying anything, boy. Doc Walters knows how to keep his mouth shut good and tight. Always has. Always will."

"Thank you, Doc. I 'preciate knowin' that."

"Hell, even if I weren't a medical man, I wouldn't say anything anyway. That's just the way I am, by nature. I'm sort of the naturally secretive type. And my Rosie won't be saying anything about it either. You can count on that. No, your Redwater Fever secret is completely safe with me. So how long do you think it'll take for you to get to that trading post way out there on the flats? I've never been to the place."

"Only a couple hours more or so. We got an account there. For sure they'll have more bullets than town will."

"I doubt you'll be able to get enough bullets anywhere to complete a job that big. Ninety-five out of a hundred will die on their own anyway. So the best thing is probably to wait and kill off the healthy ones and the ones that seem to recover."

"'N how long do ya figure that'll take?"

"Depends. Some'll die quickly. Others won't. Might take upwards of two weeks or more."

"What if we keep food 'n water from 'em? Won't that hurry things along?"

"No, you don't have to worry about that. Once Redwater sets in, they won't get hungry or thirsty. Most of them will just stand there in a stuporous state. Then they'll get feverish, their intestines will dry up and they'll piss blood. Nature's got a bit of a mean streak in her."

"Alright, thanks, Doc. Watch out for those Injuns, hear?" Colt said, heading his horse toward the northeast-running Fork Road leading to the trading post.

"That was just drunk talk back there, boy. Indians are the last thing on my mind."

"And be sure to keep everything to yourself, okay?"

"It's really not necessary to remind me of that again, boy," the vet said, becoming obviously offended. "As a lad, I was known by all my teachers as Stoney Walters. And do you know why that was?"

"I don't know. 'Cause ya couldn't learn too good?"

He's doing it again. This arrogant boy is making sport of me, the vet thought.

"You ignorant juvenile! Goodbye and perpetual good riddance to you and yours," Doc Walters said in bitter farewell then rode off southeast on Camptown Road to town.

Colt took several moments to watch the veterinarian riding away. "'N be sure to keep it to yourself, Doc!" Colt called out before leading his horse off Camptown and onto Fork Road.

Doc would be in town before Colt reached the trading post. Not only was the town half the distance but the veterinarian would force his horse to move at a faster than usual pace as he drunkenly fantasized about being ambushed by scalp-hunting Indians.

Colt walked part of the way and hoped that Doc Walters would be true to his pledge and remain silent about the Redwater Fever outbreak. He knew if word got out, it could destroy the ranch's reputation and ruin Mama Helen's bank credit.

Having temporarily relieved his horse of a passenger and feeling himself sufficiently exercised, Colt climbed back onto the saddle and resumed riding.

Several miles down the road, Colt got to thinking about Doc Walters' vow of silence and remembered hearing the vet say, "I'm sort of the naturally secretive type. And my Rosie won't be saying anything about it either." At that instant, Colt realized the doctor had admitted to intending to violate his promise by telling Rosie. *I hope she knows how to keep quiet,* Colt thought, at the same time faulting himself for having been too tired to pick up on Doc's remark at the time of utterance.

The young man tried to consider others things but his thoughts kept returning to an imaginary conversation in which Doc Walters pled with his beloved Rosie to: *promise not to tell.* Colt now regretted not having forced the veterinarian to make his commitment at the end of a gun barrel. The more Colt mulled over what Doc Walters had said, the greater grew his ire with that "pony up fifteen now and fifteen after I examine the herd" alcoholic veterinarian. Colt resolved to keep his temper in check before reaching the trading post, reminding himself that it was probably too late to do anything about what Doc Walters or Rosie might publicly discuss. Nonetheless, Colt clung to the hope that the veterinarian would be a man of his word and able to maintain tight rein-control of his mule mouthed "truly-fair."

17

ZEKE'S TRADING
POST BULLETS

Zeke's Trading Post was a well-established, commercial outpost located on the miles-long, valley floor. The building's desolate, flatland presence stood in arrant contrast to the neighboring hills and mountains and, despite its far-flung location, the store had long managed to be profitable. The business had been handed down to Zeke by his father – a man named Buzi but also called Zeke – and this sameness of name added continuity to the transition.

While the valley's inland watershed drained seasonal rains through mineral-rich soil and out to the Pacific, creating lush grasslands and an abundance of plant life that attracted wildlife to the area, it was guns, ammunition, foods, feed, traps, dry goods and assorted supplies that drew people to Zeke's store.

Colt arrived at the trading post around 9:45 AM that day. He tied his horse to a post out front and walked inside.

"Hello, Zeke," Colt greeted the man behind the counter.

Zeke, who was standing behind the counter and writing something on a piece of paper, had already been informed by his son that a rider was on the way. He glanced up. "Young Barnett," he acknowledged in his usual perfunctory manner then glanced back down at the paper.

"Need some ammunition," Colt informed Zeke.

"What kind and how much?" Zeke asked, still keeping his eyes on the paper.

"How many rounds you got for the Winchester '94?"

"Right off hand...I'd guess six and a half cases." Zeke answered, knowing exactly many cases he had in stock.

"Put it on our bill."

Zeke looked up curiously. "You want to take all of it?"

"Sure do."

"Why so much, Young Barnett? You got troubles out there?"

"No, just the ordinary goings-on. Coyotes. Mountain lions. Bobcats."

"Thousand rounds per case, six and a half cases, that's sixty-five hundred rounds. Your place must be chockfull of mountain lions," Zeke noted with some suspicion.

"We get our share. Anyway, it's always good to have ammunition on hand," Colt said, poker-faced. "Also gonna need to borrow one'a your wagons. Get it back to you in a couple'a days."

"No hurry. You can just take it into town. We're droppin' off a load there next week sometime, and we'll pick it up then. What else you need?"

"I should pick up some extra grub. Maybe a few bottles'a whiskey for the men."

"Whiskey? You never bought your hands any whiskey before. Sure everything's alright out there?"

"Couldn't be better. They been workin' extra hard 'n I wanna reward 'em."

"Whatever you say, Young Barnett; you're ranch boss now. Bullets and whiskey for cowprods. That's some fine mix."

Zeke was right. Colt had never bought the ranch hands whiskey. But, on impulse, Colt wanted to give the men alcohol to help them through the unpleasant task of killing the herd. Still, Colt felt insulted to have his judgment questioned by some lily-handed, indoor-hibernating, store clerk. "You're gettin' paid, ain't ya, Zeke?"

"Yes, I'm getting paid. Didn't mean to offend you, Young Barnett," the store owner backed down. "The McKenna Ranch has always been good to me. Always paid on time. Good customer. No harm meant, Young Barnett."

"No harm taken, Zeke," Colt responded. "Put ten bottles'a whiskey in that order. 'N give us the usual grub, enough to take us through a few weeks. How long afore I'm able to load it up?"

"Not necessary for you to do that, Young Barnett. I got my boy workin' here now. He does every bit of loadin' these days. Ezekiel!" Zeke shouted. "Ezekiel, you get out here now!"

Zeke's nine-year old boy came running out from the backroom. "What do you want me to do, Pa?"

"Get your lazy tail out there and hitch up a wagon, and bring it 'round front. You got goods to load."

"Yes, Pa," the boy said politely.

"And take care this man's horse."

"I'll do it right away, Pa." The boy rushed to the entrance door, flung it open and bolted outside.

"That boy!" Zeke said exasperatingly, "Too stupid to shut a door. Ezekiel, you get back here and shut this door! I swear that boy's gone deaf. You mind, Young Barnett?"

"No, I don't mind." Colt walked over to the door. "If you ain't gonna need me for nothin', I'd like to rest on your porch if ya don't mind."

"Course, you can. You go right ahead and rest, Young Barnett. You rest and I'll take care everything."

"'Preciate it."

Colt stepped outside and closed the door behind him. He sat on the porch with his back against the building and stretched out his legs. Soon he was deep asleep.

The dreaming began almost immediately: Colt's brain concocted a fantastic vision of malevolent Indians chasing a horrified Doc Walters and his darling Mule Face through acres of dead cattle. *Indians pushin' us into the red river. Little Big Horn. Mama Helen's dyin'. We're surrounded. Ole Smoke, get the men! Give me a rifle; my pistol won't fire!*

Colt thrashed about during a short period of anxious dreaming activated by exhaustion before he physically and psychically calmed down to a state of near perfect rest. About thirty-five minutes passed as Colt slept soundly on the wooden porch of the trading post.

Zeke's boy walked onto the porch and stood over Colt. Ezekiel was in awe: Never before, had he seen any living being in such utter stillness.

"Hey, mister," Ezekiel said, "I got your wagon ready and horse watered. Mister, you're alive, ain't ya? You still breathin', mister?" The boy shook Colt's shoulder. "You better get up, mister, 'cause my Pa sure won't like nobody dyin' on the porch."

Colt woke up, moved his hat from over his eyes and looked at the boy. "Who died on the porch?"

"You did, I thought. Your wagon's ready, mister. And I watered your horse real good."

"How long I been sleepin'?"

"I don't know. Three or four hours, I think."

"Three or four hours!" Colt said in a raised voice. "Why didn't you wake me up, kid?"

"I just did," Ezekiel answered.

Colt jumped up and stormed into the store.

"Hey, Zeke, what's the idea'a lettin' me sleep three or four hours out on your porch? I ain't got that kind'a time to be wastin'."

"But we just finished loadin'." Zeke looked at his watch. "And you only been asleep little over a half hour."

"But your boy said...."

"Oh, don't listen to that simpleton. He's too stupid to tell time. It's only been a half hour...forty minutes or so."

Colt took off his hat and rubbed his forehead with his arm. "We all set then?"

"Everything's loaded. But be very careful with all that ammunition. One good fart's liable to set it all off."

Zeke laughed as the still tired, unamused Colt put his hat back on.

"Yeah? Well, ya better tell it to that oated-up dray horse'a yours. I rid' back'a him afore 'n he's notorious for it."

"You have a good day, Young Barnett," Zeke goodbyed. "Always good doin' business with you McKenna folks."

Colt walked outside and was tying his horse to the back of the wagon when he noticed Ezekiel sitting at the end of the porch and petting his dog. "You better learn how to tell time, kid. I got cattle to tend to."

Ezekiel didn't look up. "Mister, do dogs go to heaven?"

Colt climbed onto the wagon and seated himself. "I don't know. Why?"

"I want Bloomie to go to heaven when he dies."

"Bloomie? S'that your dog's name?"

"Yeah, I named him after a flower. You think he'll go to heaven?"

"I don't know, kid. I ain't even sure there is a heaven."

"No, you're wrong, mister. There's a heaven for certain. Reverend told us there was."

"He did, did he? 'N what'd he tell you about your dog goin' there?"

"He won't answer me on it. He says I should quit chatterin' so much. But can you tell me, mister?"

Ezekiel's remarks induced Colt to think about the ranch's many thousands of diseased and dying cattle. Thoughts of that undeserved misfortune triggered an impulse in Colt's tired brain that adhered to Ezekiel's present question of dogs in heaven. Colt's mood flashed momentarily spiteful at any idea of Divine Providence.

"Tell me somethin', kid: That dog'a yours ever get any ticks on him?"

"Of course. All dogs got ticks on 'em."

"'N do you think God lets ticks into heaven?"

Ezekiel looked up. "Ticks in heaven! No, mister; that's crazy talk! God wouldn't never let no ticks go to heaven!"

"Then there's your answer, kid. No ticks in heaven, no dogs in heaven."

Colt's righteous-sounding verdict was accepted by the boy as an adult's authoritative word on the matter, leaving Ezekiel slack-jawed and staring into space as Colt drove off.

The sky was uniformly clear and the air was cool, and Colt anticipated an uneventful ride back to camp. As the wagon rolled along, he thought of Mama Helen and wondered how she would take the news of Redwater Fever. It deeply worried him.

Colt observed Zeke's horse and knew it to be a fine, strong animal that could pull a heavily loaded wagon with ease. He had been merely engaging in tit-for-tat repartee with Zeke when he implied that this equine was overly farty. It wasn't. But then, for the first time, the question arose in Colt's mind: *Do horses catch Redwater?* Realizing that he already had more than enough to deal with, he pushed that inquiry out of his thoughts and concentrated on the trail-road ahead of him.

From the trading post, there had been no sign of storms but, a few miles out, the ground patterned moist from rain-formed drainage that coursed down from the high country. During the drive, Colt had noticed that the wagon was creaking near continuously. And out here, on the mud and rutted ground, Colt thought he had detected a little play in the right, front wheel. Recognizing too late that this vehicle was old and definitely not one of Zeke's best, Colt became concerned about its state of maintenance and ability to hold up during the entire drive back to camp.

"This thing might be good for short hauls but it don't seem much good for where I'm goin'. Wonder if that stupid kid's been workin' on it? That fool Zeke!" he said to himself.

"Rut!" Colt called out to the horse as he tried turning the animal so that the right, front wheel would take less brunt from the road. He managed to miss the hazard but, after encountering several more potentially wheel-damaging depressions, Colt understood that similar efforts at maneuvering would be largely in vain since it was practically impossible to avoid all the pitfalls of this road.

Colt stopped the wagon for a short period to decide whether or not to turn back in favor of obtaining a better vehicle but concluded that he'd take the chance with this wagon and continue on in the interest of time. Yet, it was all he could do to put those concerns out of his mind.

It was wet, bumpy and slow-going for a spell but eventually the ground dried out and the horse seemed to be trying to make up for lost time by automatically picking up speed for a distance. Colt fought drowsiness and would sometimes dully sense the wagon veering off trail. At one point, the left wagon wheels rolled off the road and up onto a rocky mound, and it was all Colt could do to keep the vehicle from tipping. He was finally forced to admit that he could stay awake no longer and needed a break.

Colt stopped to inspect the wheels. Everything looked fine. Even the right, front wheel had proven to be firmly in place. He wondered if his tiredness might not have caused him to be imagining the wheel's gyrational problems. But, imaginary or not, one thing was certain: He had a great deal of soreness in his back and legs. So, he walked back and forth along the trail to try easing the discomfort.

As he exercised by pacing to-and-fro, Colt felt some remorse for having spoken so callously to Ezekiel, and this led to him wondering how his cowhands were getting along. Rewarding the men with whiskey at the end of a hard day's killing had seemed like a good idea back at the trading post but now he remembered what Zeke had said: "Bullets and whiskey for cowprods. That's some fine mix." The store keeper's comments plagued him, and he wondered if the act of putting down cattle all day long might not narrow the distance between killing animals and murdering men.

Colt walked to the back of the wagon, pulled out a bottle of whiskey, opened it and poured its contents onto the ground. "Temperance," he said as he watched the liquid spilling upon the ground. He did the same with the other nine bottles, each time returning the empty container to the wagon. Regretting the wasted expense but confident in this decision, Colt re-boarded the wagon and rode off.

It was sometime after 3 PM when Colt, who was by then well along Camptown Road and only an hour or so from camp, recognized that he could go no farther. So he stopped the wagon and climbed into the back. He lay supine on some full bags of flour and shut his eyes. Too tired to be uncomfortable, he was soon asleep.

Colt was thoroughly oblivious to his surroundings for approximately three hours until being awakened by the nearby cries of a large cat. *Cougar*, he thought, sitting up and scanning the environment.

He noticed the fading light and knew he would have to leave immediately to minimize the time driven under full dress of darkness. He disliked the fact that he hadn't been particularly considerate of Zeke's horse but figured it wasn't far to camp and that it would be better to let the creature get its water there.

"Let's go, Oatie," he ordered the horse and slapped down the reins. "We don't wanna be out here at night with no hungry painter around. Anyway, it won't be too awful long now."

Relying on the horse's ability to see through the ever dimming light, Colt negotiated cuts in the ridgelines and slopes as best he could. It was a dangerous wagon ride uphill and into the full gathering of darkness but he trusted the horse to find its way as it had done so many times before.

When he reached the top of the ridge and saw the flickerings of campfire, Colt stopped the horse and praised him. "Good work, Oatie. You done real good. Now all you gotta do is get down this hill alive 'n we'll be set. You'll drink good then, I promise ya."

The horse looked back at Colt as if to say, "Wish me luck!" before beginning its descent on that inherently dangerous slope.

Colt preferred to take this route by wagon when there was available daylight. But now that the sun had completely set, Colt knew he was entrusting his life to the good workings of this horse's eyes by light of an unclouded coyote-moon.

For the most part, Colt did nothing to either direct or misdirect the horse in its downward traversal along the cliff's edge. And so, being unable to control the course of the wagon, Colt was forced to rely on personal courage and considerable confidence in the animal. *Sure hope I ain't gonna find out too soon if horses go to heaven,* he thought on the way down.

When they did succeed in reaching the bottom in one uninjured piece, Colt breathed a sigh of relief and drove the horse to the roadside where he let it rest a bit.

"You got us down alive, Oatie. You done good," Colt spoke appreciatively to the animal.

Colt wanted to let this horse breathe easy for a good, long while before moving it on to camp. But horses sometimes have a way of telling humans exactly what it is they want. And when this horse turned its head back and gave Colt the "let's go" look, Colt complied and drove on.

"Hey, look! It's Colt!" one man shouted, seeing the wagon driving toward him.

"Hey Colt!" another man hollered.

All the cowboys were glad to see Colt arrive back at camp.

"How you men been?" Colt asked, bringing the wagon to a complete halt.

"We still got lots'a stubborn cattle on our hands," a cowboy said.

"Refuse to die, do they?" Colt asked.

"Sure, wouldn't you?" the cowboy remarked.

"You bet I would," Colt answered. "Got all this ammunition and supplies from Zeke's. You men mind givin' me a hand with this?"

"Sure thing, Colt."

"Let's help him out, boys."

The men began removing the goods from the back of the wagon.

"Looks like ya got enough bullets here to gun down the Daltons in Death Alley," one of the cowboys humorously remarked.

"Prob'ly do. But still won't be enough to take care all our cattle. I have to go to town tomorrow 'n see if I can't get us some more. But, for now, this'll have to do."

"Hey! What are all these empty whiskey bottles doin' back here?" a cowboy shouted.

"Guess the town drunk must'a been sleepin' in the wagon," Colt replied.

"Least ya could'a done was to fill 'em up for us," the cowboy fussed.

"Nope. Ain't got no kind'a money for that," Colt said, walking over to the campfire. "So what's happened here today?" he asked the men who were sitting on blankets on the ground.

"Nothin's happened. We jus' been waitin' for you is all," a cowboy said.

"This thing's gonna go on awhile; might last a couple weeks or more the doc said. But we gotta wait it out to make sure they're all dead. So we gotta use our bullets smart. Tough ones that won't die, them's the ones we gotta drop. Tradin' post had a goodly amount'a ammunition but I'll go into town in the mornin' to see if I can't get more. I'll be back tomorrow night sometime if their supply's good. Otherwise, I might be a few days."

"Don't worry, Colt, If that store ain't got 'nuff, we'll jus' make do," Ole Smoke said.

"Good. Now I got some horse work to be done," Colt said, walking toward the wagon. "Any special eatin' here tonight?"

"Beans," Cookie said, "same as last night 'n the night afore that. Now, if some'a you boys'd find us some rabbit or a few snakes, I'd throw it in. Bawlin' shame: All this cow on the ground 'n we can't eat one single bite."

"Beans's been good 'nuff with me," Ole Smoke commented.

"Good enough with me too," Colt agreed, walking away to unhitch and tend to Zeke's dray horse and to take care of his own cow horse still tied to the back of the wagon.

18

QUIETING THE QUACK

Colt left camp around 7:30 that morning and arrived in town just before noon. He had taken Zeke's wagon and dray horse to the stables and left them for one of Zeke's hirelings to pick up. His own horse had been watered and fed and was being given time to rest before taking to the road again. He figured that, if he could obtain enough ammunition from the general store, he'd borrow another wagon from the stable and head back to camp around 4:30 PM, approximately two hours before sunset. Colt wasn't overly concerned about driving the stable horse in the dark and knew his personal mount was capable of safely making its own way, if need be.

Colt had consumed some hardtack and water before falling asleep in the livery. He knew his old boss wouldn't care if he rested there so he didn't bother to ask. After sleeping on a soft pile of straw for a couple of hours, he walked to the general store.

"How ya be, Colt?" the store owner asked.

"Fine. Got any bullets for a Winchester '94?"

"Yes! Yes!" the owner said gleefully, "It so happens I just got in a big shipment! Big shipment! Ten cases! You interested?"

"Ten cases? You never had more'n a couple cases on hand afore. How'd you get so much?"

"A dealer came through, and I bought everything he had. Big demand. Top quality bullets. You interested?"

"Yeah, I'm interested. Put all ten on our account."

"That'll be twelve hundred dollars; cash upfront. Anything else?"

"Twelve hundred dollars? For ten cases'a bullets? That's what? – a hundred 'n twenty dollars a case!"

"That would be correct, sir."

"Twenty bullets in a box...fifty boxes in a case...how much is that by the box?

"Two dollars forty a box. Still a good price, Colt."

"Two dollars forty! For a single box! But a box'a twenty never cost me more'n seventy-six cents."

"Yesterday's prices I'm afraid."

"I even saw where a fella could get hundred to a box through Sears Roebuck catalog. 'N that box is only three dollars thirty-five. If you broke that down to twenty to a box, that'd come out to be somethin' like uh...," he calculated in his head, "...sixty-seven cents for a box'a twenty. 'N here you are askin' two dollars forty! What's goin' on?"

"We ain't no Sears Roebuck catalog, Colt. This here's a real-life store."

"I know you ain't no Sears Roebuck catalog but why so dang much?"

"Right now, thirty-WCF is hotter'na whorehouse on nickel night. And thirty-thirty smokeless in this amount's hard to come by. These're top-shelf, high-quality bullets, Colt. You don't get good quality like this through no catalog."

"I don't care what shelf you keep your dang bullets on; I ain't payin' no two dollars forty a box."

"Bang-up stuff, Colt. You won't find this much thirty-thirty Winchester nowhere."

"How about cuttin' the box price in half to a dollar twenty? That's still more'n I ever paid."

"Can't do it, Colt. Sorry. Just can't do it."

"A hundred twenty dollars a case is downright criminal!"

"No, I said. Congress passed the Gold Standard Act last month, and I paid government guaranteed gold certificates for these bullets. If I was to cut below one hundred twenty a case, I'd be chancin' the poorhouse."

Colt thought about it. "I could maybe buy a few boxes. Maybe a case even. But I can't buy no ten cases at that price."

"But you ain't gonna find this much thirty-thirty nowhere. Not nowhere. Tom Horn only uses a Winchester '76 to shoot down them cattle rustlers. But, if he'd go to usin' the '94, he'd pay anything to have this much smokeless."

"Tom Horn's a good shot 'n all but what's he got to do with the high price'a your bullets?"

"Nothin', Colt. I'm just sayin' the '94's better than the '76 any ole day; so naturally its bullets are gonna cost more. Besides, you never know when you're gonna need all those bullets out there on the McKenna range – things bein' what they are n'all."

"What do you mean things bein' 'what they are'? Why should I be needin' this many bullets'?" Colt asked defensively.

"No, I didn't mean you personally, Colt. I'm just sayin' that sometimes a fella wants to do an extra-special lot'a hunting or target practicin'. Folks can go through bullets mighty fast when they're target practicin'."

"Well, I ain't target practicin'. 'N if I wanted to buy bullets by the storehouse, I'd ride out to Zeke's Trading Post. I'll take one case; no more," Colt said with definiteness.

"Alright, but they'll still be here should you change your mind. That'll be a hundred and twenty dollars, cash on the barrelhead."

"What do ya mean 'on the barrelhead'? We always use credit here."

"I know that, Colt, and your credit's good. But I just paid out a heap'a good money for these bullets, and I can't afford to be lendin' out no credit right now. Right now I need actual."

Colt pulled a wad of bills and counted it. "I ain't got nowhere near a hundred 'n twenty dollars. I'll have to go out to the ranch 'n have Mama Helen visit her bank. But I'll be back tomorrow. 'N you save that case for me, hear?" he said, heading toward the door.

"Oh, don't you worry, Colt. This case has got the honorable McKenna name writ' on it. It ain't goin' nowhere; I promise you that. And if you come back tomorrow early, you still got a real good chance'a pickin' up the whole ten cases. Got to take cash though."

Colt looked back at the man and sneered. "Dirty son of a....," he said, walking outside.

Hardtack crackers never did much to fill an agitated stomach, and Colt's gut had begun to react accordingly. He remembered that Jingle Bob's Eatery was only a few buildings back and decided to try easing his hunger and sense of discouragement by patronizing that business. He walked to the restaurant and went inside.

Colt had never been in a restaurant before and, even though the place had an air of shabby magnificence and there were rows of empty tables, he was mightily impressed.

"Where do I go sit?" Colt addressed an obese, moustachioed man wearing a clean, white shirt with a standing collar and well-knotted bow tie.

"Sit any place you like. It don't matter."

Colt picked the nearest table and sat at it. The bow tie attired man handed him a menu. "What's this for?" Colt asked.

"That's a menu, sir," the waiter answered.

Colt opened the menu and looked it over. "Criminy, look at all this! I can't make out what half this stuff is. You just got any plain ole bread 'n beans?"

"Plain ole bread 'n beans? Is that all you want?"

"No, I'd like some coffee to wash it down with. You got any coffee here?"

"Yes," the man haughtily answered, "Of course we've got coffee. Jingle Bob's Eatery is a high-class, dining establishment, sir."

Colt realized that he had unwittingly offended the man. "No, I didn't mean nothin' by it, mister. I'm just new at this kind'a thing. You must be Mister Jingle Bob."

"Yes, that would be me. Mister Jingle Bob, at your service."

"So how much's all this gonna cost me?"

"Our prices are very fair. Have you ever been in our high-class, dining establishment before?"

"Nope, I ain't never been in no kind'a dinin' establishment afore, high-class or otherwise. This here's my first time bein' in one."

"Seventy-five cents, sir, and I'll throw a steak on top."

"Seventy-five cents for steak, bread, beans 'n coffee? Alright, I know I got that much on me."

"Very good."

Jingle Bob walked into the backroom kitchen and came out shortly with beans, bread and coffee. "The steak will be out in a little bit. It takes my gourmet-cook wife some time to prepare it." He walked away then turned and said, "Did I mention that my wife is a gourmet cook?"

"I believe you did, Mister Jingle Bob."

"Well, my gourmet-cook wife will have your steak ready shortly," he added before walking away.

Too ravenous to wait for his gourmet cooked steak to arrive, Colt immediately began to eat. In a short amount of time, his plate was empty and he sat there, relaxed, outstretched and looking about the room. As he sipped the coffee, he was amazed at its unusual taste. "This coffee tastes kind'a different," he said to himself, "'N just look at this fancy coffee cup. They ain't got no drinkin' bowls in this place. This is one fancy eatery; that's for sure."

Jingle Bob overheard Colt. "Did you say something, sir?"

Colt looked up. "No, I was just admirin' your place. It's real nice."

"Thank you, sir. Everything here is specially prepared by my gourmet-cook wife."

"Ain't that somethin'."

"Yes, we think so."

"Ya know, I'm just sittin' here thinkin' that seventy-five cents prob'ly ain't too bad for a fancy meal like this, considerin' the risin' price'a ammunition in this town."

"What rising price of ammunition, sir?"

"Sam Hill, Mister Jingle Bob! Ain't you been to the general store lately? I just came from there 'n they're sellin' thirty-thirties, two dollars forty for a box'a twenty. Case'a a thousand costs a hundred 'n twenty dollars. You ever heard such craziness afore?"

"Two dollars and forty cents a box? No, no, sir, not for you they're not. That store owner special ordered those for some high-toned ranchers he hates. Seems all their cattle came down with something called Redwater Fever and every one of them has to be shot and killed. That store owner's a real chiseler. He's high-priced me on supplies, and now he's trying to make extra off those people."

"High-priced? But why would he wanna do that?"

"Because he's a no-good chiseler, that's why. And because he despises them rich McKenna people. Yesterday, I heard him call Mrs. McKenna – she's the rich woman who owns the place – a highfalutin', mean talker."

"Are you sayin' he's sellin' those bullets at two dollars forty – but only to particular people?"

"That's exactly what I'm saying, sir. The man's a chiseler."

"But when I was in there a week or so ago, he didn't have too much thirty-thirty. How could he get ten cases over night?"

"Easy. That chiseler's got a cousin at the depot who's also quartermaster in the Army. His cousin fools around a little with the paperwork and can get most anything he wants at government prices. Truth be known, those bullets probably didn't cost him anything."

"S'that right?"

"Yes, sir, it is. And when that store owner learned about them McKennas having cattle problems, he hurried and sent his clerk over to the depot. Course, it's none of my affair – and I don't care too much one way or the other – but the way our sheriff tells it, that McKenna woman's a real devil."

"You don't say."

"No, I'm not saying it because I never met her. But Sheriff Hagger says she's 'meaner than a starvin' barn rat.' Says he wouldn't go back there if those people was murdering each other with butter knives and the whole place was burning down. Our sheriff really hates those McKenna people."

Colt could feel his face getting warm. "So how'd you find out it's Redwater?"

"Wasn't just me who found out; the whole town knows it. Our blabby-mouth vet Doc Walters was out there and tended to the whole thing. Mean, rich McKenna woman or not, I sort'a feel sorry for those people. Way I hear it, that spread's sky-high over its head in debt and'll be going up for auction soon."

"The vet said all that?"

"Most of it, except for the auction part; that I heard from the banker boys themselves. They was all in here talking about it. And those money men didn't waste no time neither. Once they learned how sick that herd was, they rode out to the McKenna place and are getting ready to set an auction date."

"They're really gonna auction off the ranch?" Colt asked with startlement.

"That's right. Those McKennas are gonna lose the whole kit and cargo. Take some advice from me, young man: You ever meet Doc Walters, don't go telling him anything personal. That Doc Walters has got one, big mouth on him."

"Biggest ever was."

"Bigger than that even. And, just between you and me, I think he talks way too much for a man who's not even a real vet."

"Not a real vet? How do you mean?"

"Old Doc Barnes told me that just before he died. Doc Barnes was getting ready to expose Walters and have him run out'a town."

"You're sayin' Doc Walters ain't even a real vet? You sure'a that?"

"Yes, I'm sure. Course, I can't prove it. But Doc Barnes was no liar nor gossip. That man had integrity and wouldn't say anything that wasn't true. Doc Barnes was a wonderful human being. Everybody truly misses him."

Colt's face felt red hot. He stood up. "Here's your seventy-five cents, Mr. Jingle Bob. I gotta go."

"But you haven't had your steak yet?"

"No, you can go ahead 'n eat it. My way'a sayin' thanks."

"Thanks for what? I don't even know your name."

"Name's Colt Barnett. My Mama's Helen McKenna."

Jingle Bob was dumbfounded. "McKenna? You're a McKenna! Jesus H. Christ! What'd I say now!"

Colt stepped outside the restaurant. From there, he could see Doc Walters' horse tied out front of the brothel. So he walked across the street and went inside.

The same middle-aged lady was now seated in the red parlor. "What's your pleasure, junior?"

"Where's Walters?"

"He's busy right now, sonny; can't be bothered. Oh, I remember you! You're the kid with the emergency. You ever get it fixed?"

"No, I'm still workin' on it. He back there?" Colt asked walking toward the backrooms.

"You can't go back there, kid. I told ya; Doc's busy."

"Yeah, I know. But I wanna surprise him," Colt said, opening the door and stepping through into a hallway.

"But surprises are against the house rules," she protested, following right behind him.

Colt reached in his pocket and pulled out a five dollar bill. "Here," he said handing it to the woman, "Go buy yourself some gourmet steaks at Jingle Bob's."

"Oooooo! Thank you," she said, taking the money and backing away.

"Which room's he in?"

"Number three," she whispered.

Colt walked down the hallway to Room Three. Outside the door, he could hear Doc Walters laughing and a woman saying, "Coo coo coo coo coo coo coo!"

He tried turning the handle but found it had been locked, so he backed away and gave the door a good, solid kick. When the door swung open, he saw the two surprised people sitting up from under the bedcovers and looking at him.

"Having fun, Doc?" Colt asked, walking forward, pistol in hand.

"Whaaaaa...!" the woman screamed, "...the hell are you doing here?" She waved a long peacock feather at Colt. "You can't come in here, you fool kid! You get out! Get out naaaaaoow!"

"Hobble your lip, Hoss Face!" Colt demanded.

"My name's not Hoss Face, dumbass!" protested the long-jawed woman with the big, red bow in her hair. "It's Mule Face!"

"Yeah, I can see that. Now shut your mouth afore I turn it into No Face."

"Colt, my boy! It's you!" Doc said with faux friendliness. "My, what a pleasant surprise! But as you can see, we're kind of busy right now. So why don't you just leave and close the door behind you? You and I can meet up later for a little drink."

"S'that what he pays you extra for?" Colt asked Mule Face. "Playin' tickle feather?"

Mule Face looked at Colt's pistol then looked at the decorative iridescent feather and let it drop from her fingers.

"Colt, it's really good to see you again, but let's make it some other time, hear? Right now we're both a little busy...."

"Doin' what?" Colt interrupted the doctor. "Just talkin'?"

"Yes, of course just talking. Rosie and I often like to take our clothes off when we talk. It's more conversationally relaxing that way. But for now, we're going to need you to...."

"Shut up!" Colt ordered, walking closer.

Mule Face began to tremble and whimper.

"You too, Hoss Face."

"Colt, what is it you want here? Do I detect some little animosity in your voice," Doc asked nervously. "You know, I tried my best to save your cattle. Lord knows I gave it everything I had!"

Colt stuck the gun barrel in Doc's mouth. "One more word out'a you 'n I'm splattin' those lyin' brains'a yours into the next room."

Doc's eyes grew unusually big.

"You had us kill off our herd, Walters, 'n now I find out you ain't even a real doctor, you phony playactor."

"What do you mean he ain't no 'real' doctor'? He most certainly is. Why, I've been lettin' him work on my cat for over two months now."

"I told you to shut your gills, Hossie."

"Yes, yes, I'll shut up! I'll shut up!" Mule Face trembled.

"Uhhhhhh. Uhhhhhh," Doc unintelligibly articulated, provoking Colt to remove the gun from Doc's mouth. "But I never said I was a 'real' doctor, Colt my good friend. I'm what is known in the West as a life-experienced veterinarian; and there's a whole different medical standard for that. Experience is everything out here, my boy, and I've got years and years' worth of experience. Now, you take those cattle of yours; I figured out they had Redwater sure as you're standing here. No, it sure didn't take a degree-man to figure that one out."

"Maybe not, Stoney. But does it take a degree-man to know how to shut his big bazoo?"

"Wha...what are you talking about?"

"You just had to go 'n tell everyone, didn't you. Now we're ruined 'cause'a you."

"No, I didn't say anything! Honestly I didn't!"

Colt aimed the pistol at him and cocked the hammer.

"Well, I might have inadvertently misspoken a few times. But I mean...if I did, I must have done it when I was paralyzed, hare-crazy drunk. Because I sure don't remember ever telling anybody, do I, Rosie?"

He looked to Rosie for help but she was too frightened to respond.

"Fact is, I don't remember even being there when I was telling those folks! Remember, Rosie? Remember when I was in the lobby talking to those two cardsharpies, and we were all sitting there and they plied me with alcohol... against my will? I didn't know what I was doing then, did I, Rosie? I was talking drunk out of my mind. Too drunk to even know what I was saying, wasn't I, Rosie?"

Colt glanced at Rosie, and she kept sensibly quiet.

"What are you going to do to me?" Doc Walters asked with distress. "I'm not wearing any clothes."

Colt stared at him and said nothing.

"Look, Colt, It doesn't matter what I did or didn't say. Those cattle of yours still have Redwater and that had nothing to do with me. I didn't cause their disease. I'm not to blame. I just went out there in a professional, life-experienced capacity and tried to help as best I could. All I ever did was help you, Colt, and now you're here threatening me with a gun – when you're way too young to be shooting anybody anyhow."

Colt stared intently at Doc.

"Please, I'm not wearing any clothes!"

Colt uncocked the hammer and let his arm drop to his side. With his pistol barrel aimed toward the floor, he began backing away. "You're rum-dum pathetic, Walters." He turned to walk outside.

"Somebody get the sheriiiiff!" Mule Face screamed out.

Colt turned and aimed the pistol at them.

Doc Walters instinctively held his hand over Rosie's mouth. "No! No! We won't say anything about this incident, will we, Rosie?"

Rosie nodded in the negative.

"See? You don't have to worry about us saying anything. We know how to keep quiet, don't we, Rosie?"

Rosie nodded yes.

Colt extended his arm straight and aimed the pistol directly at Doc Walters. "You open that big mouth'a yours about what happened here 'n afore this day's done, I'll kill you, your little Hoss Face 'n that lyin' sheriff too."

"No! No! We won't say anything, will we, Rosie?"

Rosie kept nodding "no" non-stop.

"No! We won't say anything! It's already been forgotten!" Doc Walters insisted.

Colt walked out of the room.

"No, we won't say anything at all, will we, Rosie? No, not us! We won't say a thing," Doc Walters tearfully promised.

"Not my little Rosie and me! We know better than to say anything. No, we won't say a word. Not a one! Not even one single word we won't say!"

The eavesdropping madam moved away from the hallway door to permit Colt to pass.

"You just make sure she keeps that big, hoss mouth shut," he instructed her, "not 'less she wants to be buried next to Doc Hornswoggle there."

Colt walked outside and to the livery where he saddled up his horse. Having been unable to acquire any thirty-thirty ammunition, Colt figured the next thing to do was ride the Town Road out to the ranch and check on Mama Helen.

Still angry, Colt left town certain that he would regain composure sometime during the four hours or so it would take to reach home. But, in his heart, Colt knew he'd been but a hair's breadth away from ending that fraudulent veterinarian's life. He knew also that, should the maligning, gossipmongering Sheriff Hagger ever come looking for him, he was prepared to take mortal revenge.

19

MCKENNA RANCH NO MORE

In accordance with the recent debt settlement agreement, all the horses had been removed from the ranch save two: Lucas, the small and amendable, buggy-pulling Banker Horse given by Henry McKenna to his dear wife Helen; and Samson, the well-trained, 18-hands high, gray, Shire stallion used for pulling heavy wagonloads. All the rooms of the house had been emptied of furniture except the kitchen and living room. For the most part, all the items that Helen McKenna had contractually retained were packed away and made ready for the move.

Although Mrs. McKenna had lost the ranch, she had shrewdly bluffed her moneylender into believing that she planned to file federal suit under the National

Bankruptcy Act of 1898. In actuality, however, neither Helen McKenna nor her creditor's newly licensed lawyer truly understood this first-of-its-kind, modern, bankruptcy legislation that was notable for allowing a debtor to present his or her case in federal court.

The possibility that Helen McKenna's case could be tied up in court for an unaccountable period of time frightened the bank's representatives into accepting less favorable terms for their financial institution. Most terrifying to the creditor's attorney was the law's text which read: "Farmers and wage-earners are expressly excepted from persons who are subject to adjudication as bankrupts on the petition of their creditors." The lawyer further frightened his client by hypothesizing how some liberal, bleeding-heart, bankruptcy referee might somehow make allowances for natural disasters that could exempt Mrs. McKenna from involuntary bankruptcy and lead to her being debt free and allowed to keep most, if not all, of her assets. The bankers had been intimidated at the very start of the process.

Helen McKenna, on the other hand, didn't know much about the National Bankruptcy Act of 1898 except its name and never had any intention of walking inside of a federal courtroom; this, compounded by her failure to consult an attorney, prevented her from becoming aware of any part of this law which might have saved her from extensive financial dissolution. But she detected how her threats of legal action made the bankers squirm, giving her a small edge in the negotiation process, which felt like more than enough for her.

In the end, Helen McKenna was permitted to keep a little start-up cash, some items of personal property, two horses and a separate, but abandoned, forty-acre homestead that had been willed to her by Henry McKenna. Yet, this "win" was hardly enough to emotionally compensate her for the loss of the vast McKenna empire.

In the living room of her now former home, Helen sat in a bentwood, rocking chair – rocking back and forth – back and forth – back and forth.... From that location, she felt as if she could remember everything. She recalled her wedding and the youthfully contracted couple's dreams of a destined life together. Henry had been both handsome and rich, and their future implied nothing short of a vital and inspiring, new world. Unfortunately, these lifemates had never succeeded in producing any children and Henry, through no fault of his own, had become deprived of his good senses. In the present, however, Helen sat alone; thinking and rocking back and forth in her Thonet-designed, Rocking Chair No. 1, a highly appreciated, matrimonial gift shipped to her by her aunt and only known, now deceased, blood relative. Back and forth – back and forth – back and forth she rocked in an effort to gain mastery over her deep sense of aggrievement.

Hours passed, and Colt didn't reach the front gate of the ranch until around nine in the evening, some two and one-half hours after sunset.

Helen McKenna looked through the window and, aided by light of a still bright moon, saw Colt riding toward the main house. She walked out onto the front porch to meet him.

Colt rode up to his mother, stopped and paused before dismounting. Neither person rushed to speak.

"Evenin', Mama Helen. How you been?"

"I know what's happened, Colter, so you won't have to be explainin' anything to me."

Colt nodded to indicate he understood.

"So how'd you learn of it?" he asked.

"Some of Doc Walters' chitchat got back to the ranch. But I guess everybody in town's learned of it by now."

"Yep, they sure have. So what's to be done, Mama Helen?"

"Nothin' left to be done 'cept for us to leave. Lender's got the place now, and it's going to be auctioned off before too awful long."

"But how could it all'a happened so fast?"

"It ain't happened fast, Colter. It just looks that way to you because you didn't know what's been going on. But this place's been in bad trouble since late winter. My purse got light, and I couldn't make the payments. Bankers agreed to hold off till the cattle got sold."

"That was decent'a 'em."

"No, it wasn't, boy. They didn't do it out of the goodliness of their church-going hearts. Them money-grubs demanded extra interest-money, and I agreed – not like I had any choice. Still, we would've been alright if everything'd worked accordin' to plan. But now with this Texas plague upon us, we're done permanent. Come on, Colter; let's go inside. Ain't no use us standin' out here like this."

Colt followed Mama Helen into the house.

"You hungry?" she asked.

"No, I don't think I am," he answered, following her into the kitchen. "So how long we get to stay?"

"We'll be leavin' tomorrow, boy." She turned to the cupboard and pulled down the package of Arbuckle's Coffee.

"Tomorrow? But why so soon?"

Helen poured some of the ground coffee into a pan of pre-heated water. "Sometimes there's nothin' like a bowl of good, hot coffee to make a person feel soothed." She lit the burner.

"Why tomorrow, Mama Helen?"

Mama Helen paused and thought about her answer. "Tomorrow – next day – next day after that – makes no difference now, Colter. It was all my fault, and now I got to live with it. Sorrowfully, so do you. But I won't have no rain cloud hangin' over our heads and us sittin' here cryin', askin' the world to hold the umbrella. No, we leave tomorrow. Sit down, boy."

Colt sat at the table. "But tomorrow's still too soon."

"No, it ain't too soon at all, Colter. We might've got kicked out last winter 'cept for the extra interest-money I agreed to give them money-grubs. But now we're settled up and got to go. I promised we'd leave when you got back, and we will. Most everything's packed, so tomorrow's the day."

"But where we gonna go to, Mama Helen?"

Helen sat next to Colt and took him by the hand. She nostalgically looked around the room.

"I still got that forty-acre place at the edge of town, Colter. It was never used as mortgage collateral so I got to keep it. I also had a little cash-money set back; not so much that we won't have to work every day but enough to pay off the hands and start over again. But that's as far as I can think right now, boy." She released Colt's hand and brusquely changed the subject. "Coffee shouldn't take too long. Water wasn't that far from boilin' when you came in. All I had to do was put in the coffee and add a little heat. You do want coffee, don't you?"

"Yeah, coffee sounds good to me right about now."

"Nothin' better than a bowl of hot coffee. Shouldn't take too long. Water was already good and hot when I put the coffee in. And that pan it's cookin' in, I had that since

Henry and I first got married. We always cooked coffee in that pan. Ain't never used it for nothin' else. You did say you want coffee, didn't you?"

"Yes, I'd like some coffee, ma'am."

She looked at the pan on the stove. "Shouldn't be too awful long now," she said, appearing distracted while unconsciously clenching her hands together. "Water was real hot when I put the coffee in so it won't be too awful long."

They waited quietly till they heard the water boiling.

"Coffee's done!" Helen McKenna said.

"You sit there," Colt said, standing up. "I'll get it."

Colt removed the pan from the stove and poured hot coffee into Mama Helen's bowl. Next, he poured coffee into his bowl then returned the pan to the stove and resumed his seat next to Mama Helen.

She waited for the coffee to cool before sipping it. As she held the bowl in her hands, she had a somewhat befogged look, as if she were peering into some vast, new world of uncertainty.

"You daydreamin', Mama Helen?"

She abruptly snapped back to the present. "No. I mean… maybe a little. Mmmm, that pan makes some good smellin' coffee, don't it, Colter? Nothin' like a good workin' pan of cooked coffee to make a body feel secure. And that pan always did work good for us, Colter. That pan right there's always been one of my favorite pans. Henry and I wouldn't never use that pan for nothin' else but coffee makin'. It was strictly our coffee-makin' pan. But I think I told you that already, didn't I? Might be a little too hot though. You think it's too hot?"

"Maybe a bit. I'll wait awhile afore I drink it."

She took another small sip then placed her bowl down on the table. "Next week or so, you should go and pay the men their wages. Maybe we'll be able to keep one or two on to work for us. That'd be nice, wouldn't it?"

"Mmm hmm," Colt agreed.

Colt didn't drink his coffee. He just gazed at the wall and thought.

They both sat there in that dimly lit room for nearly forty-five minutes, neither speaking a word.

Finally overcome by fatigue resulting from a long day of self-beleaguerment, Helen McKenna yawned, rose up out of her chair and stretched. "I'm tired, Colter. I need to rest a little before we leave tomorrow. I'm going to lay on the floor by the fireplace."

"No, don't lay on the floor, Mama Helen. Why don't you go to your own bed? You'll be more comfortable there."

"Can't. Bed's already been taken down for the move. I'm okay on the floor. I got a nice blanket to rest my head on. You better get some rest too, Colter. I want us to get an early start. We still have a little packin' to do before we load up."

"I'll be okay, Mama Helen. I can sleep here just fine. But I wanna stay up awhile 'n finish my coffee."

They said goodnight to each other, and Helen went into the living room to repose by the smolder of logs and dim glow of the fireplace. Colter, meanwhile, sat in the kitchen, staring at the wall and slowly drinking his cold coffee. Sometime after he finished his beverage, he nodded off, with no difficulty whatsoever, into the depths of otherworldly conceptions and slept the natural, rest-giving sleep of youth.

20

SEPTEMBER 1900: CHURCH SCHOOLIN'

Carlos Perez and three other youngsters sat in God's Learning Room, the backroom of the small church that lay just beyond a grove of centuries old, white oaks and a half-mile's distance from the southwest edge of town. The boy's grandfather had recently passed away, making Carlos a temporary and unofficial ward of the church.

The good Reverend Branson had written to The Children's Aid Society and The Children's Home Society in his effort to find a good home for the "poor, little, Mexican waif" as the good reverend liked to refer to him. to refer to him. So anxious was this evangelical minister to adopt out the eleven-year-old, that he had even written to "those heathen Catholics" at the New York Foundling Hospital founded by the Sisters of Charity of Saint Vincent de Paul.

It's not that Reverend Branson wouldn't have liked to keep the boy. "Don't be silly!" the reverend bristled at any suggestion to the contrary. According to the cleric, this boy was "God's little angel sent from above." However, the good reverend was also apt to add comments about how his church had long planned some necessary building alterations which were presently not being accomplished due to valuable church resources being "drained" for the boy's upkeep. And so it seemed to the reverend that sending the boy away was not only the proper, moral decision but the correct financial one as well.

One afternoon, Reverend Branson sat at his desk, anxious to read a letter that had traveled to him all the way from New York. His hands shook somewhat, and he could barely contain his excitement while ripping open the envelope.

"Dear, Reverend Branson," the letter read, "Thank you for your correspondence regarding young Carlos Perez. As you may know, our charity, The New York Foundling Hospital, sends orphans out across the country on Orphan Trains in hope of placing orphaned children in morally upstanding, Christian homes. As far as I know, the Orphan Train does not travel to your immediate locale nor does it pick up any young orphans along the way; our intention is to drop them off. We believe you will find greater success in adopting young Carlos yourself or in seeking out some loving family within your own church community. However, should you ever be in the area of Manhattan, we will be delighted to meet with you and give you a tour of our facility. Placement of orphans is, and shall always be, a most holy priority for us. Maintaining orphans, as you are no doubt aware, is a very expensive undertaking so any contributions you may give to us will be gratefully accepted. In caritate Christi, Sister Mary Maria, Sisters of Charity of Saint Vincent de Paul, The New York Foundling Hospital, 175 East 68th Street, New York, New York."

"Son of Pope Leo!" Reverend Branson reacted as he crumpled the letter and threw it across the room. "That nun thinks I'm going to send them money! I should have known better than to write to the Catholics!"

Along with Bible studies, Carlos was supposed to learn to read and write and do basic math. And he was not permitted to speak Spanish at any time. "English only!" was the rule, a canon necessitated, and put in place, by Mr. Wiles Dingler, the pastoral aide and Bible teacher, a man who barely understood the English language himself.

Mr. Dingler, a large, heavy-set, wooly-bearded man who walked with a cane, was somewhat new to the church since his recent conversion to Christian, evangelistic teetotalism. And, although Mr. Dingler was not a particularly scholarly person and clearly had gaps in his own knowledge of the "three R's," Reverend Branson found Mr. Dingler's free-of-charge maintenance of the building and grounds to be particularly useful to the "holy cause." Whether Mr. Dingler was teaching children or digging a new location for the outhouse, Reverend Branson found him to be a quite handy person to have around.

Beyond this, Reverend Branson also had a personal "vision" about Mr. Dingler and felt certain that God had intended Mr. Dingler to be a teacher of children. Reverend Branson, himself a child of a highly educated but brutal, alcoholic father, was especially impressed with Mr. Dingler's unbridled dedication to sobriety; that alone was enough to convince the good reverend that he should place Mr. Dingler in a leadership role within the church. And this is how Mr. Wiles Dingler had been transformed from a vulgar, loud-mouthed drunk to the singular, pastoral aide and Bible teacher in God's Learning Room.

Mr. Dingler looked out solemnly across the class. A full two minutes passed as he waited for absolute silence. The children had already been quiet but he wanted the silence to be "absolute": not the squeak of a chair; not a rustling of paper; just the tremulous sound of children breathing.

Then he began his reading of Psalms 18:32-36. "It is God that girdeth me with strength, and maketh my way perfect," he spoke with enlightened emphasis. "He maketh my feet like hinds' feet, and setteth me upon my high places. He teacheth my hands to war, so that a bow of steel is broken by mine arms.'"

Mr. Dingler looked up from the book.

"Do ya know what I jus' read? God Hisself done made my arms so strong that I can break a bow made out'a pure steel. 'N my feet? They's fast as the feet'a any ole deer! So who here can tell me what that all means?"

The class was silent as the students looked to each other for help.

"Come on now, children. Try! What does it all mean?"

A boy raised his hand.

"Abel," Mr. Dingle acknowledged the boy.

"It means you can beat people up and then run real fast."

Mr. Dingle paused and looked meanly at the boy. The boy wriggled nervously in his chair, having learned firsthand what severe punishment Mr. Dingler was capable of handing out.

"Gooood!" Mr.Dingler responded, "Yeah, that's e'zactly what it means! It means if ya got God on your side, you'll be stronger'n any ole devil; 'n ya can outrun 'n kill people with your arrows; 'n hurt your enemies mightily 'n in ever' which way possible. For when God's goodliness is gotten in ya, you can run roughshod over any'a those no-good, uppity types 'n beat their warrior asses right plumb to the ground."

Their mouths agape and eyes wide open, the children stared at Mr. Dingler.

"A'course when I says 'ass,' I'm talkin' 'bout the Bible-type ass. Ya know, the four-legged kind what eats grass. We don't never 'llow no word like 'ass' to be used in God's Learnin' Room less'n they's used in the Good Book. Any other talk'a 'ass' is foul 'n evil, 'n'll get yourselfs a good whuppin' to anybody what tries sayin' it. Ain't never no foul, evil talk 'llowed to be talked here in God's Learnin' Room less'n it comes straight from the Bible. Any questions 'bout the passage I jus' read?"

Carlos raised his hand and was acknowledged. "Mr. Dingler, why would we want to beat uppity people's asses to the ground if asses are just poor, dumb animals who never did nothing bad to nobody on purpose? Why would God want us to hurt them?"

Mr. Dingler pursed his lips far outward, a pose he sometimes held when deep in thought.

"Carlos, you're jus' a Mexican, campesino boy what don't know too dang much 'bout how asses act out there. But let me tell you, from my vast experience as a hard-drinkin' range-rider what spent more'n once in the hoosegow – that was afore I got saved a'course – those asses ain't always so good 'n innocent as ya like to think they is. Those asses can get downright orn'ry sometimes 'n give ya a good kick on the chin or a bite on the arm. 'N when they do, you jus' gotta kick 'n bite 'em right back. You jus' close your fist like this 'n hit 'em square in the head, hard as ya can. I put many'a orn'ry ass down that way, I tell ya."

"Mr. Dingler!" a little girl called out.

"You jus' say somethin', Loretta?" Mr. Dingler responded.

"Mr. Dingler, my Ma sometimes gets mad 'n calls my Pa a 'lazy horse's ass,'" she stated with an honest curiosity. "Now, when she's a'doin' that, is she talkin' 'bout the Bible-type ass or the other kind?"

Mr. Dingler pulled out a ruler from the inside of his jacket, grabbed his cane and hobbled over to the little girl. The children's eyes opened wider than ever.

"You got yourself a perfectly good question there, Loretta. But what'd I tell ya 'bout talkin' out'a turn? 'N don't say ya ain't been told."

"I'm sorry, Mr. Dingler, I guess I sort'a forgot. I didn't mean to...."

"Silence!" the teacher shouted then said to the boy sitting next to Loretta, "Chester, hold out your hands."

"But I didn't say nothin', Mister Dingler," the frightened boy protested. "Them was Loretta's words what came out."

"Do as I say, boy!" the teacher demanded. "You know my rule 'gainst hittin' girls afore the age'a thirteen. Now hold out those sinful hands'a yours."

Chester held out his hands, and Mr. Dingler slapped each hand hard with the ruler.

Chester screamed each time he was hit and afterward sat there whimpering.

Mr. Dingler returned his attention to the girl, "Now see what ya done did, Loretta? Ya gone 'n made me smack Chester right forceful on the hands. Say you're sorry to the boy!"

"I'm sorry, Chester," Loretta said with great sincerity. "I didn't mean it."

"It's alright," Chester said. "You ain't did it on purpose."

"Jus' thank your lucky stars you're under the age'a Leviticus 18:19," Mr. Dingler told Loretta as he limped back up to the front of the class. "Otherwise, that'a been you what got hit."

The door opened and the elderly Reverend Branson walked in.

"Good mornin', Reverend Branson!" Mr. Dingler said. "Say good mornin', young'uns."

"Good morning, Reverend Branson!" the four children said in unison.

"Good morning, dear children," the preacher replied. "Mr. Dingler may I speak with you for a moment please?"

"Certainly, Reverend Branson," Mr. Dingler said with a smile and then sternly looked at the class. "You children all get your Bibles out 'n start readin' Bible passages. I'll be back afore long, 'n I don't wanna be hearin' no talkin' in here."

The children pulled out their Bibles as the men walked outside.

"And how is today's class coming along, Mr. Dingler?" the reverend asked.

"Real good, Reverend. Real good indeed. I was jus' talkin' to the dear, sweet, little children there 'bout God's everlastin' 'n a'ternal love."

"Excellent, Mr. Dingler! We're so lucky to have you as a teacher. But what I wanted to tell you is that tomorrow you'll be getting a new student; a blind boy."

"A blind boy, you say?"

"Yes, he's totally blind."

"A blind boy, you say! Now don't that jus' break your heart?" Mr. Dingler emoted.

"Yes, it is all so very, very sad."

"'N jus' why would any blind boy wanna be goin' to school?"

"I spoke with his mother today, and she seems to feel that the boy's schooling and religious training have been severely neglected. And now that he's gone blind, she's hoping to have him catch up a little. Do you think you'd be able to teach a poor, pitiful, blind child, Mr. Dingler?"

"Sure I can, Reverend Branson. Dang, I can teach anybody: deaf, dumb, blind, stupid; it don't matter. I learn 'em all real good."

"I think, to express it a little more accurately, it should be said that you 'teach them all very well,'" the ever polite reverend corrected teacher Dingler's grammar.

"Why, I thank you for sayin' that, Reverend Branson. 'Cause I do too. 'N if God chooses to send that little, blind boy to me, I'll teach him well as well can be. 'Cause it's doin' the Lord's teachin' work what's been helpin' keep me off that damnatatin' hoochinoo."

"Yes, it has, hasn't it. And how are you coming along with that, Mr. Dingler? Is it getting any easier for you?"

"Yes, Reverend Branson. With the Lord's help – 'n yours' too a'course – I feel I've got Lucifer firm by the eggs 'n a'swingin' 'n a'flingin' him back into the fiery pits'a Hell!"

"Good heavens, Mr. Dingler! I'm thrilled that you're doing so well but please don't talk about grabbing anything as befouled as Lucifer's hellish, deviled eggs to the children."

"No, Reverend Branson, I wouldn't never do nothin' like that. So tell me more about this blind boy, Reverend. What's his name?"

"The poor lad's name is Colter Barnett."

"Colton Barnett? Mr. Dingler turned a shade pale. "Why, that's Helen McKenna's adopted boy, ain't it?"

"Yes, that's him. But his name is Colter. How do you know them?"

"No...I jus' heard 'bout 'em is all. They's those bankrupts what used to own that big ranch southwest'a here."

"Yes, that's the McKennas alright. And so much trouble has befallen them. First, Mr. McKenna tragically died. Then, Mrs. McKenna lost the ranch. And now, her adopted son Colter has turned blind. It's all so very, very tragic."

"Young Colton's blind, you say? That's...," Mr. Dingler coughed in a way that sounded like he was trying to suppress a sudden surge of emotion.

"Mr. Dingler, are you alright?"

"Yeah, I'm jus' feelin' little overcome is all. That poor Colton child! Blind! 'N so dang young too!" Mr. Dingler coughed a couple more times and had to clear his throat and spit into his handkerchief in order to continue.

"Yes, it really is quite sad," the reverend agreed. "I'm so impressed by how moved you are by all of this. Will you be alright, Mr. Dingler?"

"Oh yeah, I'll be jus' fine. Somethin' in my throat's all. So how'd the kid go blind?"

"I really don't know the details surrounding it. I didn't want to seem impolite by prying too much. They've suffered such a great deal; it just didn't seem right."

"Yeah, they's suffered a goodly amount, aint' they. Hoooeey! Oh Lordy, Lordy, Lord-Lord! God's judgment certainly works in mysterious ways! So how ole is little Colton now? Fifteen? Sixteen?"

"He's turning seventeen on the twenty-sixth of this month; his mother told me."

"That'll be comin' up, next Wednesday I think. 'N when does he start his church schoolin'?"

"I'll bring him around sometime tomorrow afternoon. Best to start off slow, I believe. Maybe he could just sit in class awhile and listen. Then afterwards, perhaps, you could meet with him privately and tell him all about our little church school."

"Yes, Reverend Branson, I'd be glad to do that." Mr. Dingler coughed again. "Please 'scuse me, Reverend. My throat feels kind'a dried up 'n all itchy-like. I gotta go to the well for some water."

"Yes, of course, Mr. Dingler," Reverend Branson said, deeply moved by Mr. Dingler's discernible sympathy for the blind child. "We'll speak more about this later." The preacher said and walked away.

"Thank you, Reverend Branson," responded Mr. Dingler before turning his back to the preacher and slowly limping over to the well alongside the building.

Once at the well, Mr. Dingler didn't bother to get a drink of water. He just stood there looking down into the well's deep, dark innards. But he wasn't observing anything outside of himself at all. The teacher was, in fact, completely disoriented by thoughts of the blind Barnett boy.

When Mr. Dingler finally did return to God's Learning Room, he dismissed the class early then left for the day.

21

TEACHER DINGLER MEETS THE BLIND CHILD

Friday morning was uneventful for the students. As was his custom, Mr. Dingler "educated" the children with talk of his past, wild ways and about how his former "bad life" was now all behind him due to the Lord's loving intervention and a life-changing, bull-riding accident to his leg. On this day, however, Mr. Dingler talked with less energy than usual, and he seemed to be looking out the window a lot more.

Sometime around noon, just before releasing the children for lunch, Mr. Dingler mentioned that a new student, "a God-pitiful, blind boy," would be joining the class then read the following from Zephaniah 1:17,

"And I will bring distress upon men, that they shall walk like blind men, because they have sinned against the LORD: and their blood shall be poured out as dust, and their flesh as the dung."

Mr. Dingler looked menacingly at the class. "You all know the meanin'a what I jus' read? It says sin can make your eyes blind 'n your flesh go pyew-ee rotten! 'N that's for sinnin' 'gainst the Lord 'n the teachers'a His holy Word! So anyone what sins 'gainst a Bible teacher can suffer the curse'a agonizin' blindness." Dingler took time to observe what effect his words might be having on the children.

"Alright, you all can go eat now."

The children scampered outside to eat their lunches under the spread of majestic oaks.

Forgoing his own mid-day repast, Mr. Dingler spent the greater part of that time standing and watching through a window that overlooked the yard. From there, he observed all the children sitting on the ground and eating their lunches. But the teacher was particularly interested in studying the lone, blind boy with the bandaged eyes who sat under a tree and apart from the others.

"Mr. Dingler!" Reverend Branson called out as he walked into the room.

Mr. Dingler turned and noticed the cleric. "Reverend Branson, you done scared me. I didn't hear ya comin' in."

"May I have a few moments of your lunch period?"

"Certainly," Mr. Dingler answered and, cane in hand, walked falteringly to the reverend.

"The blind Barnett boy is outside, and I have instructed him to come in after lunch," Reverend Branson informed the teacher.

"Yeah, I saw him sittin' out there all lonesome-like. So where's the boy's mama at?"

"She drove him out here and will be back for him next Wednesday for his seventeenth birthday. I thought it might be best if he stayed at the church awhile – just to help him get used to things."

"Yeah, that's sort'a a good idea, I guess" Mr. Dingler commented. "But where's the boy gonna sleep?"

"He can stay in the storeroom adjacent to Carlos' room. Of course, it's unbelievably dirty so you'll have to give it a good scrubbing for our special, blind child."

"Uh huh."

"Come to think of it, when I was in there a few days ago, it smelled like a dead rat might be under the floorboards. Perhaps it would be better if you gave him your room and you slept in the storeroom instead – considering how sharp the sense of smell must be for a blind person."

"No, he'll be alright, Reverend. Anyway, my smeller gets real touchy when it whiffs up dead stuff, prob'ly more'n any blind person's ever could."

"Oh, I'm sorry to hear that, Mr. Dingler."

"Yeah, so I'll jus' get me some'a that hemp out back 'n burn the pyew-ee right out'a that room. The blind boy'll be jus' fine in there. When I'm done, even the rat won't mind it."

"Even the rat won't mind it! My, that's funny," the reverend said with a smile. "Yes, well, whatever you think, Mr. Dingler. I just hope it all goes smoothly. Oh, by the way, I won't be here tomorrow so you can tell me all about it after Sunday's church service."

"You goin' somewheres, Reverend?"

"Yes, I'm just now leaving to spend the night at the Winchell place. Seems Mrs. Winchell has had another one of her fretful, sadness spells and requires my special ministering."

"That woman must be very grateful to you, Reverend; seein' how much sadness-ministerin' you been givin' to her since her husband died."

"Thank you, Mr. Dingler, but ministering to folks' needs is a big part of my duties. And I always find it rather satisfying."

"Well, don't you be worryin' 'bout nothin' here, Reverend Branson. You jus' go ahead 'n get yourself a whole heap'a satisfaction with Mrs. Winchell, 'n we'll be talkin' 'bout it at church this Sunday."

"Pardon me. Did you say there might be some talk about it?"

"Yeah, 'bout the blind boy after next Sunday church like you asked me to."

"Yes! Yes, of course! Our after-church-talk about the poor, blind Barnett child! Silly me! Whatever could I have been thinking?"

"'N you be sure 'n tell Mrs. Winchell I wish I was there too so I could give her my big hahdo face-to-face."

"I'm sorry, Mr. Dingler, your...'big hahdo'? Just what exactly is your 'big hahdo'?"

"My big hahdo, Reverend. You know; like in: Hahdo, Mrs. Winchell! 'N hah ya doin' this nice, fine day?"

"Oh yes, of course! Your big hahdo! I can be so dull sometimes. Certainly I'll be glad to convey your 'big hahdo' to Mrs. Winchell for you. But time is swiftly passing, and I really must be leaving. Take care, Mr. Dingler. You and the children have a blessed, blessed school day."

"We always do, Reverend Branson," Mr. Dingler responded.

The teacher waited until the preacher left the room before returning to the window to make further observations of Colter Barnett. He was surprised to see Carlos Perez standing near the seated blind boy.

"What in the devil is that campesino boy sayin' to Barnett?" Mr. Dingler asked himself.

Colt raised his head. "You say somethin' to me?"

Carlos looked down at the bandages covering Colt's eyes. "Si, I was just asking if it hurts much?"

"'N just who wants to know?"

"My name is Carlos Perez. Our teacher told us that you're going to be in class today. What is your name?"

"My name's Colter but most folks call me Colt. No, my eyes don't hurt all that much. They itch a little, but that's about it."

"How'd you get all blind like that?"

"Don't know for sure. Think I rubbed my eyes when I was out workin' out in the field. Must'a got somethin' in 'em. Doc guesses it was poison oak but it might'a been itch weed or somethin'. He don't really know. But I gotta wear these bandages to keep it from gettin' any worse."

"So what is it like being blind?"

"Danged if I know. I ain't blind – least not true permanent-blind like a fella what ain't got no eyes. Doc says I should get all my vision back afore too long if I take care'a my peepers. I can see light but it's awful blurry."

"So why are you coming to school if your eyes don't work right? Shouldn't you be home in bed?"

"Bed ain't never been no place for me. Anyway, my Mama says I ain't no good around the ranch right now 'n the best place for me is in school. She figures I can use the extra learnin' time. You Spanish? You talk with a Mexico accent."

"Si, Señor Colt, I am Mexican. I've been in this school since my Abuelo died."

"Your abuelo's your grandfather, right?"

"Yes. He always wanted me to get educated. I think his blessed spirit has led me here."

"His blessed spirit, huh? Well, as long as your abuelo ain't hangin' around here right now listenin' to us, I'm okay. Not that I got anything against your dead relatives. He was prob'ly a nice abuelo 'n all, but I don't like bein' around no ghosts, not even my own ghost I wouldn't."

"No, I don't think he's here right now, Señor Colt. At least, I have never seen him."

"That's good. 'Cause right now, everything's lookin' kind'a ghosty to me anyway so I wouldn't be able to tell your abuelo from campfire smoke. 'N please stop callin' me Señor Colt 'cause I ain't no dang señor. I'm just plain Colt"

"Si, I will just call you Colt."

Mr. Dingler rang a handheld bell, his signal for the children to return to God's Learning Room.

The children scurried to the building but Carlos remained behind with Colt.

"Do you want me to help you find your way to the classroom?"

"Yeah, I'd be obliged if you'd let me hold on to your arm. I might never find my way there otherwise."

Carlos waited for Colt to stand then led the new student across the yard and into the classroom. The other students were already seated when they arrived.

"You can sit here," Carlos directed Colt. "No one ever sits in this chair."

"Thanks, I sure 'preciate it."

"De nada," Carlos responded.

Mr. Dingler looked at the class and waited for everyone to "absolutely" quiet down. Several minutes passed.

"Children, as you can see, we got us a new student today. His name is Colton Barnett, 'n he's wearin' those bandages 'cause his eyes can't see good like yours 'n mine can. He's what is known by the good, hard-workin', God-shudderin' folks as bein' 'blind 'n helpless' 'n a 'duty-burden' to society. But no matter what you call 'em, blind people like Colton here ain't normal like all us regular folks is. So we gotta feed 'em 'n take care'a 'em 'n keep 'em out'a the rain, jus' like they's little, helpless babies. It's our Christian duty-burden."

The teacher looked up toward heaven and paused for dramatic emphasis.

"Now sometimes folks's born blind as a way to pay for the sins'a their parents. 'N sometimes they go blind 'cause'a somethin' they themselfs done did what was bad in the eyes'a the Creator. But either way, the Lord is a mighty Lord: always fair 'n upright in His punishments 'n 'forgivenesses.' So I want you all to always feel real sorry for young Colton here 'n always treat this poor, useless, blind boy jus' like he was some good, worthy 'n proper member'a society. You young'uns understandin' me?"

"Yes, Mr. Dingler," all except Colt answered.

"Good. 'N now it's time for us to have today's math lesson. Now who can tell me how long it took for God to create the heavens 'n the earth the way he did? That 'n ever'thin' in it?"

Loretta raised her hand, and was acknowledged by Mr. Dingler. "Six days, Mr. Dingler. And on the seventh day the Lord rested."

"Very good, young missy. 'N thank you for raisin' your hand 'n not causin' Chester to get hand-slapped again. Yes, children, God did create ever'thin' in only six days. Only six days to create the world! Can you imagine that? Now who can tell me, how much is six plus six? Who can tell me that? Anybody? Yes, Chester."

"Six plus six is twelve, Mr. Dingler," Chester answered.

"Very good, Chester. It's exactly twelve! 'Deed if it ain't! Now here's another math question for you all to answer. In Isaiah 6:1-2, the seraphims stood above the throne'a the Lord, 'n jus' how many wings did each seraphim have?" He paused. "Anybody?" He paused again. "How many wings they got? Anybody here know?" He paused a third time. "Nobody? The answer is 'six.' Each seraphim had six wings."

Mr. Dingler opened his Bible, outstretched his right hand and read: "In the year that king Uzziah died I saw also the Lord sitting upon a throne, high and lifted up, and his train filled the temple. Above it stood the seraphims: each one had six wings; with twain he covered his face, and with twain he covered his feet, and with twain he did fly." He looked up from the Bible and stared at the class. "So the answer was 'six.' Now who can tell me, how much is six and twenty? Chester?"

"Six and twenty is twenty-six!" Chester answered.

"Very good, Chester! Six 'n twenty is twenty-six! I'm right proud'a you, Chester. Not that I can say that for the rest'a you shirkers in this class. Anybody got questions? Yes, Loretta."

"Mr. Dingler, what's a twain?" she asked most sincerely.

Mr. Dingler stared sternly at the little girl.

"Missy Loretta, I don't know nobody who rightly knows what 'twain' means e'zactly, 'n it don't make no difference nohow. No 'twain' is ever gonna put meat on your table nor apples in your pie. So you jus' never mind what a 'twain' is. But do you know how important math is in your ever'day workaday life? Why, you can't do nothin' without knowin' no math. Like if you wanna buy somethin' at the general store, you gotta know math. Or if you're gonna build yourself a good, sturdy hogpen, you gotta know math. Math is ever'thin', 'n it don't matter if it's six stones, six wings on a seraphim or six toes on a duck, you gotta know math. 'N that's why you all need to be studyin' your Isaiah too."

The class grew silent from the chastisement.

"Now let's move on to our proper Bible studies. Any'a you ever get any bad dreams?" he asked the class.

Chester's hand quickly went up but just as quickly dropped when it became obvious that none of the other students had ever had any bad dreams.

"Well, I sure do," Mr. Dingler freely admitted. "'N that's when it's nice to have the Bible to console me. Jus' last night, I had me one'a my bad dreams. So I got up, opened my Bible 'n guess where my finger done landed? It was pointin' right here at this verse here: Job 33:15. 'For God speaketh once, yea twice, yet man perceiveth it not. In a dream, in a vision of the night, when deep sleep falleth upon men, in slumberings upon the bed.' Did you hear that?" he asked the class. "It says in a vision'a the night!"

No one, save Mr. Dingler, understood what he had just read.

"What an amazement it is to have the Bible to show us the way. 'N then I found this here verse in Genesis 46:2. 'And God spake unto Israel in the visions of the night, and said, Jacob, Jacob. And he said, Here am I.' See?" he asked the students. "It's talkin' 'bout 'visions' again! Glory is the knowledge'a the Lord!" Mr. Dingler added with happy excitement.

Still, no one knew what Mr. Dingler was talking about.

"'N then I found this one here in Proverbs 29:18. 'Where there is no vision, the people perish: but he that keepeth the law, happy is he.' Praise 'n glory!" Mr. Dingler shouted and began bouncing up and down. "Vision! Vision!" he called out. "The answer is vision. I jus' had to read it for myself!"

By now, every child in the room was totally mystified.

"Today, children, we're gonna end the class a little early. Ever'one may go except poor, blind-child Barnett. Class dismissed!"

Mr. Dingler turned away from his students to arrange some items on the floor behind his desk.

Carlos approached Colt. "Do you want me to wait outside and help you find your way around?"

"Yeah, if you want," Colt answered.

All the children left, and Mr. Dingler made sure the front door was closed then lumbered over to the window and looked out.

"So, young man," Mr. Dingler asked while peering outside to make certain no one was about, "how do you like our class?"

"It's alright, I s'pose. Kind'a shorter'n I expected," Colt answered.

Colt heard the sounds of a cane hitting the wooden floor and a chair being dragged across the room as Mr. Dingler limped toward him.

"Tell me: You ever gone to studyin' the Bible afore today?"

"No. I never been to any school afore today. This here's my first one."

"Can you read?"

"Yeah, I can read as good as necessary."

"You can, can you? 'N who taught you to do that?"

"Nobody taught me. Far as I remember, I picked it up all on my own."

"All on your own! My, oh my, my, my!" Mr. Dingler pulled the chair in front of the boy and sat down. "You are a bright boy, ain't ya Colton. Yeah, I can see that. But now I'd like to read you some scripture, if ya don't mind."

"No, I don't mind. But my name's Colter."

Mr. Dingler opened his Bible to Luke 16:19-23 and began reading: "There was a certain rich man, which was clothed in purple and fine linen, and fared sumptuously every day: And there was a certain beggar named Lazarus, which was laid at his gate, full of sores, And desiring to be fed with the crumbs which fell from the rich man's table: moreover the dogs came and licked his sores. And it came to pass, that the beggar died, and was carried by the angels into Abraham's bosom: the rich man also died, and was buried; And in hell he lift up his eyes, being in torments, and seeth Abraham afar off, and Lazarus in his bosom."

Mr. Dingler paused. "Hah!" he amusedly exclaimed. "There's a powerful message in there, boy. You know who God is talkin' 'bout in that passage?"

"No, I surely don't."

"He's talkin' 'bout those high-'n-mighty folks! You know, those uppities what likes to live it up 'n lord it over all us poor people. But then, you know folks like that, don't you, Colton?"

"No, can't say as I do."

"You don't? Sure ya do, Colton. Jus' think 'bout it. Don't that there rich feller remind you'a someone you know real personal-like? Someone in your ever'day personal acquaintance maybe? Maybe someone in your family even?"

"No, I sure don't know anyone like that personal."

"You certain, Colton?" Mr. Dingler asked sardonically. "Think on it for a spell. There must be somebody."

"No, I'm certain. I ain't never knowed nobody like that ever."

"But now, ain't your mama one'a those high-'n-mighty McKenna people?

"'Scuse me?"

"'N wasn't those McKenna people all livin' it up on that big, fancy ranch'a theirs; eatin' their sump'shus foods ever' supper; 'n your mama always wearin' her fancy, royalty clothes; 'n those McKennas actin' all rich 'n snooty-like?"

"What's my Mama got to do with this? I'm not followin' your meanin', Teacher."

"Those McKennas. They's all rich, wasn't they?"

"I never knowed any McKennas; only my Mama Helen. Yeah, she had land but, from what I heard, the McKennas wasn't nothin' but plain ole, workin' folks. They sure never ate no sump'shus supper foods nor wore no fancy duds I ever learned of."

Mr. Dingler became agitated. "Oh come on, Colton! Don't you lie to me now! Didn't you hear what the Bible's sayin' 'bout all you uppity, rich folks? You're all gonna end up burnin' for a'ternity in the flames'a Hell!"

Colt hesitated. "What in blazes are you talkin' about? Who are you anyway?"

"Who am I? Why, I ain't nothin' but some low-down, cripply-legged teacher who used to work at the McKenna Ranch 'n who now goes by the name'a Mr. Wiles Dingler."

"Wiles Dingler?" Colt thought about the name. "Is this Dingles?"

"No, you disrespectful, blind boy, you may not call me by that name no more. You may got away with callin' me Dingles back at the ranch but I don't work for you highfalutin' McKennas no more. From now on, Mr. Wiles Dingler is your teacher 'n your better so you will only address me as Mr. Dingler, understand?"

Having no doubt whatsoever that this was Dingles, Colt instinctively slid his chair back several feet.

"Oh, don't worry, Colton, I ain't gonna hurt you. I should oughta break your neck. But I won't. What's done is all did in the past now, 'n today I'm brand new in the Lord: a sinner no more. 'Repent!' Acts 3:19 tells us. 'Repent ye therefore, and be converted, that your sins may be blotted out, when the times of refreshing shall come from the presence of the Lord.'"

"I don't believe this," Colter said.

"You know what that means, Colton? That means I – Mr. Wiles Dingler - forgive you. I shouldn't but I do; I truly do. I forgive you for sneak-hittin' me in the head with that log 'n for givin' me this permanent, cripply leg. I forgive you the pain I went through 'n for the cane I gotta use each 'n ever'day. For I have found the love'a Jesus 'n I have repented! I am a new man, Colton, 'n I'm walkin' in the ways'a the Lord. So I forgive you."

"I don't believe it. Dirty-mouth Dingles? A Bible teacher? How could that be possible? You had the rottenest mouth on the range."

"Please don't say that, Colton Barnett. Don't you be sittin' there judgin' me 'n castin' demon doubts upon my Lordly conversion. It makes me mad when uppity folks like you get to talkin' that way – 'specially after all those bad things you done did to me."

"Well, there's a reason for all them bad things I done did to you, Dingles. Remember them nasty things you was sayin' about my Mama Helen?"

"Course I remember! 'N don't you never be callin' me Dingles no more! As boss teacher in God's Learnin' Room, I absolutely forbid it!"

"Boss teacher? How many teachers you got workin' here to boss over, Dingles?"

"I jus' told you never to call me that! I worked hard at forgivin' you, boy. So don't you go makin' me change my mind. I prayed 'n I prayed 'n I prayed. 'There is therefore now no condemnation to them which are in Christ Jesus, who walk not after the flesh, but after the Spirit.' Romans 8:1. Yes, I become permanent cripply 'cause'a you! Yes, my knee hurts me ever' second'a ever'day. But I forgive you, Colton Barnett. I forgive you with all my heart. Can you believe that?"

Colt hesitated. "Is this a joke? Is this really you, Dingles? It just don't seem true."

Mr. Dingler rose up to his full height and began to cry.

"Damn you, boy! I done warned you 'bout callin' me that! My name is Mr. Wiles Dingler now, 'n you will respect me! Oh Lord, help me for what I'm 'bout to do in accordance with Thine good 'n holy Will. Yes, I prayed, n' I prayed, 'n I prayed; but it ain't done much good. So on this day, You hath sent to me the little mutton-puncher. Thine enemy You hath delivereth to me, Mr. Wiles Dingler, Thou true 'n lovin' servant. For in Thine wisdom, Thou desireth complete 'n righteous revenge 'gainst those evil McKenna uppities. 'N now this demon uppity has entered into Thine holy house 'n Thou demandeth me to smote him'a all sins. Yea 'n verily unto You!"

"What kind'a crazy talk are you doin' there, Dingles?"

But Mr. Dingler ignored Colt and continued on his rapturous rant. "Ever'day, I secretly prayed 'bout facin' this McKenna whore-spawn what made me cripply-legged. 'N now You hath delivereth him to me. For as it says in Hebrews 10:17, 'And their sins and iniquities will I remember no more.' 'N also in Nahum 1:2, 'God is jealous, and the LORD revengeth; the LORD revengeth, and is furious; the LORD will take vengeance on his adversaries, and he reserveth wrath for his enemies.'"

"Look, Dingles, I 'preciate your learnin' all this holy-roly razzle-dazzle. But maybe you should consider doin' your religious blubberin' in private. It prob'ly ain't somethin' most sane folks wanna hear."

Mr. Dingler looked angrily at Colt and said lowly, "You cursed infidel."

"But, if it helps," Colt continued, "I'm willin' to admit that I was prob'ly wrong to go wailin' on you like I done. I prob'ly shouldn'ta been so quick to go guff-bustin' ya 'n just fired your worthless butt instead. So if it makes you feel any better, Dingles, I say I'm sorry for what happened back then. It was wrong."

"You're damn right it was wrong, you blind beast from Hell! Now I've gotta walk with a cane all 'cause'a you, you misbegotten progeny'a McKenna whoredom! Your kind ain't even worthy in the eyes'a the Lord. For as God says in Deuteronomy 23:2, 'A bastard shall not enter into the congregation of the LORD; even to his tenth generation shall he not enter into the congregation of the LORD.' So you're not even loved by the great 'n heavenly God Hisself."

Outside the building, Carlos Perez had climbed atop an American Radiator Company, cherub-ornated, cast-iron radiator that someone had donated by anonymously setting it against the building – a convective item which Reverend Branson had hoped to install along with the purchase of "some type of a coal-fired boiler" once the costly orphan expenditure was eliminated. Instead, the living "expenditure" now peered in through the window and was becoming distressed at observing Mr. Dingler's threatening actions toward the new, blind student.

Carlos was well aware of Mr. Dingler's holier-than-thou meanness but the man's present level of dangerousness seemed beyond terrifying. This Mexican boy's fears were compounded by the fact that he had once witnessed his grandfather being severely beaten for "practicing medicine without a license." It was, in fact, that beating which had led to the old man's overall loss of health and eventual demise. Carlos' internal wounds made viewing Mr. Dingler's menacing behavior all the more unbearable.

"Hold it right there, Dingles; you brought your cripply injuries upon yourself. You shootin' off your filthy clap-trap out on the range was one thing but when you went to insultin' my Mama Helen like you done, well, you just bulldozed one step too far. So maybe it's time for you to start admittin' you was wrong too, Dingles. You may be a Bible spouter now but you still ain't convinced me you're some kind'a saint."

Mr. Dingler began to sob uncontrollably.

"My poor leg! All that cattlin' work! My pride! Ever'thin' taken from me by that blind, little mutton-puncher! 'N for what? – so he could look all biggity by beatin' me up with that log 'n shamin' me in front'a the men? Oh Lordy, Lordy, Lord-Lord!"

Feeling some little sympathy for the hysterically weeping man, Colt became uncharacteristically "conciliatory." "Look here, Dingler, I ain't one to mollycoddle nobody, especially no loose-gobbed swine what insulted my Mama

Helen. But you can stop your boohooin' now 'cause I already admitted it was prob'ly wrong what I done to you. I wish I hadn't gone to bashin' in your leg that way. It was wrong. 'N now that you likely changed for the better – you bein' a Bible teacher 'n all – I feel kind'a sorry about it. So if you're willin' to forgive me, Lordy, I sure am willin' to forgive you."

"You! Willin' to forgive me! I'm crippled up 'cause'a you, you runty, little mutton-puncher! You high-'n-mighty, McKenna bastard child! You cow poodle! You blind little....!" No longer able to contain his hellfire anger through the power of the sacred manual, Mr. Dingler surrendered to his internal apocalypse, exploded and charged at Colt.

"Hey!" Colt shouted as Dingler locked his powerful, right arm around the boy's neck.

Colt struggled to get free but Dingler was much too large and robust and the chokehold was too strongly braced. Colt thrashed around and jumped out of his chair but Mr. Dingler only further tightened the stranglehold by pulling his muscular, left arm with his massively strong, right hand.

"I'm gonna kill you, you little, McKenna bastard, whore-child! I done killed afore 'n – Lord or no Lord – you're as good as dead!"

His upper airway dangerously compressed and finding himself unable to breathe, Colt pulled desperately on Mr. Dingler's right arm. But to no avail. Colt pushed back hard with his legs, forcing Mr. Dingler off balance and knocking him against the wall, but that didn't work either. At core, Mr. Dingler was a cruel, brutish creature with a strangulation grip that several innocent victims had also discovered to be inescapably fatal.

The struggle continued for minutes until, feeling the life force withdrawing from his body and beginning to lose consciousness, Colt swung his fist upward and back, trying to hit Mr. Dingler square in the face. But Mr. Dingler was too tall and Colt's blows failed to reach their mark.

The last thing Colt remembered before passing out was falling and crashing through a chair with the enormous weight of Mr. Dingler falling on top of him.

Colt lay unconscious for several minutes.

"Are you alright?" a young voice asked. "Are you still alive? Wake up, Señor Colt! Wake up!"

Colt could feel someone shaking him, and it felt like he was being pulled back from the frontier of death. Becoming aware of his surroundings, Colt discovered that he was unable to move under the dead weight of Mr. Dingler.

"I am glad you're alive. I thought he had killed you."

Colt coughed as he tried to regain his breath. "Who's that talkin' to me?" he asked.

"It's me, Carlos! Mr. Dingler went insano and tried to murder you. So I had to hit him in the head with a hammer to get him to stop."

"Thanks, Carlos, you saved my life. Help get Charlie Sampson off me, will ya?"

Colt used his back to lift as Carlos pulled Mr. Dingler up by the back of the shirt. Working together, and with some difficulty, they were able to free Colt and move Mr. Dingler's body to one side.

"Muchas gracias, Carlos. My goose was cooked. Where'd you find the hammer?"

"The farrier dropped it last week when he was shoeing Reverend Branson's mare." Carlos moved one of Mr. Dingler's legs out of the way. "His nail hurt the horse so bad that it kicked him and he dropped it. So I borrowed it afterwards and hid it by the steps. I know I'm not supposed to borrow things but it turned out good this time, si?"

"Dang right it turned out good. Your borrowin' that thing saved my life. But my legs don't feel right. Can you help me up?"

"Si," Carlos said, helping Colt to stand.

"Dingles dead?" Colt asked.

"What's a 'dinglesdead'?"

"Dingles? Is he dead?"

Carlos looked at the body. "Ah, entiendo; you mean Mr. Dingler! No, he is not dead. I think...I mean...I hope he's not dead. I did not try to kill him."

"Feel his wrist, Carlos. See if you can get some kind'a pulse."

Carlos bent down and felt Mr. Dingler's wrist. "¡Madre de Dios! ¡Soy un asesino! (Mother of God! I am a killer!) I have killed him! Now I will be put into la cárcel!"

"Put into jail? No, that won't happen. They don't put people in jail for protectin' themselves against murderin' Bible-pigs."

"But I wasn't protecting me, Señor Colt! I was protecting you!"

Colt thought about it for a second. "Yeah, you're right. You might-could end up in jail at that."

"¡Este es la mala suerte! ¡Ah Dios! ¡Vine aquí para aprender, y ahora voy a ser ejecutado! (This is bad luck! Oh God! I came here to learn, and now I am going to be executed!)"

"Wait a minute. Try slow talkin' some. No entiendo when you jabber so fast."

"I must leave this place now, Señor Colt, before I am arrested."

"Yeah, that'd prob'ly be the best thing to do. Can you get some horses?"

"Reverend Branson has some extra horses in the church barn, and he's not here. I saw him riding off in his carriage."

"Good. Saddle us up a couple'a good horses. First, we'll ride out to the homestead so I can tell Mama Helen what's happened. She's gotta know. Then, we'll take to the backlands. From there, maybe head south."

"You are going with me, Señor Colt?"

"Course, I'm goin' with you, Carlos. You just saved my life, amigo."

"But you are blind, Señor Colt."

"Please quit callin' me señor. And you're right; my eyes ain't what they should be but, in a week or so, they'll be fine. 'N now we need some supplies. You got any money?"

"No tengo nada. (I have nothing.)"

"Nothin' eh? Well, I got two dollars Mama Helen left with me. You got anything at all you could sell at the general store?"

"No, I own nothing of value." But then Carlos remembered. "No, no es verdadero. (No, that is not true.) I have a silver picture frame my Abuelo gave me before he died. He told me that someday it would bring me luck."

"Your abuelo gave it to you? You sure you wanna sell it?"

"Si, I am sure. Ever since I got it – solamente mala suerte (nothing but bad luck.) I think it might be possessed by an evil of some kind."

"Well, ya better get rid'a the dang thing then. We sure don't need no bad luck picture frame anywhere near us. How much you think you can get for the confounded thing?"

"I don't know. It's made out of real silver so it must be very valuable – maybe one hundred dollars or more."

"One hundred dollars! That much? That is one valuable piece'a bad luck ya got there. Here," Colt said reaching out to hand Carlos the money, "Take this two dollars 'n sell that evil picture frame'a yours 'n see what you can get for supplies. Do you know what to buy, amigo?"

"Si, I would often buy supplies for my Abuelo. And Reverend Branson sends me for supplies too. You wait here, and I'll be back as soon as I can."

"Don't worry none; I'll be right here alright. I ain't goin' nowhere. Just make it 'ruhpeedoh,' understand?"

"Sí, rápido. I will go now. But this could take a while." Carlos pulled a chair over to Colt. "Here. Sit, por favor. And please do not leave the building."

Colt reached out and grabbed the chair. "No, pretty sure I won't be leavin'," he said and seated himself.

Carlos walked to the door. "Tenga cuidado. (Be careful,)" he said before closing the door behind him.

All became quiet.

Time passed and Colt began to think about sharing the room with Mr. Dingler's dead body. This was the first time he'd ever been alone with a human corpse, and he didn't particularly care for the feeling. He tried not thinking about it.

"What did Carlos mean, 'You wait here'?" Colt asked himself. "Just where in the heck else would I go?"

Nearly two hours went by and Colt spent the time humming and talking to himself as a way to distract his thoughts from Dingler's body. Time seemed to pass slower than usual for Colt, and he was concerned that Carlos hadn't yet returned.

"Sure hope he didn't have no problems along the way," Colt wondered aloud.

The wind began to blow, and Colt heard some slight hitting and scraping noises on the roof and against the sides of the building.

"Must be tree branches," he said, "or it might even be squirrels." He couldn't keep from listening but tried not worrying about the continuing sounds.

Eventually Colt's nervousness concerning otherworldly matters broke through.

"I just hope that noise ain't you, Dingles, you no-good, Bible versin', son'a the devil," Colt called out. "It ain't really you, is it, Dingles? If it is, make some sort'a sign."

The noises abruptly stopped.

"Oh Lordy! It is you!"

Colt took a deep breath to calm himself.

"See here, Dingles, if it helps any, I'm really sorry about what's happened to you today. When I got up this mornin', I sure wasn't plannin' on runnin' into you much less havin' you get whomped in the head 'n die on me. For certain, if I coulda known in advance what was gonna happen, I woulda stayed home."

The room remained eerily quiet so Colt decided to speak directly to the body which he knew lay several feet in front of him.

"Mr. Dingles, you know I can't change things. 'Cause if I could – hocus-pocus abra-cadaver! – I'd bring ya back to life right now. But I can't do nothin' about things any more'n you can. So there really ain't no use in you hangin' around here no more. I know I'm gonna leave soon as Carlos gets back 'n you should get goin' too – sooner the better, I think."

It was still eerily quiet.

"Can't be no fun, Dingles, your body laid out on the floor like that with your head all bashed in; that's gotta be uncomfortable even for a dead man. So why don't you just gather up your spirit or whatever 'n get the heck out'a here? You seemed to love the Bible a whole bunch, so why don't ya just hustle on out'a here 'n go meet the Guy what wrote it?"

Colt waited for a response but none was forthcoming.

"To be honest, Dingles, I don't like bein' in this room any more'n you do. Sooner we get out'a here, the better.

But since we're both here right now, let's try makin' the best'a things, alright? There ain't no point in us harborin' hard feelin's toward each other. What's done is done, Mr. Dingles."

The room still seemed unduly quiet, especially to a person whose vision had been so recently and greatly attenuated. Straightaway, as if in response to Colt's attempted "beyond the pale" communication, the roof started to crack loudly. Colt was startled and interpreted it as Dingles' spirit making physical communication.

"Look here, Dingles, I think it'd just be best if you got your boisterous, upscuddlin' ghost out'a here lickety-split. So I'm willin' to do whatever it takes to help you on your way to the other side. How about me sayin' a goodly prayer for you? You think that might help? Alright, I'll say some kind'a prayer for you then. Just let me think about this a second."

Colt collected his thoughts for several moments before beginning to speak with a tone of unfeigned solemnity.

"Lord, I would like to tell you a little bit about Mr. Dingles – I mean Mr. Dingler – sorry about that Dingles; just a habit I gotten into. Lord, if you can help him on his way to wherever it is he's s'posed to be goin' – Heaven? – Hell? – wherever he's bound for – we'll both be gratefully thankful for it. Just kindly make it sooner'n later 'cause we'd both like it that way, please."

He thought a short while before continuing.

"Dingles was a – sorry, Dingles – I mean, Mr. Dingler was a man who uh...who used to work for us out at the ranch. 'N uh...that was afore we had that big fallin'-out, that is. But that Dingler was one good talker; Dingles was. Why he'd just be yappin' away all the time he was out there. Seems like you could hardly shut Mr. Dingles up once he got to workin' his big bazoo. 'N Dingles was a...he was a...."

More thinking was required.

"'N Dingles was a smart person too...kind'a, in a way... least not near as stupid as most people thought he was. I mean, the man had to have somethin' in that fat noggin to go studyin' the Good Book like he done. So at least we know now that Dingles wasn't the illiterate loudmouth everybody made him out to be."

Colt wanted this all to be over with but he went on with the "prayer" only because he deemed it necessary.

"Sure, he'd sometimes cause trouble, shootin' off that big, dirty mouth'a his like he always done. But at least he wasn't no crafty, smooth-talkin' con man like them medicine show fellas are. No sir, God, Mr. Dingler wasn't never that smart to be connin' people out'a their money 'n stuff. So, I guess you could say that makes him a good man too, in a way."

"Sure, Dingles was a vulgar, uncouth galoot out there on the range but that's just the way Dingles was; couldn't be helped. 'N there was those few times that he actually did some pretty good work too. So you could say he was kind'a a halfways good worker, when you was watchin' him. There it is, Lord: Dingles in a nutshell. So I say 'Amen,' Lord, 'n please let Mr. Dingle's soul pass out'a this room 'n into that other place whatever it is. Amen again to you, Lord, 'n goodbye to you too, Mr. Dingles...I mean, Mr. Dingler."

Fifteen seconds passed.

"Are you gone now, Dingles?"

Colt listened intently for another fifteen seconds.

"Yippee! It worked! What a relief," he sighed.

It was another twenty seconds or so before Colt heard the door open.

"Dingles? Is that you?"

"No, it's me. Carlos. I bought the supplies, and we have two horses from the barn. We can leave now."

"How much'd you get for your silver picture frame?"

"Not so much as I thought."

"How much?"

"A sack of sugar."

"One measly sack'a sugar? But you said it was worth a hundred dollars."

"It probably was; I don't know. But the man wouldn't give me nothing for it but a sack of sugar. What could I do?"

"Nothin', I s'pose," Colt said with a shrug. "Well, at least you got rid'a that bad luck thing."

"We must leave now before somebody comes here and finds Mr. Dingler's body. I will help you to your horse, amigo." Carlos took Colt by the arm. "Walk along with me, por favor."

Colt and Carlos went outside and climbed atop their horses. Carlos rode in the lead with Colt's horse walking naturally alongside.

"Did you get a big sack'a sugar or a little sack?" Colt asked as they rode away.

"I don't know," Carlos answered. "It was just sugar."

They rode five miles to the forty-acre homestead where Colter informed Mama Helen of all that had transpired. She insisted the boys should stay there and that they would "all fight it together." But Colt said they couldn't because Carlos might end up getting convicted and that he owed Carlos his very life. When Helen McKenna came to understand that Colter would otherwise have been dead, she praised Carlos' brave intervention and agreed to Colter's plan. She then told Colt not to worry because she could run the homestead "pretty well" with some help from the hired hands. But she made Colter promise to return home as soon as possible. He said he would when the situation "cleared," and that seemed to put Mama Helen at ease somewhat.

Helen McKenna gave her son some food and what little money she had on hand, and they separated with no little sadness. And, as she stood in that doorway, stoically watching her son ride away and knowing that she may be seeing him for the very last time, a single tear streamed down her face.

The two boys rode for several hours after sunset before making camp beside a small, seasonal stream hidden within a thicket of mature oaks. Since the following day was Saturday, they believed Dingler's body wouldn't be discovered until Sunday Sabbath. Carlos told Colt all about Mr. Dingler's merciless teaching methods, and they discussed how the horrified parishioners might react when they first detected the disagreeable sights and smells of Dingle's decaying corpse. Colt wryly commented that he didn't think it would be "a sensible way to start off church service" and that he hoped Loretta would remember to "raise her hand afore screamin'." Even Carlos had to laugh.

Just to be safe, the boys agreed not to have a campfire that first night and redeclared this decision at the end of every day for nearly a week. And they always rode south.

Thus and hence, marked the end and beginning of the lives and adventures of Colt and Carlos, two new friends tied together by murder and an unseen influence spirited through the sympathetic mediumship of a "bad luck" silver picture frame.

EPILOGUE

Our terrene world is basically a hostile place, and good and evil are intrinsic parts of our lives; it's as simple as that. No matter how hard we try, sin, wickedness and human error can never be avoided. No one is free from high moral judgment or far from the onus of trial and harsh punishment. Innocent or otherwise, judgment and punishment were the very things Colt and Carlos had been determined to keep from encountering. And what empathetic person could really blame them for running away?

The characters in *Rattlesnakes, Ghosts and Murderers, Volume 1: McKenna and Barnett* have already lived and died within the consciousness of the author. They moved upon his psyche like winds across desert sands; above and through but never settling sufficiently to fall completely earthbound. Although their "bones" have been buried and left to decay over time, the actors themselves will never be found in any graves, phantasmic or otherwise.

The histories of Helen McKenna, Colt Barnett and others have already been chronicled in the author's ethereal envisagements and his written records, and it is this author's intent that their stories unfold in future volumes.

We live in a dream of all we have done.
We are one and we are many; we are nothing else.
Len Francis Monahan

NOTE

Rattlesnakes, Ghosts and Murderers, Volume 1: McKenna and Barnett was completed on February 20, 2012 (prepublication edit, May 8, 2012; copyright submission, May 12, 2012.) The setting of *Rattlesnakes, Ghosts and Murderers, Volume 2: The Curse Continues* follows Volume 1 by more than a century – and yet the books are intimately connected; so much so, Volume 1 should be read prior to Volume 2. Although the latter volume can be enjoyed entirely on its own – and while I personally like to comprehend newspapers from back to front – I don't recommend such reading practice in this case.

CONSIDERATIONS AND ACKNOWLEDGMENTS

First and foremost, I want to thank my wife Elaine for her wise counsel and her artwork in the interior of this book. We have worked together in this way on musical projects. I wrote, produced and performed music while Elaine created the record covers and related art. Elaine is the first person to have read this work and was its sole editor.

I also wish to thank Kathy Gillen for reading the pre-publication materials and my friend John Sanders (Sanders Canyon) the cowboy-artist who created the outstanding picture for this book's cover.

Excerpt from

Len Francis Monahan's

RATTLESNAKES, GHOSTS and MURDERERS

Volume 2: The Curse Continues

51 Months, 9 Days, 13 Hours, 28 Minutes Ago: (12:28 AM) The Daniels

The inside of the cabin where Frank and Josephine Daniels were vacationing was warm and cozy. The Daniels had been married for just over forty-seven years. Their four children were grown, and they had nine grandchildren and one great-grandchild yet to be born. They knew the still-developing fetus was a girl and had purchased some pretty, pink, baby clothes during this vacation.

The Daniels had worked hard and rose from impoverished beginnings to reach the comfort of middle class. They had always found solace in religion; and, during those times when their travails sluiced downward and through life's deepest valleys, they continued to look to each other for support and weathered their hardships stoically. In due course of time, as they had always believed would happen, it all paid off for them. After years of working six or seven days a week, Frank was finally able to retire; and Josephine's health problems had gone into remission. This was the first vacation by themselves since their honeymoon weekend more than four decades ago. Yes, life was good indeed.

Unawares to the Daniels, however, just off the dirt drive that led to their small, rental house, three corrupt men sat in a stolen car and drank tequila. The driver craftily kept the vehicle's lights off to avoid detection.

"Do you want another sandwich?" Josephine asked Frank.

"No, I'm not hungry," Frank called back from his chair while admiring his wife's appearance as she stood at the kitchen counter.

"I'll make you one if you want."

"No, I'm not going to eat any more today. You know what the doctor said. So what's with this 'second sandwich' you want to make for me? You usually tell me I eat too much and have to cut back. Now, here you are, pressuring me to have a second sandwich! What's behind this; the insurance money?"

"Don't be funny, Frank. And I'm not pressuring you. We're on vacation. We can worry about our diets when we get home."

"No, I think you mean we can worry about 'my' diet when we get home. You're still trim as the day I met you."

"Stop it, Frank. You and I both know that's not true."

"It most certainly is true. You're still as beautiful as the day you walked down the aisle."

"So do you want a sandwich or not?"

"Of course I want it. But I'm not going to eat it and let your next husband spend my life insurance money on some wild, Las Vegas honeymoon."

"Alright, that does it. I'm putting the bread away."

"Thank you. You're finally beginning to make sense."

"Speaking of beautiful: it certainly was a beautiful day today, wasn't it – all those flowers and fresh air. It was simply lovely."

"Yeah, it was kind of nice. Too bad I didn't have my gun with me. I could've shot a deer for sure."

"No, you don't need any gun out here. I'm not going to let you spoil our vacation by killing animals."

"Well, how about fishing? Fishing doesn't hurt anything."

"No. No fishing either. You can catch your smelly fish when you get back home."

Frank got up from the dining room chair and stretched lazily. "That's fine with me. I'm too darn tired to go out and catch those stinky fish anyway. Any-hoo, my back's still hurting. I'm going to bed. How about you?"

"I'll be there in a little bit. I want to stay up and do a crossword puzzle."

"Even on vacation, you're doing crossword puzzles. You better stop before you get too smart for me."

"Oh, Frank, quit."

"Good thing you married me just for my dashing, good looks."

"Right, you just keep telling yourself that."

"You should get to bed now. We have to get up early to deliver those family 'heirlooms' to your sister. I still don't know why we had to bring all this stuff with us on our trip. It's just a lot of old junk."

"I told you, Frank; it's not junk. There are some pictures of my aunts and uncles and distant cousins. My sister needs all that for her ancestry research."

"I wasn't referring to your family pictures. I was talking about the old dolls and cups and saucers and that other worthless stuff. Oh, never mind; at least we're getting it out of the garage. But couldn't you forget about your crossword puzzles for just one night and come to bed? I won't be able to sleep with you wandering around this place, making all sorts of noise and leaving the lights on."

"Oh, alright," Josephine reluctantly agreed, while putting away the food. "You have really turned into some kind of insufferable, old coot."

"Thank you. But you forgot to mention 'adorable.'"

"No, I didn't forget to mention anything."

Outside, Loco sat relaxed in the driver's seat of the car. Guillermo sat next to him, and José sat in the back.

"How long we gonna wait, Loco? We been here over an hour already," Guillermo complained.

"We go when I say we go," Loco declared.

"Just a couple old people in there," Guillermo noted, "They can't be nothin' to take down."

"We ain't gonna hafta kill doze ole geezers, is we Loco?" José asked.

Loco looked into the dashboard mirror and shot a look at José. "We're just here to rob the old nacos is all. But who knows? It goes down how it goes down."

"But how can you be sure they're rich?" Guillermo asked.

"Look, man, I told you. I saw what the old dude had in his wallet back at the gas station. Must have been three or four hundred dollars in there. And rate that ride of theirs. They're driving a Lexus that looks like it could be brand new. No, they got money alright."

"Afterwards, let's get us some good dope, dog, and get this party poppin'," Guillermo said, moving back and forth to some imaginary music. "But first I gotta go outside and take a piss."

"No, you ain't going noplace; not until after we finish this job," Loco said.

"But I gotta piss bad, primo!"

"Shuts up, Guillermo," José said. "You heards what da Loco man said. You holds dat piss till everythin's done."

"Hey look, man. That light just went off," Guillermo pointed out.

"Let's go," Loco ordered.

"But dough'n you think we should waits awhile till after dey goes ta sleep?" José asked nervously.

"No, man, I gotta piss, "Guillermo anxiously stated. "Let's do it now and get it over with."

"We go now," Loco ordered. "No sense us sitting here all night waiting for two, rich, old gringos to take a nap. Now it's time to get burglar."

Loco opened his door and stepped out. The other two followed.

"You think we mights hafta hurts dem, Loco?" José asked lowly as they moved silently toward the cabin.

"What's with you?" Loco reacted. "You growing man boobs?"

Although José had grown up in a quiet, suburban neighborhood just outside of Fresno, his early associations with criminal types made him a virtuoso in the art of gang-slang, which he tended to use heavily when under duress.

"No, primo, I'm juss be askin'," José asserted defensively. "We gotsta do what we gotsta do. Whutevah!"

"Let's get this over with, man. I gotta piss so bad I can taste it," Guillermo said, holding tightly to his crotch.

As they neared the cabin, Loco whispered. "I'll check the windows in front. You each take a side and check around back. If you see either of them gringos walking in their sleep, you make some kinda bird noises or something. When we get inside, I'll go for their wallets. You two grab whatever looks valuable. And don't be seen. Otherwise we gotta do permanent damage."

As the men walked away from each other, José asked himself silently, "Bird noises? Who be makins bird noises? What da hell kinda plan s'dat?"

Loco moved stealthily to the west-facing front of the three-room, vacation home and peered in through a window. José took up a position on the left or northern side of the cabin and waited before acting. Guillermo, in the meantime, had moved to the side of the building facing south, rushed past the bathroom window and hurried to the back where he immediately unzipped his pants and began to urinate.

"I don't care what that Loco says. I gotta piss," Guillermo said to himself, and he urinated on the ground next to the bedroom window. "Ahhhhhhh!"

"What's that?" Josephine sat up in bed and asked her husband. "Did you leave a faucet on outside?"

"What faucet?"

"No, it sounds like something peeing outside our window."

"Go to sleep, will you. It's probably a deer or raccoon or something."

"No, Frank, it definitely sounds like peeing. Something is urinating just outside the window. Go take a look, Frank."

"Are you kidding me? Who would be standing outside our window taking a pee at this time of night? Bigfoot?"

"Will you please just go look! And be careful."

"Oh, alright," Frank agreed. "But first let me put on my slippers."

Frank kneeled at the side of the bed and felt around the floor for his slippers. "Ooh, my back! I can't find the darn things anywhere."

"Forget the slippers. Just go look."

"Wait a minute. Here they are!" Frank said with mild surprise.

Hearing the Daniels talking but not knowing what was being said, Guillermo hurriedly finished his business and zipped up.

"By the time you get there.... Wait. It stopped," Josephine discerned.

"Just a second. I've got to put them on."

"No, listen. I don't hear anything."

"Well, not even Bigfoot can pee forever. Okay, I've got one on. Just let me put on the other one. I should be wearing socks. I could catch cold."

José, who had just walked around the rear of the building, saw Guillermo pressing close to the cabin as if to avoid being seen. Taking that as a cue, the frightened José bulled through and into a nearby bush to conceal himself.

"Did you hear that?" Josephine asked nervously. "It sounded like branches."

At nearly the same moment, the sound of a window being slowly opened at the front of the cabin could be heard.

"Do you hear that?" Josephine restated. "Somebody's opening a window in the front room!"

Wearing only one slipper, Frank moved to the bedroom door, opened it a crack and peered out. Then he quickly shut the door and said, "Somebody's breaking into this place. We're being burglarized."

....continued

www.ingramcontent.com/pod-product-compliance
Lightning Source LLC
Chambersburg PA
CBHW071510260626
47170CB00002B/324